The Menagerie: An Anthology

Short Stories

CURTIS ORLOFF

THE MENAGERIE: AN ANTHOLOGY

Short Stories

BY

CURT ORLOFF

ISBN: 978-1-967375-16-5 (Paperback)
ISBN: 978-1-967375-17-2 (E-book)

Library of Congress Control Number: 2025912018

Printed in the United States of America

Published by:

info@thequippyquill.com
(302) 295-2278

SHORT STORIES

TO CLIMB A MOUNTAIN

Dawn licked a mountainous skyline red. Tentative shafts of light peaked over the summits, one by one lighting the valley below, sparkling the dew. Birds shook off sleep to begin singing. Rodents scurried about in blurs of motion, afraid of the predators who hugged the shadows. Winds rushed down the exposed slopes to rustle the naked hemlocks on the foothills before shaking the skeletal spruce and alder on the valley floor. It was late summer, high up on the Continental Divide.

The sunlight washed over a campsite. Situated in a depression between a dirt road and a winding stream, it was a simple affair, comprised of a rock pile filled with charred ash and a sleeping bag covered by a frosted poncho. A flashlight, canteen, matchbox, and a paperback lay on one side of the bag. A log with an ax embedded lay on the other.

With the sun climbing in the sky, melting the frost and evaporating the dew, the sleeper should have been up and about, building a breakfast fire. Still, the camper slept.

A sudden breeze dislodged a precariously balanced faggot. The burned-out campfire. toppled. The sleeping bag quivered, then rose up.

A hand appeared. It reached for the ax and tugged at the handle. The blade remained fast and refused to become dislodged, regardless of how violently shaken. A gesture of frustration ended the matter.

The camper had been in the throes of a nightmare. A "National Geographic" magazine had warned of bears: the burly black bear that still populated the high country, the kind that lumbers into camps to wreck and ruin on a whim. The man had thought nothing of them when he had read about them; they were so foreign to his life. He had thought nothing of them when he had pitched camp. Only with the oncoming of night had he began thinking about them. They had disturbed his sleep, causing him to periodically shine his flashlight on the ax, to insure it was close at hand.

A strong breeze shook a nearby bush.

The man curled up in his sleeping bag, then peeked out. Seeing his worries were unfounded, he oozed out of the bag, gathered himself, and stood upright, rubbing the sleep from his eyes. He chuckled in self-recrimination.

He reached down for the canteen and had lifted it close to his mouth before he became aware his fingers had stuck to it. Only after he blew on them could he remove them.

"Last night must have been chilly," he said.

He knew he should be more reflective; that's one of the reasons he went camping: to improve himself, acquire a competitive edge.

His poncho crinkled as he folded it. His unshaven face crinkled as he ran his hand over the stubble. He longed for a hot towel to massage his face and hot cream to help him shave it. He wished he had some coffee to warm his belly.

He congratulated himself for grabbing the ax, hoping to warm himself by chopping kindling. Just wrenching the ax free warmed him, though he didn't realize it, so frustrated was he trying to free it. Chopping the wood wound him as badly as it had last night. A glance at the odd purple sky while gulping for air did not cause him to contrast it to the light blue skies of previous mornings. He had only looked at the sky. He had never seen it.

The match he removed from the damp matchbox refused to ignite the wood he managed to chop. He vowed not to let them get wet again, wrapped the box inside his jacket, and patiently waited until they dried. The fire that eventually blazed was a tribute to that patience. He was not a quitter.

The sun cleared the mountain tops by the time he had finished breakfast. He took off his jacket and took deep drafts from the canteen. The few bits of remaining ice chilled his teeth.

He prided himself on his fastidiousness. It was a matter of course for him to wash the cooking gear. Holding the pan in the rushing water almost sprained his wrist. *Oddly, the water should look so inviting*, he thought as he blew onto his numb extremity.

After reassembling his dining kit, he drenched the fire, scattered and covered it with dirt. His camp gear ended up under a conspicuous tree. The man surveyed his cleaning with satisfaction, having broken camp as the paperback book he was reading detailed. The author would have evaluated him favorably.

It was getting toward late morning. Most shadows were gone. Passing clouds provided the only shade. A wall of granite commanded the far side of the road. Not until a bird he was watching flew in front of it did, he take notice. He whistled as he leaned back to take it all in. *No man could climb that*." He mused. The elevations that flanked it were almost as impressive. They looked like bookends, squeezing an imposing set of tomes.

The range on the near side of the road did not look half as imposing. Two peaks rose above the foothills. The shorter, more colorful one looked far more accessible than its muscular, steel-grey neighbor. It was the one he chose to ascend. He was a practical man, and he congratulated himself for being honest about his limitations.

He was also a careful man, given to taking his time, weighing all the options and possibilities. He figured four hours were adequate to reach the summit. At most, two hours would be needed to walk down. That would make it five o'clock if he started at eleven. Night does not fall until after seven, so two hours should be enough cushion. The logic seemed irrefutable.

To be on the safe side--if worse came to worst-- and something did happen, he put the matches into his jacket. He didn't let go of them, however. He pulled them out. The warm air seduced him into discarding the jacket. He was sure it might impair his reach at a critical juncture. The box wound up in his shirt pocket, and the jacket under the tree. He considered and rejected taking accessories like his knife and poncho on the ground; they, too, might prove more hindrance than help.

A glance back at his car made him think. The late-model Buick suddenly meant a great deal to him. It was his security, a lifeline to the world he knew. His stomach tightened when he saw how much the western ranges dwarfed it. The events that had led to his trading safety for adventure flashed back to him.

Told he deserved a vacation for having closed an important deal, he jumped at the opportunity. He'd lose vacation time if he didn't use it up. His company's policy about taking days off was very strict. He also knew his arthritis was degenerative. He knew he didn't have much time left to get in touch with nature.

The idea of adventuring in the Rockies thrilled him. It was something he had never done. Vacations always had been spent with his family at theme parks, in motels and restaurants, not by himself, eating out of a backpack, hiking up mountains. He was proud of the courage he had shown to rise above his wife's objections. He had never been so unyielding before. He had never wanted to do anything so badly before. Everyone else who had done it had raved about it.

He hadn't planned an itinerary. He intended to take things as they came. That was how rugged adventurers used to do it. He would show his colleagues he was as much a free spirit as they. Nowhere in his past had he experienced such an overpowering sense of freedom. He likened himself to Jack London.

In anticipation of his trip, he had taken out a subscription to <u>Colorado Magazine</u> and ensured that copies were displayed in the firm's waiting room. Talk about his plans had reverberated around his office. "Don't go hiking alone. Can't tell what might happen" was the unheeded advice of several critics. The man had to get it alone, "Climb every mountain" (as the song went). He had something to prove.

As he neared it, the shorter peak he chose to hike up appeared to be merely a large hill. It was unfair to the other formations to call it a mountain. Mountains should be colossal. He'd need all his gifts of salesmanship to convince people that this Bunker Hill had been Pike's Peak.

A diagonal fissure separated a steep, inhospitable slope from a mild, vegetated slope. A carpet of shrubs guarded an inverted cone of talus.

The man's schedule had not taken into account the time it took to hack through an unexpected thicket. The shrubs were, in fact, the tops of trees that crowded a depression. The shrug of his shoulders on the near side of the depression became an honest sigh of relief on the far side.

He grimaced when he looked back at the camp. It appeared so close. He could still see his possessions. Matted and charred weeds made a mockery out of his efforts to erase signs of the campsite, so it would blend into the environment as "Outdoor Life" said it should.

Sweat coursed down his face when he reached the talus. He didn't stop to consider why the cobbles were of uniform size. It turned out he didn't have to, once he came upon a flume. He walked up it to the yawning mine shaft it led to. If he weren't so overheated and it looked so cool inside, he wouldn't have entered it. He wasn't all that curious. The match he lit to see his way illuminated a chaos of deteriorating hoses, support beams, a rusted pushcart, and twisted tracks that vanished into an abyss. The history of an era came and went in the time for one match to burn out. He did not light a second.

The damp mine had been refreshing. He wished he were back in it soon after he began climbing the fissure above it.

In a squat, he shuffled forward, his palms flat against the roof. He continued to lean forward--for balance--as he strained to prove he hadn't erred by tackling the fissure rather than the lower slope. Progress was slow and exhausting. Waddling was more fatiguing than running, and he never had been much of a runner. He had never been all that athletic, preferring to shine in the classroom rather than on the playing field, as it was more beneficial to one's career.

Because resting would be too hard on his knees, he had to continue up the incline. Crawling over to the slopes above and below was out of the question. Both became much steeper than they had at first appeared.

He did not speed up when the fissure leveled off. Instead, he sat down, turned halfway around, dangled his feet over the side, performed several mental calculations, and lowered himself onto a convex slab below. Enough tiny indentations existed to enable him to reach a stunted tree. Looking back, he shook away an amazement. The slab had been a trick of perspective. He had stood upon a nearly perpendicular face, its bright sheen an indication of smoothness. It was beyond him how he could have traversed such a face. The footholds and handholds were almost invisible. He had learned a reassuring lesson: the most unpromising thing could support him.

For a thousand feet, he shambled over loose dirt, fallen limbs, and crumbling rocks. A breeze cooled the sweat that drenched his shirt.

The wind picked up. Dead trees grated against each other, making ominous sounds. Gulped air didn't fill the man's lungs. His chest heaved. He grew dizzy.

He could not see the summit and wondered whether he had misjudged the height. The wall of granite still dominated the other side of the canyon. But formerly hidden sierras appeared behind it, and from distant hues and colors hinted there were others behind them.

He could not see the summit and wondered whether he had misjudged the height. The wall of granite still dominated the other side of the canyon. But formerly hidden sierras appeared behind it, and from distant hues and colors hinted there were more behind them.

The ghostly woods ended. The man had to make a decision. He could either climb up, across dangerously weathered rocks, or go right, up a pot-marked wall, then left, over loose slats. He chose the latter. He seldom equivocated whenever he made up his mind.

Finding trustworthy indentations to insert his extremities proved difficult. His pudgy fingers weren't nimble enough to fit into as many as he expected. He slipped from some and, for terrifying moments, slid downward, each time ending his slide by finding those he could claw deep enough into to break his descent. Spotting the less steep avenue up (the one he eschewed for not being challenging enough) he scrambled to it with all the will he had left, and extracted something from deep within to clamber up, to rest where it leveled out, where he wondered how he could have been so wrong about the difficulty of the climb when he had started.

Straining himself was no fun. He always hated to strain himself. That was one reason he had gotten into sales. He knew how things worked. Hard work is no longer guaranteed success in today's business world. A facile tongue and a gift for spotting opportunities were far more important. Women didn't care about muscles. The world had advanced to where physical attributes were anachronistic.

A momentary slip turned his attention back to the task at hand. Inch by inch, he concentrated upon the cold, lifeless rock, mistakenly thinking he had to press himself as closely as possible when he should be leaning back…something he would have known had he read the technique articles as closely as he had those that had merely praised the outdoors.

A large crevice came into view. It was a goal, representing safety. He slipped while hurrying toward it. For dearest life, he pressed himself into the rock. The few yards lost seemed like miles, scaring him into being more deliberate.

One hand soon appeared on the floor of the crevice. The other followed, clawing at the stone, ripping off fingernails. A foot appeared. His body rolled over, into the cul-de-sac. He turned on his back. A breeze carried the sweet smell of pine. He opened his eyes, sat up, and looked outward.

He had made progress. He was even to half the granite wall. The background range had grown and changed colors from yellow to purple. A lake separated the range from the wall. The body of water seemed inaccessible and might be one of the virgin lakes he had read about.

"It might not have fish. It might not be known," he said aloud…to his embarrassment. (Only addled people talk to themselves.) He silently vowed to see about naming it upon his return.

A delicate flower flopped down as he stuck his head out to see what was above. He knocked it out of his line of sight.

Shiny slate separated the crevice from a surface ravaged by handholds. Despite his experience on the last shiny surface, it still looked daunting. The eerie howling of the wind as it tunneled through the cul-de-sac unnerved him.

He believed himself to be a wise man. He would have to retrace his climb. Resolutely, he descended, with former handholds and footholds, until reaching a position where he could challenge the weathered grade. Momentary traction was all he needed to keep from slipping.

He took a deserved break on a jutting shelf. From it, he intended to plan his next move but was distracted. The panorama absorbed him. It was nonsense to conceptualize the canyon as a stadium. It was too unimportant to be much of anything. Many peaks were reflected in the lake. Cordilleras stretched from the northern to the southern horizon, collecting into endless vistas of purple and grey. He could not make out his camp. He could barely find the stream. The thicket appeared level with the ground. The talus was a tiny cone, his car, a white dot.

The sun was overhead. The sky was deep purple. The wind had increased, causing him to shiver. Turning back, an hour's climb went by in a minute. He was too busy to sight-see. The plant and animal community changed without him being aware of it. He had to step on a snow drift before he realized it was there. No trace of snow could be seen from below. It had been visible only on the top of the adjacent peak.

As the sparse foliage gave way to moss and lichens, larger patches of snow became the norm. A confusion of two-toed tracks was everywhere. Several nanny goats and kids had stood on the drift watching him begin his climb. They had fled when he had closed to a range where he could shoot them.

The higher he climbed, the more the summit telescoped out of sight. It looked the same distance away as it had much lower down.

He long since had abandoned all thoughts of having fun. His damp shirt clung. His chilled fingers weren't efficient. His lungs hurt. Muscles he never knew existed ached. If he wasn't convinced the top was around the next bend or over the next rise, he'd turn back.

As if it were alive and exceedingly malicious, the summit remained out of reach until he was thoroughly frustrated.

He was so exasperated he didn't care when he reached it. Its bleakness repulsed him. Primitive plants provided the only color. All the rocks were sculptured into grotesque shapes. No birds, butterflies, or crickets tied the land to the man's soul. Only flies.

The summit was stark. But as he rested, regained his composure, he found it also could be engaging. Looking beyond mere appearances, he understood it to be one of the most significant places in his life. He had won a personal dare. He had proved he could hang tough. He was not a quitter.

Looking out, he noticed that the wall of granite wasn't large at all. It and the lake were dwarfed by the edifices that surrounded them. Even the canyon was insignificant, a trivial hollow among vast uplifts.

His accomplishment was thrilling. He plucked a queer weed and inserted it in his mouth. Perhaps he was the first to ever have been there. He hadn't seen any signs of a man.

Still, if he could do it, so could others. He was a rational man. No matter; life is made up of disconnected, private milestones. This, to him, was one.

While exploring, he observed an unforgettable sight. Gigantic elevations frowned upon his puny Olympus. His mountain was as unimportant as the canyon.

A sigh was a disappointment. Frustration had followed him out of the city and into the wilds. Only when he reminded himself that start-up companies no one thought much of had turned into Wal-Mart, Toys R Us, and 7-11 could he reconcile himself to his minor achievement. From the tiny seed does a great oak grow. He would move on to grander expeditions.

It was getting late. Shadows were long, and the light was of an orange hue.

"My God!" exclaimed the man after looking at his watch. Too much time had slipped by. An easy slope had to be found immediately. One walks down a mountain one had climbed up. The man had read that. What he didn't read was the fact that one looks for descents during the ascent.

He sped down a littered draw, trading caution for quickness. Rocks he jarred loose followed him down slope. He became hot. A crippling fall or, as he reentered the tree line, a bad cut were real possibilities. Yet, when the draw abruptly ended, he leaped into a tangle of branches, thinking they would gently give way under his weight. That they broke his fall without inflicting a single scratch was sheer good luck, not good planning. The drop-off they lowered him down was more severe than he had figured.

Regaining his balance and composure, he moved down an animal trail, castigating himself for the tremendous chance he had taken. Onto finding sure footing, he noticed how far down he had traveled. The lake was at eye level. Thoughts of a consoling campfire, a big supper, hot coffee, and being swallowed in his down sleeping bag played across his mind. The amenities of a motel tomorrow would be a delicious reward.

Perhaps the reason for adventuring was to appreciate what is normally taken for granted. He reflected.

Another drop-off slowed him down. He was someone who learned from his mistakes and did not blindly jump into them. He very deliberately knelt and, on all fours, tried to find a way down. No matter where he looked, it was at least twenty feet to the next lower level.

No big deal. He thought. I'm not a sales manager for nothing.

"When the going gets tough, the tough get going," he asserted.

A shadow crept over the fissure he had used on his ascent, denying him use of it for orientation. Shadows were hiding everything. Fortunately, none hid a series of overhangs, one below the other. Nor did they obscure what looked like a gentle slope at the bottom of them.

A pebble dropped to ensure against a trick of perspective bounced off the first overhang, arched into the air, and did not hit until several seconds later. There was no room for error.

One look back at the draw where he had descended was all the man needed to realize there was no turning back. Swathed in darkness, the odds against finding an alternate route if he retraced his steps were slim. As an investor rather than a speculator, he was adverse to taking risks. Nevertheless, he knew that you could get burned no matter what you did.

Facing the mountain, he slithered feet first over the precipice, dangled, dropped, then jumped into the rock when he hit, clutching for any handhold. Turning around when he felt stable enough, he noticed how wrong he had been about the lower slope. It wasn't gentle at all. It was, in fact, the rock face he had avoided during the climb up.

Having no choice, he lowered himself to the overhangs and then angled over to the slope. Every jutting rock or indentation was considered a godsend if employable as a handhold. Like cologne, the odor given off by the stone crept into his nostrils, becoming familiar. An environment alien to him yesterday was not alien to him today. He became as used to the crystals, matrices, hardness, textures, and structures as he was with the dials on his car's dashboard. He regretted no one saw his display of agility.

He shuffled to a protrusion where he could survey his next move. It gave way, leaving him dangling by his fingertips.

The horrors he'd expect to come to mind didn't come to mind. He was just experiencing something different, that was all. Only the consequences were exceptional. Defying death wasn't as dramatic as he thought.

Trifles irritated him. His hair blew into his eyes and tickled his ears. The wind chaffed his skin and caused his injuries to sting. One affliction soon overcame dozens of minor complaints. His fingers began to tremble, mimicking sewing machines.

The gain grew unbearable. Seizures wracked both arms. He regarded letting go as a release. That way, the anguish would end.

All the aspects he didn't like about himself and had kept secret rose like bile from his stomach to his throat, choking him. The thought of glowing testimonials in his honor nauseated him. He knew the few average grades he had received in school could not be cancelled until he had become a vice president. The papers he had paid a ghostwriter to author had only fooled people into thinking he was a gifted writer. He still couldn't read a contract as well as he should. The need to correct his faults made him hold on. He had to survive. He was so incomplete.

He desperately felt for a foothold. Knowing he could smear his foot into the tiniest crack, when he found one, he trusted his life to it. Using it and one arm to support him, he could shake his free arm, restore life to it. Continuing the strategy enabled him to reach a slope so mild he could sit down. He rested. Like the proverbial pot of gold at the end of the rainbow, he had earned the right to relax. He was a firm believer in just desserts.

He found it difficult to force himself up. His sore muscles held him back. But with only a few shafts of light left, he was going to have to race against darkness. Not that he had used the diminution of light to tell time. He used his watch to find out he was behind schedule. His clock radio was the real hero behind his legendary punctuality, not the shy emergence of dawn. In his world, yellow lights preceded red lights, and whistles warned of danger. He was immune to subtle transitions. Without mechanisms to inform his eyes and ears of change, he had no eyes and ears. Certain he had paid his dues, had experienced more than his share of terror, he failed to be as careful as the situation warranted. Once up, he boldly stepped forward, and immediately came to grief. His foot slipped into a small crack. Rather than gingerly remove it, he jerked it up, wrenching it. Trying to walk away from the pain only aggravated the problem. His ankle ceased being reliable. It buckled on gentle inclines, and when half again its normal size, proved useless on steep grades. Much to his consternation, he had to stop.

Night had caught up with him. He could not fool himself about being able to see. Under a starless sky, he couldn't see a thing. He dared not move. He might fall off a cliff. He was a captive.

The wind whistled balefully through chutes and caused the naked trees to moan. Malevolent noises encircled him. One made him wheel about, twist his ankle. A stabbing pain raced across his body. He could not move. He should not move. It was too dark, too dangerous. He was stranded, for the first time in his life, beaten.

He was a reasonable man. Certain people get stranded from time to time, but he did not panic. Someone would see his car. His colleagues would get someone to look for him minutes after he was supposed to return to work. He was that punctual. They also knew he was a realistic man. It wouldn't take a genius to deduce which route he had taken into the mountains or which mountain he'd have traversed.

An increasing wind drove down the temperature, compelling him to hurriedly build a fire. He yanked on a waist-high branch. It unexpectedly gave way, showering twigs on the matchbox he set down. A calm search degenerated into a frantic search. Twigs and dirt filled the air. His inability to find it made him fear he might have pitched it.

He calmed down. Thrashing about was foolish. He was a logical man. Proceeding intelligently, he assumed that the box had to be close by and (for his peace of mind) was all right. While stacking the wood according to size, he uncovered the prize.

Getting the fire started proved difficult. Had he brought the knife, he'd be able to cut kindling small enough to burn easily. As it was, he couldn't keep the wood lit, regardless of how well he protected it from being blown out. He was a man given to detail and, as such, was able to get the fire going.

He felt safe within the sphere of light, in control. Out of inquisitiveness, he took off his boot to see what he had done to himself. His puffed-up ankle was pink and tender. Purple splotches on his instep indicated a break. It seemed unfair to him that such a minor mishap could result in something so debilitating. Then he found out he couldn't put his boot back on.

A drop of rain on his back went unnoticed, as did the sound of distant thunder. More drops fell on him, forcing him to admit it was beginning to rain. "It'll blow over. They always do," he said.

Moving around the fire alternately singed and chilled him. Smoke followed him no matter where he sat. Keeping it going proved to be an all-consuming chore, one he gave his heart and soul to.

Wet snow soon slopped down. The man cuddled the endangered flames. Smoke accompanied a hiss wherever the flakes breached his defenses. The fire popped and sizzled. He spread his shirt over his shoulders and leaned over the flames. His eyes teared. His nose clogged with smoke. In addition, his arms began to ache. When he tried shifting positions, his bad foot hurt so badly he flinched, letting the storm in on the fire. An eruption of smoke accompanied a loud whoosh.

The quick removal of the dampened kindling salvaged what was left of the fire. Although his good foot was asleep, he arched himself over the tiny flames. The fire continued to spit and crackle.

He became a contortionist, prezelling himself to remove a match from the matchbox. But he couldn't become the magician he needed to be in order to light one. His stiff fingers wouldn't cooperate. Dropped matches plugged into the accumulating snow. Match heads struck too harshly, darted into the night. Flames would creep up the shaft to burn his fingers before he could apply them to the wood.

With only a few remaining, he devoted as much care to them as surgeons do to their instruments. He ignored his foot, the incipient pain of frostbite, and the aches resulting from holding his shirt over the fire. He lost track of time, absorbed as he was with the task at hand.

A white light twinkled from down below. The hum of a motor and the crunch of compacted dirt indicated the presence of a car. It stopped. A door opened and closed.

The shadow of a man passed through the headlights. A tinkling sound was heard, whereafter a tiny red light preceded a burst of yellow light. A red streamer trailed into the dark. When the form had finished his cigarette, he returned to the car and drove off. The taillights soon disappeared.

The entire event had taken place without the man uttering a sound. He had been too embarrassed.

The storm had ended. It had ended before the appearance of the car. The man had been so preoccupied by relighting the fire that he hadn't paid attention.

After arranging several sticks into a tepee, he found it a relatively simple matter to get the fire going again. While simultaneously tucking in his shirt and positioning himself more comfortably, he accidentally kicked the structure. It tumbled into the wet kindling he had neglected to clear away. The rest of his matches failed to restart.

Turtle-like, he bunched up inside his clothes, alternately blowing into his hands and rubbing his extremities.

Many thoughts raced through his mind, none alighting for any appreciable amount of time. He thought of his incompleteness, the white lies he told his family concerning all the time he promised to spend with them in the future, knowing very well he'd be even busier. He thought of several women and girls he could have conquered had he been more forceful or more attuned to their needs. He had many regrets. Not one success came to mind.

He practiced the Zen Buddhism learned during a youthful flirtation with the Beatnik movement. He willed himself to be at peace.

The sensation of warmth crept outward from his chest to his limbs. He could feel himself sweating. The trance seemed to be fruitful. He must have tapped a hidden reservoir. His foot quit pulsating. He sensed dawn. His mind reached across time and space to see his wife hugging him and his colleagues offering hearty handshakes.

The heat became unbearable. He took off his shirt and stretched, trying to cool down. Overhead, the stars danced, whizzing and whirling, streaking across the sky. Many climbed into the heavens, reached an apogee, then dove straight at him, crashing into his foot.

He screamed and dragged himself to the nearest tree to wait, watch, ready to flee upon the slightest provocation.

He was not an imaginative man.

Strange sensations pummeled him. The need to sleep chewed at his insides. Keeping watch on the stars taxed all his willpower. He did not want to sleep. It was dangerous and could prove embarrassing if rescuers caught him unawares. But mostly, sleeping would be a sign of weakness. He prided himself on always getting the job done regardless of the personal costs. He held his eyelids open with his fingers and kept his mouth open to gulp in as much air as possible.

Sleep overcame him.

A timid light peeked above the eastern ridgeline, tinting the snow pink. Snow periodically cascaded from bowed trees. One by one, diagonal shafts of light sprang to life, sparkling the white landscape and illuminating crazy patterns of animal tracks. Movement and contrasting colors soon were detectable.

A spot of yellow stood out as it moved across a steep, grey slope. A pungent odor had taken a mountain goat's mid-off its early morning feeding to lead it to a tiny campsite surrounded by gnarled trees. The animal sniffed the bulging eyes and sneezed in the gaping mouth of the body, which emitted the smell. Nosing the corpse's legs aside, the goat renewed its grazing on a patch of edibles underneath.

APOSTASY

"Mind if I walk with you?" asked Doug to a Berkeley co-ed.

"He'll make her think?" asked Doug's Street partner, Barn Hippie, to his girl, Shenandoah.

"No way. He hit her up yesterday."

The pert blond clutched her books and, fixing her eyes straight ahead, hurried along, ignoring him as best she could. By turning left into the languid morning traffic of Telegraph Avenue, she eluded him.

"Ugly as a mug, man," said Barn Hippie, trying to cheer up his friend as he handed him a joint. "Take a hit."

"Fuck yeah, might as well."

A bay breeze blew the smoke down the sidewalk. From the alleys and behind vendors' carts, street people appeared, wearing glad rags and sporting the same kind of headbands as the two friends. Once spotting where the smell originated, those on agreeable terms with the two advanced. Those who didn't retreat. The joint, several cigarettes, and beer were shared. A bearded policeman strolled by without showing the least interest, even after Barn Hippie invited him to join them. "Just for a minute."

"Hey man, what the fuck you doing?" scolded Doug.

Barn Hippie mumbled something about how different Berkeley was from Austin—the city where the police harassed his old lady so relentlessly she killed herself.

Shenandoah stepped between her man and Doug before anything serious happened. "You watch yourself!" she roared. Doug's upraised arms floated down to his sides. He lost his sinister expression. "He ought to watch himself," he whined.

People let Doug sulk by himself. Nobody tried to reason with him. That had been tried too often without any luck. His thick head was infamous.

An exodus of students returning from early classes crowded the "Avenue" (as Bob Dylan called it). The street came alive with vendors hawking everything from hot dogs to eggplants, with street people hitting up pedestrians for spare change, and with unrelenting Californian traffic. The funky cultural center swung to life. The sidewalk vibrated. The street symphony, composed of wash tubs, kazoos, and fiddles, put all the sights and sounds to music (and attracted money from passers-by). Eddies of people stopped to browse, to listen, to talk, to have their portraits painted, to enjoy themselves.

Among the afternoon crowd, a dark-haired, lissome girl strode toward Doug, her arms gaily swinging. With his head bent, shuffling his feet, Doug wasn't watching where he was going as he moved toward her. He was feeling sorry for himself, having suffered another rejection. They didn't collide, but brushed by just enough to catch each other's attention. Doug read more into her smile than she intended.

"Mind if I walk with you?" he asked.

"Sure. I'd love to talk with you. I just love Berkeley. I've never loved any place as much. The people, the bay, the hills, the weather, everything."

"You've got good vibrations. You're special."

"I haven't seen a lot. Work too much in the city to see much of Oakland, let alone Berkeley."

"I bet you're a Leo. Leos are sensitive."

"Hassles at home can't bother me here. Can stay here forever."

She made a right at Ashby. "This is where I turn. Thanks for the talk."

"Yeah, sure…come back if ya want," he said to her while thinking women were put on earth to torment him.

Kathy skipped home. A real Berkeleyite lad paid attention to her. Such friendliness! Back home in the suburbs, people had never been so open. The affluent middle class is inhospitable. She reflected. Penniless outcasts are more spontaneous, more decent. My family here doesn't hold to conventions like the family I was born into. It understands me. It trusts me, treats me like an adult, and assumes I have an adult's sense of responsibility and good sense.

"What is it!" she shouted to her roommate instead of knocking on the door of their walk-up.

"It's live!" exclaimed Victoria.

"Bad, real bad," said Kathy as the door swung open to expose a menagerie of cats at Victoria's feet. Wicker furniture and plants filled up the apartment.

"Guys from downstairs are coming up for dinner. Hope you don't mind."

They frequently had their neighbors over. Kathy considered them part of her new family.

'Raw daw. Totally."

The rear steps groaned with heavy footsteps.

"Door's unlocked!" Victoria bellowed.

Three bearded, gaunt figures in fatigues trudged into the kitchen. Saying very little, they fell upon the zucchini drop cookies and persimmon pudding cake laid out on the kitchen table. The scabrous inner elbows of two of the guests limited their reach. Kathy could tell by their expressions that, although it hurt them to stretch, it hurt them more to admit their problem—a stoic trait she ascribed to their experiences in Vietnam.

They were enigmas. Kathy avoided thinking about what they did for a living. She and Victoria had agreed not to pry into other people's business. The three were sweet and kind. That was all that mattered.

"This is for you, Kathy," said the one with the tattoo: "Born to Raise Hell" on his forearm. "I worked on it for weeks."

"It's beautiful. Oh, you're so wonderful," she said as she admired the elaborately carved bong. A syrupy look warned the veteran of an enthusiastic hug.

"Your meals are gifts enough," he said.

"My ma can't do any better," said another. "Your zucchini's far out."

A supper of meat loaf, mushroom quiche, corn, and pumpkin chiffon pie washed down with white wine was accented by table conversation that ranged from how Eastern ideologies were the salvation of Western political problems and whether Joni Mitchell was America's unofficial poet laureate. The christening of Kathy's present put an end to serious debate.

When daylight outshone the indoor lights, which had been left on. The guests got up from where they had passed out and left.

"Had they stayed, I'd have fixed them breakfast," said Kathy while she prepared for work. "I can't remember when I had such a talk, certainly not at home, or in school, even in the debate club. The topics were always so dull."

"Kathy, this is where it's at. Revolutionaries, sophists, pantheists, Libertarians...everybody like that gravitates here. It's as far from suburbia as you can get."

"It's where I belonged all along."

"It's where you'll have a hard time remaining if you don't hurry up for work."

Her job as a store clerk in San Francisco took a large chunk out of her day. It was the sacrifice she had to make to remain in the niche she was beginning to carve for herself. Having to work overtime to take bimonthly inventory particularly irritated her. It gave her only the nights to enjoy her self-imposed exile.

She was more familiar with Berkeley at night than during the day. In the weeks she had lived there, she hadn't gotten to know it better than she would have had she been on a brief vacation. Except on her days off, Berkeley was no more than a dream city, as Oz saw in a blur from B.A.R.T. during the day and as an island of yellow and white lights at night.

The local hills were her command posts, her getaways where she'd plot, dream, and hope the future would be all it could be. They'd elevate her above daily affairs and the trivia that threatened her well-being. Different observation points uniquely influenced her thinking. The certainty she had about the decisions she arrived at on the summit of the highest hill (above the city), she often lost when she descended. Only when she stopped by a maple similar to that she had climbed as a child did her resolve return to remain with her back in town.

Under its bought, she concluded what would be best for her. Certain that street people were more real than the stuffed shirts she had known, she decided to get to know them. How else could she explore Berkeley if she didn't immerse herself in it? She had come to taste other lifestyles, comprehend other frames of reference, and do what the paralyzed people back home couldn't.

"That chick's checking you out. Doug," said Barn Hippie the next morning. Doug slowly looked in Kathy's direction. He looked away when their eyes met and backpedaled when she advanced.

"Hi, remember me?"

"Yeah, sure…sure! Can get concert tickets. This dude 'n I gotta thing going. Get tickets for free. Wanna come?"

"Live, totally live."

"Tonight, if that's okay?" He looked at her quizzically.

"Kathy Martin. And what's your name?"

"Doug. That's all. Doug. Two names are fucked. Enough people know me, so I don't need a second name."

He talked throughout the morning and saluted the afternoon with his first beer. All else he did from then on was subordinate to his drinking. Kathy pretended not to notice. She also looked the other way whenever Doug's friends panhandled.

"You're a pretty lady, you can sell it when the depression hits," said Shenandoah to a woman who snubbed her.

Barn Hippie was more decorous. He had tact and was able to orchestrate his approach to the kind of person he hit upon. Their walk, dress, and demeanor clued him in to what tactic he should use. He'd intimidate weak-willed people by sticking his face into theirs and bellowing. And he'd challenge the intellect of the strong-willed ones, play mental games. "You'd lose less money by giving me eighty cents than giving a charity a dollar and deducting it from your taxes. And it'd be just as ungratifying."

A quarter conned from a simpering, red-faced businessman slipped from his hands into a pool of chewing tobacco. Picking it up, he wiped it off on his jeans and, along with those from his pocket, handed it to Shenandoah. She counted the take before dropping it into her embroidered shoulder bag.

Shenandoah harvested more money than her partner. Her angelic face and big bosoms more readily lured change from men than her skinny lover could from women.

"The stupid sucker," she remarked to Kathy after scoring a dollar from a cigar smoker who swatted her behind. "Tits and ass. Get rides, get money, get anything. They get fucked. Tits and ass run the world."

"Whaddya want?" she hissed as Barn Hippie crowded close.

"You know."

"She reached into her bag, scooped out a fistful of change, counted it, and gingerly gave him a share. He hurried off to return in the middle of an anecdote

Shenandoah was sharing about the sugar daddies she had known. He apportioned the fried pies and French fries he had gone after equally.

"You hang out a lot with them?" Kathy asked Doug.

"When not going to school."

"I wouldn't have guessed you were a student. Junior college or Cal?"

"Cal."

"What year?"

"Third."

"How many hours do you have?"

"Uh, five. Want a beer/"

"No thanks."

The activity along the street slowed and virtually stopped by mid-afternoon. The transition from day to night dragged on. The heat pressed upon them. Kathy fought against drowsiness. Unable to initiate a stimulating conversation and feeling too uncomfortable to read a book, she gave in to Doug's offer to take a beer.

Refreshing breezes heralded the evening and its accompanying return of activity. People with names like Butch, Daytripper, Edgar High, and Midget Jesse wandered by to trade wine, pot, and cigarettes for beer from Doug's seemingly bottomless cooler. Talk ran the gamut from the merits of different kinds of grass to the talents of the groups that jammed at the free concerts.

"When is the next concert?" Kathy eagerly inquired.

"Tonight," replied Shenandoah.

"Then we won't need to get the tickets. I'd just love to see a free concert."

"What other concert?" asked Edgar High, before receiving a signal from Doug to be quiet. "Okay by me," answered Doug.

Kathy could not tell whether people congregated around her and Doug to eye her or partake of his generosity. Nevertheless, the discomfort that afflicted her when she had barged into their lives no longer remained. Finding the people likeable and honest (more honest than the jerks back home) helped her feel comfortable around them. She was even more comfortable around Doug, regardless of what he said about being a student. He wore well on her. He was good medicine.

There were no strings attached to the beers he gave out. His friends' pleasure was his pleasure. It was obvious he'd have been the center of attention if he didn't have a cooler. He had charisma. Besides, he was a fox.

The jazz band featured in Provo Park kept the night mellow. The musicians communicated their love for their music and how right, how natural it was to be happy. Most listeners kept their lids and rolling papers in their pockets. Kathy and Doug did. They didn't need them. The justice the band gave to the music of Miles Davis, Chick Corea,

George Fenson, and John Coltrane provided all the stimulation two impressionable persons could want.

The soft harmonies stirred the natural resonances in both their bodies. Their fingers intertwined. Behind her closed eyelids, Kathy could see what she had been searching for. She knew she would no longer call in sick to have a day off. She was going to quit work.

She could not get the idea out of her mind. It was too delicious, more impetuous than anything else she had ever done. She was tired of being reasonable all the time, for as long as she could remember. What had she gotten from working after school? Passes from grubby old men and grief about lower grades. She refused to sacrifice herself for a few moments of pleasure. Enough was enough. She had money saved.

The music she heard that night would become her anthem.

Doug needn't have felt rejected when she removed his hands from her back pocket or didn't allow him to escort her all the way home. He held a firm place in the new life she intended to lead.

"Come in, Kathy, meet some friends!" shouted Victoria from the first-floor window.

Smiles appeared from three huge, hairy faces which, like Cheshire cats, seemed to fill the room. Patches on their leather jackets identified them as members of a local motorcycle gang. Kathy was amiable to them. She tries not to judge them, valiantly striving to concentrate on their good qualities. What she couldn't overlook, however, was the strange smell and glassy look in their eyes once they finished visiting the washroom. The sight of a scorched spoon scared her enough to excuse herself and withdraw upstairs.

She agonized about calling in to quit the next morning. Once she did it, she rushed off to spend the day with Doug.

He was not among the sleepers along the sidewalk. Nor was he among the flood of students heading toward campus. He ambled by at mid-morning, carrying a cooler.

"You've been here long?" asked Kathy after they had hugged.

"Just got here."

"From where?"

"Bernard's. Sleep there."

"What's rent?"

"Nothing. We got an understanding."

"He gave you the beer?"

"Pay for it."

"With what?"

"S.S.I....Social Security Insurance."

"For what?"

"Fucked up on thorazine The Man always gave me in my foster homes, 'til I got thrown out of the program."

"How many homes?"

"Shit lot of them. Said I was too hyperactive."

"How much S.S.I. do you get?"

"Enough. Can get you on it. Know a doctor."

Like that, her money problems could be solved. But she couldn't rationalize her way into accepting it, not when she had crusaded against hypocrisy back home. She had scruples. And she had compassion. Doug's past excused his actions. She doubted she could have dealt with his past as well as he.

The absence of the look he had manufactured when lying about his being a student and when bragging about getting concert tickets free confirmed he was telling the truth. His child-like obviousness was endearing. Because of his background, she would judge him leniently. His value system was different. The challenge of understanding it excited her.

The monotony of Doug's life did not distress her. She accepted it, like she accepted Shenandoah's sharp tongue and Barn Hippie's slyness. She blamed all derogatory observations on her bourgeois upbringing, with all its prejudices and narrow-mindedness.

Her presence was like a catalyst. By throwing herself into their life, remaining curious and uncritical about everything they did, she gave them recognition no one else from her class ever did.

Her profoundest effect was upon Doug. He soon became animated, rambling on about anything, showing Kathy how wide-ranging his interests were. He talked through a late afternoon drizzle and showed no indication of quitting when it stopped.

"Aren't you going to put on something dry?" asked Kathy.

"Don't have anything else to put on."

Down the street staggered Midget Jesse, looking battered.

"Daytripper mugged me, ripped me off."

"Sure, man?"

"Fuck yeah. Took every fucking thing."

"Ugly as a mug. Going to go to The Man?" asked Shenandoah.

"Fuck, fuck, fuck The Man!" yelled Doug.

"Go to The Man," Shenandoah whispered as she slid her bulging purse out of sight, behind he back.

Seeing her, Doug yanked off his shirt and handed it to Midget Jesse. "Here, man, take it. I care."

"Raw, daw."

"Have a seat. Scarf a brew, as many as you like. We're partners. Nobody fucks a partner without fucking me. This is all the bread I got now; take it." He turned all his pockets inside out to prove he was telling the truth. He then nursed the victim, going so far as to forsake beer as he did so.

The care and concern he lavished on Midget Jesse endeared him to Kathy. His altruism was fetching, reminding her of the poor woman who gave Christ all she could. He was awesome.

Once Midget Jesse was taken care of, Kathy set about cajoling Doug to her walk-up. Seducing him was no mean feat, for it wasn't until recently that she had learned about love. She hadn't wanted to arrive on the infamous West Coast inexperienced. That would have put her at a psychological disadvantage and might have been dangerous, considering how often she got propositioned.

At home, she slithered around Doug, devouring him with affection. Only when he started to take off his clothes did she recall how much sex hurt. She momentarily cringed at the lust which disfigured his face but recovered well enough to perform as a paramour. Yet he immediately went from hot and passionate to frigid and removed. Lust left his face. He backed away from her. Not knowing what to do, she remained stationary and watched, trying not to come to any conclusions as he began to play with himself. She gave up the exotic dance she thought would lure him to her. He was too intent upon reaching a climax.

Luring him into the shower to prevent his falling asleep after he had come, she tried to coax the intimacy she knew he possessed into the open. To a certain extent, she succeeded. They played with each other, lathering each other up and scrubbing down, applying more pressure on each other's genitals than anywhere else. His playfulness encouraged her. Even though he retreated into his shell once they toweled off, she still considered herself to have accomplished something.

Snuggling up to him in bed was more romantic than snuggling up to her Snoopy doll. But Snoopy didn't snore, sweat, need a share, or toss and turn. Unable to sleep, she moved to a mattress in a back room when he began to snore steadily.

"Damn bitch!" Doug bellowed. "Get the fuck back where you belong."

Kathy rushed back, wrapped herself around him, making sure their genitals touched in the hope that something would come of it. Nothing did.

"Aren't you going to work?" asked Doug the first thing upon arising.

"What for?" she replied as pleasantly as possible, considering his morning breath. "Would rather spend time with you."

"You be my lady?"

"For all time," she cooed. She started to pet him, applying more and more pressure, arousing him. She sucked and played with him until he took over the lead.

It hurt. God, it hurt. His member was like a knife, scrapping, gouging, drawing blood, throwing her this way and that, causing her to dig her fingernails into his back, emit animal noises, and pretend she was in the throes of ecstasy, not torture.

Once he got started, he wouldn't slow down. She had triggered a side of him she hadn't seen before: an animalistic side she knew she had to contain. He could tear her apart.

His huge thrusts seized her, lifted her off the bed, and terrified her. She unknowingly had consented to be brutalized.

She experimented. Resistance only enraged him—it was taken as an affront. Riding him out, moving as he moved, proved to be her only recourse. She outlasted him. His seizures were brief, or at least they were when properly handled. When he settled down, she composed herself well enough to ask if she had satisfied him. His falling asleep answered the question better than a verbal response.

"You just nap. I'll get breakfast," she intoned as she hobbled into the kitchen.

Pancakes smothered in syrup, overlapping fried eggs browned on the edges on a plate fringed by muffins, accompanied by orange juice and coffee on a tray, she slid in front of him when he awoke.

He reacted as if he were expecting the meal. "Thanks," he said without emotion.

"Scarf up, you're good people."

He ate punctiliously. Kathy noted how adroitly he handled his napkin and didn't smack his lips.

"Why don't you move in?"

"Live. But I can't. Bernard would freak. Owe him too much to split."

"Let's meet him. I mean, look, I want to know all about you, who you know…everything."

"Let's book."

Bernard lived in a row house that, like most Berkeley row houses, was recovering from the neglect of the sixties. The convergence of gays like Bernard, seeking a Mecca, saved the Victorian structures. Unlike the Chinese before them, when they arrived, they didn't reconstruct their new homes to mimic what they had left behind, but restored what was already there.

The remarkable resemblance of Bernard's décor to her décor made Kathy suspicious. Hanging plants and tapestries complemented the safari shirt and khaki pants he had on when he greeted them.

"Oh, so charmed to meet you," Bernard said, letting her shake his outstretched hand.

"A friend of Douglas' is a friend of mine."

Kathy's eyes were attracted to a half-naked man who strolled across an interior room.

"That's Harold, don't mind him. He's not comfortable around strangers," said Bernard.

"Who's not comfortable?" Harold whimpered as he stepped forward to hook a finger in one of Bernard's belt loops. "Bernard's always saying things to get my goat."

"Harold means well."

"You're just too kind."

"Does Doug live here for free?"

"He'd pay Doug to live here if anything could come of it," Harold remarked.

"Harold's so impulsive, aren't you?" Bernard remarked while uncoupling Harold's finger.

"I'd love to see the house," Kathy blurted out.

"I'll show you," said Harold. "I doubt Bernard can break himself away from Doug long enough."

"I'd love to learn where this vase came from," she said, referring to the only ugly artifact in the otherwise tasteful assemblage of decorations.

Moving on to other items, she inundated the two quarrelers with so many questions that they soon forgot their argument. After the tour, it occurred to her she hadn't seen a room in wild disorder. A house inhabited by a young man has a messy room in it; that was a law of nature. The only evidence of Doug's presence was some camping equipment.

"Where's your stuff?" she asked once they were alone.

"Stuff you saw is it. Don't need nothing else."

Back on the street, Kathy started to view pedestrians with a jaundiced eye. They became faceless, robotic. The inhabitants of the streets became the only real people around. She devoted herself to ferreting out and cherishing their uniqueness. They colored the pavement with a distinction all their own. By bits and pieces, Kathy learned their culture, finding it to be all that the middle class wasn't. It was laid-back and friendly, a real alternative lifestyle. Its attributes far outweighed its faults. The ubiquitous cigarettes were balanced by their vegetarian diets. Their weak speed and pot were no worse than the alcohol, which drowned suburbia.

"I've never been so happy," she whispered to Doug one morning before planting a big, wet kiss on his lips. Her tongue plunged so deeply into his mouth that he gagged. More than their lovemaking, the kiss consummated their relationship. Doug, henceforth affectionately called her Deep Throat. He thought so much of her that he shared with her his most prized possession: Tom Wolfe's <u>Kandy-Kolored Tangerine-Flake Streamline Baby</u>.

Kathy's happenstance familiarity with it was a plus. By debating whether Wolfe did justice to the subjects he treated, she lured out of him his gift for dialectics. The exposition of an unsuspected part of him made Kathy glow.

None of this changed Doug's habits. Come mid-afternoon, beer would begin to slur his speech. By late afternoon, he was incoherent and, if Kathy wasn't careful, violent. He'd insist she drink, belch, and compliment him for his ability to chew off the tops of cans.

It was obvious she had to wean him off alcohol. To do that, she had to separate him from Bernard, as she was certain his drinking had something to do with their relationship.

Her meeting with Bernard quickly degenerated into a shouting match. Doug retreated to the television.

"I took him out of the gutter, you cunt!" screamed Bernard. "No one else was willing to sponsor him in cashing his Social Security checks. He owes me his life."

"And you're not satisfied until he gives it to you!"

"He owes me."

"He owes you shit, you kidnapper."

Harold watched the argument with unmitigated glee. He trailed the quarrelers to Doug.

Kathy found it hard to pry Doug from the flickering screen.

"The precious loves T.V. He is as mesmerized by it as R.C.A.'s little dog," said Harold.

Not until she blew in his ears did Doug respond to her.

"Let me alone."

"Let's go. I'll explain later."

"After the show."

She blew into his ear again.

"Bitch. Fuck off, after the show."

"You've got a problem there," said Bernard.

"I'm going. You know where I'll be. You go there only when you no longer intend to come here again." Kathy flashed her middle finger at Bernard and stormed out.

For the second time in her life, she called the bluff of someone close to her. The last time, her parents hadn't taken her seriously.

The rotating lights stop several squad cars washing through a thicket of motorcycles by her walk-up in reds and yellows. Policemen moved jerkily in and out of the lights; their authoritative voices rang out. Their prisoners just mumbled.

Several officers held shotguns, acting like their tough shit, enforcing laws Kathy was sure only protected citizens from themselves.

From a hedge, she watched a cruiser patrol the streets, looking for anyone who might have escaped. She also noticed a stroller. Rushing to him, she wrapped herself around him, so that they looked like two lovers when they were bathed by the police car's headlights.

Kathy breathlessly explained her actions once the car had turned the corner. Doug wasn't interested.

"You crushed the rose I brought for you."

"I'm sorry," she composed herself well enough to say. Knowing the emotional upheaval he must have experienced to turn his back on Bernard, she explained the situation diplomatically. She conducted a thorough reconnaissance of the neighborhood before going home.

Both suffered quite a start when they pulled the shower curtain back to find Victoria huddled up, asleep.

"Fucking pigs busted us. Had great sugar," she said.

"That's dead. Totally."

Victoria's disturbing insistence that the police barged into a private affair made Kathy suspicious. When Victoria and Doug were asleep, she sneaked a peek at a hollow floorboard she had discovered earlier. In it was a bag of white powder and a nylon stocking holding more money than the occupants of the house would see in a year. None of them had the jobs they told her. They had blown their credibility.

Kathy chastised herself for being so naïve. She did not listen to Victoria's harangue about police harassment the next morning and planned to move out as soon as possible.

Luckily, the veterans moved out soon after they were released on bail, taking Victoria and the stash with them. The bikers never returned, and Doug moved in.

Except for his continued drinking, their relationship became idyllic. She took to spending time in the university library, satisfying her curiosity about several subjects. One day, she returned home to find three malnourished teenagers as houseguests.

"Runaways from L.A.," Doug explained. "Tried to get a Grey Rabbit bus for them, but it's after hours. Don't mind; do you?"

A hug answered the question. Kathy became a surrogate mother, a counselor, and a companion to the adolescents. She understood where they came from. When they left after a week, she wished for another batch of kids to straighten out.

'These represent all the parts of you I dig," said Doug about the rose petals he placed on a windowsill as they watched the youths depart. "Tenderness, intelligence, friendliness, cuteness, helpfulness, and wiseness."

"I've never gotten a nicer present. You're a wonderful person," she said. "Like I knew you were all along," she whispered to herself.

In bed that night, he was more tender and responsive than he had ever been. They lightheartedly played with each other, giggling, tickling, cutting through their inhibitions.

Doug ushered in the morning by fixing breakfast. Although not as well-appointed as Kathy's had been, it was more joyously received. They luxuriated in bed, giving Kathy the courage to ask Doug about looking into Alcoholics Anonymous.

A lot of urging led to his making a phone call...which turned out to be a big mistake. Kathy didn't have to hear the other party to know that whoever answered the phone had no business working at the center.

"Hey man, it's not that easy," was Doug's first scornful comment.

"You can say anything. Talk is cheap. You were an alchy, too. You should know." His eyes started to flame.

"You don't care. No one cares. Want to quit for my woman. Want to hold on to the only good thing I ever had." His grip tightened.

"Getting her was the only good thing I ever did. Going to lose her if I don't sober up." He was shouting.

"Can't do it myself. Get off your fucking high horse. You don't know shit. You stupid fucking motherfucker!" He slammed the phone down, breaking the cradle.

"Them dumb fuckers. They don't know their ass from a hole in the ground."

"It was only one person."

"Fuck them all. They're all the same."

"Be reasonable."

"Reasonable fuck. Everybody's against me. Can't win. Nobody'll let me. Fuck. Fuck everybody." He stomped to the refrigerator to furiously pop open a beer.

Kathy helplessly watched him down can after can. She started to cry. She remained silent as he drank and drank, almost into a stupor that would have knocked him out had a pain not first seized him. Vomit spewed out of his mouth.

Blood followed, deeper and more vicious until it was black and solid.

Wracked by convulsions, covered by slime, he was horrified but did not immobilize Kathy. She burst out the door, took the stairs three at a time, and leaped through an open window into the downstairs apartment. Words weren't necessary to convey the emergency to the new renters. Both rushed upstairs in a flash. The sound of slamming bodies and broken furniture moved from room to room to the stairs, where Doug was bundled to the bottom. Dirt shot out from under the mag wheels of the Chevy Malibu he was thrown.

Although the local hospital was closer, it was bypassed in favor of the free clinic: the place where the two locals were more comfortable, if they were products of the sixties. The staff knew street people. Their expertise in psychology was indispensable. Doug suffered no embarrassment or shame from having his stomach pumped. When he was released, he left behind people who would gladly see him socially.

Kathy mistook his placidity for a change of personality. The adept handling of him at the clinic had only cancelled the ineptitude of the A.A. receptionist. It hadn't changed him. Kathy shouldn't have been so aggrieved that they had a spat about her co-signing his Social Security checks.

"But I'm not twenty-one," she said for the umpteenth time.

"Change your I.D."

"I can't."

Once he realized she wasn't going to back down, he became mad and rushed out of the apartment. He returned an hour later, lugging two cases of beer. His bitter tone of voice and aloofness clued her into who co-signed the checks.

Self-hate entered the picture to darken his psyche. The generous, shy soul who had attracted Kathy existed only rarely. Doug would lash out at her in bed, during meals, and in public. He punished himself by jeopardizing their relationship.

She stoically took the abuse and looked the other way whenever he committed indiscretions, of which smashing bottles and being publicly obscene were typical. She smothered him in love and understanding. The only thing she didn't do was sign his checks.

She planned to get firmer with him when the time was right.

He was improving when she carelessly let him see a paycheck from her new job. Recalling the abasement he had undergone at the hands of Bernard because she withheld all that money from him infuriated him. The argument that erupted ended with Kathy bruised and bloody, Doug gone, the apartment in shambles, and the police being called by concerned neighbors.

"Haven't seen anybody much," said Barn Hippie in response to Kathy's question about where Doug was. "Me and Shenandoah fixing to go to Eugene."

"Oregon?"

"Gotta get outta here. To where the air is fresh, where good people are. Can't trust anybody here. That's for fucking sure."

"Any ideas where he might have gone?"

"No idea," replied Shenandoah.

"But you're his friends."

"Nobody's got friends. Too much shit happening. Stinky raping everybody. Daytripper ripping people off. That's why we're splitting." Barn Hippie turned to Shenandoah to ask about taking a dog along.

No one else along Telegraph Avenue was helpful or too concerned about his disappearance. Midge Jesse's offhand remark about how he'll show up somewhere, sometime, particularly angered Kathy.

"In the bay, face up, and you don't care."

"That's his business."

The first few days after his disappearance, she was beside herself with grief and guilt. She was on the verge of calling the police. She also felt betrayed by her former friends. But she recovered, much to her amazement.

The men she met at work helped. However, the sense of independence she started to feel helped much more.

Making her way was very appealing. It might have been the reason she had run away in the first place.

Doug was so much out of her mind that she didn't immediately recognize his voice when he came calling. His angry tone caused her to lock the deadbolt and keep it locked when he called out her nickname. It was obvious he was in a drunken fit. Reasoning with him was impossible. He began slamming himself against the door, loosening pins from the hinges. She reached for the phone.

The battering stopped. One pin tinkled as it quit whizzing around. The louvered window exploded in a thunderous tumult. Kathy jumped. The phone slipped from her hand. She was pushed away while trying to retrieve it.

"It's cool. Nothing's wrong," Doug nervously said into the receiver. Rather than hanging up, he yanked the phone off the wall.

"You bitch!" he shouted while pushing her. "I've seen you with other men. You slut. I've been watching."

"I can do what I want with my life," Kathy replied as nonchalantly as she could, wishing she hadn't gotten hold of the police.

He unleashed a barrage of insults. Unimpressed, she shifted her weight, so her hips displayed her disconcert. The knife he pulled did not change her attitude. She saw through his histrionics. A downstairs occupant needn't have rushed to her rescue. Doug never would have hurt her. The melodrama embarrassed her.

"Stick me if you have to stick someone," said her neighbor.

Doug made an incoherent sound.

"Let me have the knife," said the neighbor, extending his hand. "I'll see no charges are pressed."

"This is stupid," Kathy had the composure to say, even though Doug held the knife at her throat.

Sirens screeched to a halt in front of the building. Doug bolted to the rear. Two loaded-down policemen clambered up the stairs and hurried through the door Kathy opened for them. They disappeared into the kitchen. Sounds of a struggle were heard from the rear. Obscenities rent the air. Kathy raced toward the noise to find Doug handcuffed between two other policemen who must have come up the back way.

"Joe Blow," Doug answered.

Kathy was interrupted before she could completely answer.

"I know him!" exclaimed another policeman. "He's wanted for grand theft and assault."

"And more," said another whose face brightened with recognition. "He's Peter Smith, Doug Dewitt, Alan Watts...whatever's on the credit cards he steals. He's got a record as long as your arm.

"The shit gets off all the time. Psychiatrists and social workers pet him. He's, their darling. They broke the law right after leaving their offices. Should lock him up and throw away the key."

"Fuck you, Kathy! Fuck you all!" Doug screamed while being led away.

"A real creep," reiterated a patrolman as he threw Doug into the back seat. The officer's call letters crackled over the radio. He and his partner jogged to the driver's window, leaned in, and by turns talked into the microphone; after which they slid inside and were off.

Kathy watched the traffic make way for the cruiser. She also saw three street people give the car the finger.

REMINISCENCE

The glow of light was strong on Gam-ou's face as he sat facing the westward sun. It was warm, but he was not fooled. It is always warm and bright before a chilly twilight. He was hot, but only he knew or cared. All day he had walked on the rocky, uneven ground, stumbling behind what was left of the tribe, often falling and colliding into bushes but waving away any aid, whether imagined or not. As chief, it would be the sign of weakness to accept all manner of aid. Nor did he complain, entreat any guardian god, or utter foul words whenever he lost his equilibrium or lost his vision. He had fallen behind and remained behind, yet continued on in the direction of the weakening noises to his front.

Then he ceased trying, relying on his husband's strength. He knew what they were doing. Long ago, he had forced acute hearing upon himself when the sharp hills lost their edges and took the form of clouds, becoming dimmer and dimmer. It was a long time before anyone knew. Olsep, his son, and Mamuk, Olsep's son, didn't know that he identified animals not by sight but by sound, memorizing each habit until his ken was second to none. Only recently did he slow the tribe in its vital wanderings, becoming more of a burden than an asset in a land rapidly filling with a warring enemy.

There had always been a strong quality for self-betterment in his makeup. That was the trait that won him the unanimous choice of the elders after it was admitted the old chief was unable to perform his duties, and his son certainly too unright in the head for consideration. Infested as he was with the evil the son was killed before it could infest others, maybe cripple the tribe as it had in former times, almost destroying it until the old chief's forefather rose, usurped sovereignty, and kept the tribe alive by cruel although necessary measures. With the passing of the chief and the end of his line, no new family would be allowed to create a dynasty, for fear of a renewal of the disease. The tribe had learned to be careful.

His life, as he now viewed it, was one of opportunities taken and beliefs firmly purchased regardless of the consequences, particularly during that time when the council was undecided about who should receive the power. By far the fairest group possible, there still were a few, three in particular, who purposely advanced an ill-fit brave destined to remain forever in their debt. These three were the most powerful, and their preference was on the verge of winning until Gam-ou bravely exposed them and their plan. Clever oratory, with cunning to match the opposition, allowed him to be heard, his judgments considered by the less strong but more numerous. An insufferable amount of time passed in debate, all of which he spent defending life and limb. By learning to sleep with his eyes open, staying constantly alert to any and every possibility, he remained alive to forward his belief. At the end of the long talks, the three conspirators were revealed, banished, and he was elected as leader. After more deliberation it was their intention not to honor his adjunct wish to award his unborn with a heritage; but so well had he conducted himself in the face of grievous odds that they relinquished and agreed that his first son would become the chief only after he proved himself the owner of a strong body by surviving five nights on an exposed hill.

It was fair, and Gam-ou was fair and accepted. Along with that, sometimes overshadowing it, was his innate energy. Everything he had started, no matter what the problem or odds, he completed with zeal. This, he remembered, had been no different...his resolves were made without trepidation, and in their propagation he had been ruthless. No one worked harder than he, for he was more than a leader, but a man whose example was worth following. Results came fast. Sodden spirits rose, the old challenges arousing them as furiously as the new. The long losing trends almost reversed themselves. The disease abetted.

In all the years, he never admitted, but always knew, that at times haste and anger superseded patience and intelligence, to an unfortunate end. But that was long ago, and he grew out of it. He must have, because few complained, and who was there more capable of containing himself than he when he buried his firstborn on the same hill where he died. And when fortunes ebbed further for him and the tribe, those unborn during the choosing ran red with criticism were ignored, while letting his actions speak louder than any verbal defense. It worked until his body, not his mind, gave out.

His hand instinctively rubbed a soft wound. He had been bruised before, many times before sight and speed crept away. His bare feet had countered incessant queries by forming a scabrous hide as tough as leather, impervious to fallen cones or pointed needles. He had no wish to see if any were now embedded.

When young, it was his pleasure to remove the sharpest objects in front of the squaws; their sympathy was his source of delight, and the more they pitied, the louder he sang his song.

He had been shamed before, before the choosing, when he was learning many skills and torn between striving for adult wisdom while rocked by youthful exuberance. It was he who quarreled with Mamel, the small, over whose arrow killed a large buck and lost that quarrel after it grew into a fight. He still carries the scar, just under his left ear, and several of the youths rallied 'round the fact in jest, sometimes in seriousness when his commands varied from their opinions after he became their chief, Mamel is gone, crippled in an attack and left behind. Because the rest who knew either preceded or followed him in death, there wasn't anyone to object to his lie when Mamuk, on his grandfather's shoulder, asked about it. Gam-ou regretted that lie since and regretted it now that he once again thought about it. Still, Mamuk was so proud.

He was fallible, of that he was certain. Others had their bows snap on them. Lose canoes because of improper repair, and so did he, although he never mistook a family of goats for an enemy band as Mamel once had. In times past, there was not one noise, be it a bleat, a shriek, a squeal, any signal, or the song of any beast that he could not immediately identify, figure the direction, perceive the distance, and understand every note.

Skills abounded in the tribe, bravery was no more than an ordinary state of affairs, as accepted as the air, the boundless land, undeniably plentiful and pure, and regarded only in a negative sense. A person without manifold courage was rare indeed. Then why were they, once dominant on both shores of the river and controlling as far up as they chose, now cowering from sight, shunted into and out of the trees, around and over the hills and rocks? The gods must have cursed them; that was the only explanation.

If only his body had held up during the darkest days of the invasion. His vow to breathe life and unity in the rest still held longer than any of those reigns heard in tales told to him by the elders. As long as he bristled with golden flame....but they ceased to listen, lost their unity in their constant bickering, and he, of all who didn't deserve it, survived to witness the end.

They were far ahead now, no longer soft pedaling on bare dirt near the prickly brush that grows by itself, but traversing the slope to the waters where hid the canoes. He heard several grabs and shakes of the brown birch tree, so often used for balance that all its bark was lost even when he was in the first years of his rule, just after he led them from the sea's side inland. Olsep had climbed it when still a boy and waved to his father from its highest top. There, too, he had won his first fight and shyly asked for the hand of Ellos, the beauty who died giving birth to Mamut. Their secret love sign, smoothed through weathering, could still be seen. There are no branches so low to the ground to cover it. Those higher up are brittle, without fine lines, but lined harshly against the evening horizon. Still, it stands, free from blight, watching other trees come up and die off. The gods themselves had tried to feel it, vainly striking with flashing fingers from a clear sky. It proudly bears the mark that looks like the underside of a cat. It's not ashamed of its age or scar—"And neither am I" Gam-ou pleaded in his native tongue to any spirit who might have tuned in to his hard won deduction...demanding that his wisdom was still good, in its way a availing as the tree is yet for balance, for dreaming, for lovers to etch their love on.

Before Olsep was there to climb the green boughs, they lived half the year by the sea, in a marshland, and just witnessed the oncoming of the enemy.

Gam-ou was young, very young then, and reticent about picking a bride. Although chosen as chief and certainly the most eligible bachelor, he, with the spirit of the young, labored under the knowledge that he must prove their choice correct.

It was the early part of the year, the worst part for the practice of stealth, as the mud clung to the feet, reluctant to give, and giving only after much noise. Only the ablest of stalkers could have won as close to an enemy encampment as he that night. It was raining and it was cold. He did not mind. For that, he could thank his tribe.

Of the many traits passed on from previous generations, they retained a few that once assured their supremacy. One of these, a minor one, was their abnormal ability to withstand the sticky cold of water. Swimming in the slow winter stream was never a feat to them, nor was the ability to hold their breaths until blue and maintain perfect vision. And it was he whose reactions were such that any snake on top of the water was in danger of being pulled under and rent before having time to strike. Gam-ou prided himself on that as well as his ability to snatch passing fish. Others caught them in their mouths, or so it seemed, as they rose to the surface with the fish all but swallowed. It took a while until he figured out they hooked them with grapples hidden in their clothes, then put the fish in their mouths before surfacing. Poor man, that Kashish, he shouldn't have hurt him so. But he couldn't stand cheaters. That's why he demanded to conduct that raid alone, where it was he against them with no room for reliance on talents he did not possess.

The prizes were sacks of down from a rare bird found only in the lands his tribe had never ventured to, as told to them by a wanderer whose loyalty was wholly to himself.

When the man said it was very light, easy to handle, slow to burn, and did not shrink or lose any warming properties when wet there was not a squaw who did not demand her brave fetch some. Gam-ou, without a squaw, was the first, the only one, to eventually go.

Rumors of monstrous scaly beasts that could snap a man's leg with a twitch of their tail, and demons that smote warriors with dread disease, daunted him not. He considered the enemy successful by the weight of their numbers, not through divine attributes. If they could thrive in such a land, he should have no difficulty in merely traversing it.

Stealthfully he came, quietly he remained, shivering all the while, until far into the night when the dogs fell asleep before moving cautiously in. That part of him was taught by his father: how to place his feet, how to look at objects askance to see them the best, and many others allowed him inside, first to slay the dogs, then the men, one by one, trading time for perfection and silence. When it was over, he took the scalps as proof of his valor (he was no fish eater, as he called those who feigned ability) and loaded the sacks on his shoulders. No sleep settled his flesh until in camp.

The light lost its shine, the white glow absents as a cool red wafted before him in still sections. His skin was beginning to feel sticky and dirty; his clothes adhered and crackled when pulled off. A wind arose at the same time two birds of dusk began their song, a raspy, unpleasant call to shelter. The noises of falling rocks and scuffed dirt were replaced by those of handling canoes, their hollow banging into the bark replaced by lower overtones of heavy cargoes.

With the success of that mission, he was acclaimed even by those who, although voting for him, did so more out of equanimity than conviction…it was his youth and all the rashness of its hurried pace that caused them to demure. Only then, after the raid, did they realize the need for boldness in the conduct of affairs- that victory went to the swift, and a wide chasm had formed between them and it.

With such support at his back, he ran off again and again seeking new honors by conducting raids so brash that those who followed did so with tremulous spirits. He was successful, but the more his exploits won their imagination, the less pronounced was the management of camp upon his return, until he realized that the rightful place for a chief was in camp, not adventuring far away. That was pointed out vividly when he returned after his third raid to find the camp rife with dispute, the elders fighting the youths over presupposed rights and adherence to old rules. It took all his ability to settle the wound to a point mutually agreeable, and it required his constant presence to uphold. That was the key—he had to be there, when he was everything was fine. When he wasn't in trouble stirred. Try as he might, he could not create, only rule, and without his guidance to follow, they were humble before any competitor.

As the years went by, he molded his tribe into the fighting force necessary not to defend but to survive as they countered the awesome numbers of the enemy. They became and remained mobile, shedding and comfortable without what many would consider absolute necessities. The old and slow, weak or lame were always the first to go at first lamented by those they had sired and raised into adulthood, but not for long, as, more and more, each day became a trial with life the reward granted to those most considered in saving themselves.

Whatever happened to those left behind? Gam-ou did not know. He never thought of it before; there was never any need because once stranded, they remained, resigned before the oncoming of night and the rites of the dark gods. No screams were ever heard. Not even from Nah- tag- he, the last of the council who chose him and who, in his last moments, wept piteously not far from camp. He had always been too full of emotion, too hungry, anxious for battle, and too kind-hearted afterwards, slow to kill the wounded who might yet have the strength to slay the unsuspecting. His was a passion quick to erupt, quick to die. Perhaps that's why he was a favorite with the squaws, siring ten braves who were now leaving Gam-ou behind.

Gam-ou did not like pain, nor did he trust those who swore they did not mind it. Before battle or on a long trek, hefting back-breaking loads while leading the rest, his soul pleading to lessen the burden, as he struggled refrained from hiding the anguish on his face.

Once, when still a young chief, he called to account a brave who refused to admit fatiguing and, ignoring his weariness, flew into the braggart and started to wrestle. The council, then in their prime, demanded it stop, and many hands reached down to quell the disgrace. Gam-ou would not have it. Through the dust and commotion, his tired voice ordered them off. He won, but not without the marks from many wounds. Worse still, like the braggart, his body was broken and tardy in obeying the slightest command. Hands that offered to carry him to the next hill where the night's camp was to be pitched, were refused and he remained intractable despite the soft cooing or giddy cajoling of the squaws, even those he, in his dreams, so lusted for. In his mind, there was much honor at stake, too much to bend under the want of another. So, the tribe camped there, on lower relief, susceptible to an easy attack from above. If any complained, then they must have only to themselves because he did not hear. Later, after the mellowing induced by years of brutal experience, did he chaff at his actions. They were those of a pup, and innocent to life. Bragging is a minor infraction indeed compared to famine, privation, and loss as were later witnessed. He had made a fool of himself and endangered the tribe with more foolishness. Why the council had not told him so was proof of their wisdom—it would look bad; there were problems enough without precipitating new ones. By swallowing their pride, they were men; by not realizing that they did, he was yet a boy. They knew he would grow out of it.

Sometimes he wished he wasn't the chief. He gave up a lot for it and the responsibility. He so enjoyed the leg matches and good-natured contests of strength and coordination and wished he could join in instead of pretending to be entertained by it all.

From below, almost parallel to him, came the chops of paddles cutting water, followed by the rush of waves upon the shore, lapping rhythmically up, too many to count.

The air became cooler, the sweat less sticky despite an increasing wind. He was comfortable. More birds began their swain songs, high and ecstatic one moment, guttural and resigned the next.

Toward the mouth of the river, on an expanse of stone that rose as a watchtower for the entire shoreline, an abrupt change in a blackbird's song had Gam-ou alerting his son of hidden dangers. And he proceeded cautiously around a blind corner on a lower slope, knife out, then instantly into the flesh of an unsuspecting enemy. The death song was more startled than frightened, thus ignored by others in his party, many more than the two could hope to handle.

Father and son had many occasions to rely upon each other. They thought the same, Gam-ou teaching Olsep all that he knew and quickening the process by warning him of mistakes he had made when Olsep was his age. Gam-ou was older than most fathers who had sons the age of his son, and his many years as chief to draw upon while they were still full of themselves gave him an advantage. This occurred because he wanted only the best of possible mothers for the best of all sons who, after the ending of the practice of the ordeal, when his time was nigh, would be the unanimous choice of the chief. What he wanted more than life itself was a dynasty.

Olsep was born healthy and able; he was lucky. The gods' curse was on many babies that year and hung close as they strove toward adulthood. It was a quick race. Those who survived did so because they gave up their youth and donned adult responsibilities. Boys took over the jobs of men. And the men carried twice the burden. The women, having no time to adorn their features, worked just as hard. They lived in a practical world, without frivolity, the adventure transformed by went into deadly seriousness.

A weak but sharp voice called his name. It was Mumit on the river, just realizing the situation and pleading for them to join. Gam-ou heard Olsep try to quiet the boy. Still, he cried. Gam-ou knew he must be in plain sight and switched his weight to get up and move out of sight down the near slope but gave it up. What did it matter? There was another appeal, swift across the water and impelling without compromise. Gam-ou did not reply or in any way act like he heard. It would be wrong to raise the boy's spirits on false hopes. If he spoke, Mumit would beg to be put ashore, and when refused, cry until his eyes refused to water, maybe giving their exodus away to some wandering party. So, he sat, like stone, awaiting the night.

It was fast approaching. The ground was starting to cool. All light was grey, without warmth. The layers of sweat lost their insulating properties and added to the encroaching chill. He shuddered; his gooseflesh was up; his ancestors were shaking him.

Like his father, Olsep put off marriage, not because he was finicky, but out of bashfulness before asking the girl's hand under the tree. She was gentle; he was shy, and Gam-ou approved of the match. Big boned and strong-willed with just the right amount of femininity, she had all the qualities of Olsep's mother.

He remembered his own wife's expression when Olsep first joined the hunting band. Sadly proud, she held back tears and watched and watched until they were out of sight. Gam-ou did not say anything, and when he felt his hand being tightly squeezed, he kissed just above the eyes of a mother losing her son to manhood. It was not fair that Olsep's wife lost the chance to see Mumit join the band. Many things are not fair.

Already, Gam-ou knew just the wife for Mumit, an innocent, round-eyed girl, gentle as the soft sunrise, entirely pleasant, and still happy. Hopefully they would unite and, later, see their brave off.

A branch snapped and fell from the old birch tree. The wind was stronger; the ground colder; the light absent. The roof of his mouth was serried with thirst. He had not drunk all day. He opened his mouth and felt inside. His tongue was puffed, the cheeks and gums dry and fat, accounting for his dizziness and why it was hard to swallow.

The birds of dusk were silent, replaced by one or two whose short songs sang of the early night. They were harsher than before, deriding the cold, the dark, the loss of sight, complaining of impending fright.

The canoes were gone, the river peaceful, just as it was that day of the tribe's last major fight. As a leader, he planned it very carefully, calling upon all the lessons he had ever learned and combining them with the best the council had to offer. Many suggestions were, or seemed, feasible, and it taxed him to combine and select the very best until, in his heart, he knew he had chosen the one most promising of victory. Even then, as he constructed the battle plan, he knew that it was a final, desperate effort with very little chance of success. The matter weighed so heavily upon him that the unanimous approval of the council did little to assuage the nagging doubt.

Abstracting the reports of the scouts, he was reasonably certain where their greatest numbers were and unhesitatingly ordered his main force against their center while, to protect his flanks, two minor forces with explicit instructions to make all the noise possible were positioned on either side. It was a ponderable chance, but proving their valor, most braves volunteered to go to the flanks, and those chosen were envied by the rest.

The land was quiet, reverently still, at peace with itself, and should not have been blighted by man bent on destroying man. The attack went well, their center folding and his stone flanks holding. It seemed luck was finally theirs.

Venting its displeasure, the land gave birth to many new warriors and, with them, allowed the enemy to bolster a weakening line, becoming so numerous that the formidable became an impossible foe, and they were beaten.

Only the bravest stayed behind to shield the retreat of the rest. Gam-ou suffered six wounds, Olsep five; both would have stayed until they, exhausted and without comprehension of the world outside their flesh, had not been dragged off by the squaws who disobeyed orders and rushed to the battle scene, banging on drums while shouting as only hysterical women can shout. That saved many others and blunted the enemy's charge by instilling in them a sizeable doubt about their apparent success. It worked well enough for the tribe to regroup and flee still further upriver.

That's where matters stood until Gam-ou's body began to wear heavily, the skin, so long in the sun, folded in ugly ridges, and his eyes began to fade.

There was no telling how long he had been there, the dark was complete, without change, and the birds of early night passed on in favor of the owl and the rapports of the Jut bird, the one imported into the upper river because of its down.

All sounds were magnified. A young tree with growing pains, a squirrel biting an acorn, and a rabbit stepping on a twig seemed inimically dangerous. He started on several of these, more puzzled at his timidity than at the noise. He never did that before. Perhaps he should be left behind. A wild noise in the night might send him screaming into the hills, giving the camp away. Yes, he should be left behind. But who would now lead? Olsep hopefully. He's able, but, truthfully, there are others just as good. He would certainly insist, and perhaps that insistence would cause further dissension, destroying the last shred of cohesiveness in the tribe. Gam-ou now wished he hadn't forced only man-sized virility. A woman's understanding should have been included.

A lump of spittle was choked down. His throat was hard, mouth was completely dry. He sucked his tongue back, hurting the base of his neck.

For a moment, he considered getting up to romp about and remove the cold coat the sweat had congealed into. It was a good idea, only he lacked the stamina. Best he save his reserve for the last, before dawn, so he may be the first of all those left behind to see the start of another day. Where did they go? What happened to them? A wave of strength passed across his body. If there was to be a fight, then whatever it was he must fight would have to reckon with a desperate foe.

The night passed. He was unable to tell whether he had slept. He heard steps, surefooted over the rocks, moving contentedly through the small bushes. Whatever it was had not seen him. Yet, how could it not see him? He wasn't in a shadow, a faint feeling told him he was in the middle of a moon-washed land, while his last recollection had him on the ridge top path, above the canopy of trees on the slopes that canted away on either side. There was more than one, all meandering about, disinterested in his presence, until, in a stroke, becoming hesitant, affrighted, then silent, forming by that silence one wide shadow that buckled the night in imminence. He braced himself for the end that was sure to come, passionately hoping it would be swift or, if it wasn't, that his senses would be equally blinded in a whirlwind fight.

Instead, nothing happened, the taut spring of opposites loosening each ludicrous moment. There was a sniff, and another accompanied by a return of the snappy steps. At last, there was a bleat and a mad rush down the same path they had entered. They were goats.

Trapped emotions relaxed in one wave, weakening him in his shame and loneliness.

Another owl hooted. He could tell it was another because its warning was lower-pitched than before. The misery of night returned and, once again, consumed his thoughts. No spittle was left to sluice down and quench his throat. His mouth began to palpitate. A new wind pasted the cold coat tighter and presaged the arrival of morning...the heaviest rains and strongest winds are perpetual signs of the dawn.

His trunk must be above the land, how else could Mumit see him? Maybe they'll return. When abandoning the members of the old council, he often had to fend against a dominating charity and twice returned to where they were left but never found them. Someone would surely do the same for him—a man ripe with lifesaving wisdom.

Yet, when confronted with the full fury of the enemy, he had called the tribe together and lectured on the subtleties of survival. And in those lectures, he had affirmed all the pragmatic ways of their ancestors, leaving the deathly sick or utterly incapable behind was one subject harped upon. If anybody would not be rescued, it was he. Those years dwelt upon it now sealed his doom. The probability of being saved was nil, he was incapable of fending for himself…what was left was the worst of fates. Capture. What fun they would have, what more fun if they found him alive, especially if they realized he was the chief. Best he goes, find a secure hiding place out of sight of any enemy, away from the winds and scenting of any large animal.—This would be his final effort, the last stance of pride.

Dawn was fast approaching. Early birds were singing the night's sleep away. Crickets were full on. One cricket wasn't and hadn't been since a giant form intruded his home, clumsily working its way in the crevice below the birch tree and struggling next to the remains of another who had done the same thing a long time ago.

OUTWARD BOUND

Puffs of white lingered above the purple and blue peaks on top of a wintery land. A many-colored mist lingered between the canyon floor and the foamy clouds. The mountain sides were deep violet, hinting more there than what could readily be seen. Milky rivulets coursed across and down the receding cordilleras that, along a central valley, ranged to a wide bowl whence the chain seemed to have been exuded in a flood long ago. Thin air invigorated the pleasantly chilled breeze to catch the top of the snow and blow it into drifts high enough to again be caught and blown. Not one sound needed to compete with the encompassing sights. North, south, east, and west were the lording tops joining the ascending slopes in subservience to that silence.

Sole speck on a commanding summit, a man could not unshackle himself from unguessed and unchecked intoxication. It shook him in spasms of tears that congealed under each eye. Grey breath puffed and disappeared and frosted his beard and mustache. Standing there, by himself, a solitary spire in a yellow ski suit, insignificance, any fear of rejection was lost to an aura of satisfaction, of belonging, of acceptance and welcome that invited from every quarter, wishing him to enjoy their offerings. They beckoned and he yearned to savor every inch, each shade, the air and quiet, not to miss a single instant or sensation, to hear and see and feel everything in an infinite invitation of good cheer.

Nothing bulged from his pockets. Neither of his two pockets were on his right rear, where his wallet belonged. He had no wallet. Nor did he have tissues, a notepad, number one or two pencils, or pens. No change jangled with keys on a steel beaded chain. No glass case could be put in a nonexistent shirr pocket. He was not wearing or in need of glasses. His eyesight was perfect. His wrists were free from a watch or a band of white to cry for a watch's return. The time frame he moved in was entirely his own.

Although he could stand and watch forever if ethereal and on top of his desires, he wasn't and was responsible for what was happening to his body. His toes were numb, and his legs were trembling from too much standing. He had to move down the slippery run. It was good there were inconveniences keeping him from what at the moment appeared a fine idea. He knew if he didn't move on, ski down the demanding slope, he wouldn't have the chance to view a different scene set at a different angle and elevation but not one bit less magnificent.

The noise made repositioning his poles did not offend the omnipresent stillness. There was no danger of sacrilege, of that he was certain. Short stepping clockwise he thrilled at the slickness, the promised onrush of speed and exhilaration. A push on the poles and he was down, racing and curving, cutting scissor sharp into the wind he alone created.

From edge to precipitous edge the cold carpet dashed underneath the tips, and replaced itself over and over, faster and faster as the man swished down and across the moguls in titillating leaps and returns that slapped the accelerating snow. The receding heights rose to touch the down-threaded clouds as he dipped deeper into the blue that was not blue at all but green and brown with stately pines spiraling up and leaning back in groves along the angled face.

Out of one grove and upon a second the last yard was saved for rooster tailing to a sudden stop, from where he high stepped it to the edge to see the heavy shadows of imposing and multitudinous shapes. As promised, every sensation, each balm and thrilling breath experienced above was revisited with the tinge of newness…as were supplementary points of observation the rest of his weaving way down.

The bottom—gained after a final burst—heralded and kept its vow to be no different. Looking from the flat floor, mountains up in august heights patterned the skyline and girded him in an imminence he knew to be even more imperial and moving. He was in a canyon a thousand dozen feet from the reaching plain seen only from above.

The dipping day colors were tired and readying for the promise of night. But there was no sad transition in the event: the exchange of the bright for the black. It's proper for him to obey the way things are. Although as tired as the hour, he was, relatively, refreshed and saw just that in his ruddy reflection on a frozen stream. A night light stayed for him to undo his skis and unbuckle the firm boots.

His suit was hardened by the snow that melted and clung after one of his two falls. It was like cardboard, not iron as the last time when he wore blue jeans and, not as skilled, tumbled so much that the universe could not help but see and ask if he was all right—a better solace than his wife who moaned about his staining his long john's blue. But the universe had no reason to worry; he was always all right. He had learned from those early mistakes so well that what once repelled him as impractical was now practical and vulnerable. Glancing up, he smiled as an assurance drifted down, predicting he would soon tackle the toughest tests. It was all so perfect…enjoying and improving at a sport reliant upon his desire to improve and performed before an appreciative audience who applauded every step of the way.

Squeaking atop the hard pan, becoming chilled and not as red as the warmth hustled closer to his heart, his muscles stiffened before gaining his cabin. There his cold toes were agonizingly warmed, a bath taken, and a steak dinner eaten. A slush lamp hanging above his cot fanned enough light for thirty pages of Kipling's poems before the book gingerly slid from his hands and onto his stomach. The bang it made falling as he rolled over did not awaken him from a deserved slumber.

Up the next morning with the first crack of light through the eastern window, he could not shed the last of his sultry dreams. It centered upon a girl, a blond beauty with features etched by Dianna. No wake-up, get-ready task could diminish its persistence. He had had enough of being alone. His desire to purge himself of people had passed, and he now craved companionship, only to have another to share an environment that gives and gives.

She had to be more than athletic and made from a classic hand...too often, he had seen the type blemished with a craggy voice or vile vocabulary. Nor could she be obsequious. No, she had to be intelligent and bright with the life that shaped her and perfect to cavort with around the spanking ranges and sugar-crested mounts. That was what preyed on him so much that it lost its fantasy as he prepared the runners of his cross-country skis for a lengthy trip.

New at the sport, he did not know which color of wax to slather on the bottom. Compensating for the indecision, the pack was made perfect and thrown on his back. Working the twisted straps flat, the man stepped out and forward, toward a mid-morning sun sitting dreamily atop the highest peak.

The going once absorbed inside the grooves got tough. His lubricant was wrong for the chosen route, and he started and stopped, unable to slide. Having to pick his feet up drained more energy than if he ran. Soon he was deep in the powder bordering the trail, finding to his misfortune its depths so confining he had to take his skis off. That, too, was a task more than manageable. So he slipped down the incline, his skis half on, furrowing a path he struggled not to make. A cushioned bump ended the unwanted progress.

Woven among low branches, the wet and cold did not deter his attempts to unpretzel himself. Up above, like a stage towering out of reach to a small boy, was the flat trail. Finding the puzzle too binding, his efforts were all out for that one key move, his tugging and yanking so comical he could not refrain from laughing. A mighty effort, and he slumped with a hilarity that did not drown the chuckling of another voice, one fringed in a singing melody. An incisive comment, the man appreciated as clever, interposed a girl's offering of advice as she came gliding down.

Helpful hands strayed from the labors as a conversation ensued, not commensurate with the service being performed. The agony was ecstasy as he was disentangled and helped up. His desire rose, and as it did, he was resolved it was shared in kind. The fact was established with his courageous look into her eyes, coying with token resistance, but resistance ready to flare if an overwrought move was made. He had to and did unwind himself before her in a way so appealing she was all over him getting him set to right. Whether she would be his companion was a question not needing to be asked.

The way was long and involved. Days were needed for the range to level so the plain where they put their winter gear away and walked, side by side, into the brown turning young and green before them. A lake was passed with Indian horsemen splashing ahead of a Spaniard, enraged at their kidnapping of his beautiful daughters. They disappeared at the same place: a whirlpool above a feeding river, first the

Indians with the girls, then the girl's father…to reappear on shore to reenact the legend of Saguache Lake. Other shades danced or stormed in the replaying of the tales that had passed through many fancies since the days of their conception. Ghost riders silently galloped to warn spectral men of impending attacks. Gold seekers, Spanish expeditions searching for the seven cities of Cibola, lovers and their loves finding unmitigated happiness or unbearable woe, and amid this were the two live lovers. Buying beaver pelts from Jim Bridger, they made the acquaintance of William S. Williams, M.T. (Master Trapper), born from a rainstorm and out of the mountains for rendezvous with lesser lights…Kit Carson withstanding. There too was Colonel A. H. Pfeiffer with his retinue of "Injun hungry" wolves skirting the camps on his revenge-soaked prowl for Apache's.

Everybody who was anybody was seen there. The known and unknown were equally delighted to share their wealth with the visitors.

They wandered northwest, days turning into weeks as both moved into a valley pregnant with honest and hard-working people just there after pushing handcarts from the east. A sea too salty to drink from captivated them with its primitive crags rising from the blue that evinced what the earth looked like when oxygen was new to the atmosphere. Around and over the land and times they went, pivoting south and returning via the mesas and river gorges of a land whose posture made for difficult going. The route traversed cut across, paralleled, crossing of the Colorado. But, unlike the fathers, the two did not want for food. And when they weren't trekking, they were discussing the mileposts of the arts, the commissioners of logic, science, and philosophy — the entire realm of meaning, both keen with and adaptable to new insights.

The grinning range opened its passes in greeting. Camp was made on the bank of a crystal, cold, and clear stream. Fish could be seen on the bottom, temporarily stymied by beaver dams. The sparkling creek invited him to drink as he dipped his canteen into the cooking water. The gurgling over the rocks encouraged and convinced him it was perfectly all right to forgo cupping his hands to immerse his lips and enjoy in the manner of the rest of nature. The water was frigid and tingling as it went down. Fantasies gave way to facts, the more his soul gripped the call to home.

"He is reacting to the solution, Cathy," said the psychiatrist-neighbor of Cathy Wentworth

"I'd better. Every sick leave is used up, and vacation time is only for visiting my folks, like I promised."

"Try not to force him."

"What he needs is a good whipping, like a little boy."

"No good. He grew that beard and mustache for a very sincere purpose."

"The fool. He knew Payton Industries didn't want their employees to wear them. It doesn't hurt to obey a dress code. Heaven knows I have. He knows I hate the way it scratches. He knows. He knows."

"Last time it was an intergalactic astronaut. Had maps and overlays, astronomical charts he made up in his universe. He's bankrupting us. You know, I had to pawn the China to pay the bills. That horrible Sue Kraus. My luck, she worked there. I don't dare show my face in public."

"I'm sorry."

"So am I. I married him because he had plans. Big plans…big deal. What can I do to make sure he won't slip back?"

"Substitution after he regains his footing."

"Again? The last time. Skiing! I knew he would break his leg. Should have stayed on the learning slopes like I told him. But how was I to know he'd take those regional books bought near Denver seriously? By the time we got home, his eyes dripped with the same watery look he's had ever since. From Captain Marvel to Kit Carson, and if we send him someplace else, introduce him to another sport, he'll just build another world. Maybe stamp collecting?"

"No, it must be physical. His life is too sedentary. And may I advise golf?"

"No! My sister's a golf widow and probably worse off than me."

"It's socially acceptable."

"Why do you insist upon substitution? Can't you cure him?"

"I'd honestly like to, but that takes money and more time than I can afford. I'm not a nine-to-five worker."

"We are friends."

There was a pregnant pause.

"Joe is my best friend."

"And the bridge games."

"Perhaps after work, when Myrtle has…"

"Fine, it's settled. We'll haggle about any fee after he's cured."

"It might not be soon."

"Oh, sure it will. You underestimate your skills. Be confident."

It was getting late and, after Mrs. Wentworth obliged him with a cup of coffee, he left precisely at ten.

There was a routine he did not vary from that; more than his skeleton was the fabric of his life. To bed late, he still had to get up early to commute into the city. H and Joe had once been members of a carpool, adding their drop to the bumper-to-bumper tide around the endless structures whose shadows hid the perpetual muck which defined the roads more accurately than the guardrails. That palled; despite the public clamor for car-pooling, neither could resist the opportunity of being by themselves, even if it was only to the train they decided was the best bet for the worst of the trip.

Although Dr. Winkler saw more of Joe Wentworth at the station than anywhere else, the crowd seldom let them close. So rarely did they find themselves in the same car. But when they did, it was noticeable they weren't like the rest, Joe losing himself in some volume of poetry, and the doctor with popular science. Never did they peruse the paper or thumb through a magazine, declaring their disinvolvement with the congestion and faceless faces.

Twice daily, the train rumbles by a smelly paint plant. No air conditioning could keep out the stench Dr. Winkler's son, clerking in the rail car plant next door, had to put up with. They see each other only occasionally and for just a few minutes. Little wonder. When at home, before graduating from college, Myrtle had him be home at ten sharp every night, no excuses. And that to a twenty-year-old. She always ran things. Disputes were always over when he got home. Her work was law and indisputable except for the one successful insurrection involving his son's trying out for the high school football. She said no. He said yes and, pressing the screws, won. But the other major requests he backed: Boy Scouts, wrestling, and baseball were lost. The boy wound up playing the piano and hating it. He hated to listen to him play. Myrtle's behests were like his own mother's—who insisted he become a doctor and threatened to withhold funds unless he changed his major from drama to pre-med.

When up for a breather from his reading, his mind covered many topics in search of refreshment, but all too often was snagged on the collisions frequent to the mass transit system. Not one aspect, from the initial shock on, was ever skipped over in his "what it would be like and how he would react to it" interrogations. He did not want to go that way, or in a car wreck, or be struck by lightning. The best way was to go gallantly at the helm of a schooner dashed by a typhoon; except he never sailed in his life. Maybe someday.

Joe was an inveterate clock watcher. He fidgets in his seat, glancing at his watch as if the train would hurry up if he were behind. Like a yawn, watching Joe made Dr. Winkler conscious of time. And he had sometimes found himself checking the second hand of his watch twice before completing the minute. There was good reason to worry. The clock was much more of a dictator to him than to Joe. Joe was in a profession not locked into rigid time frames. But him! A disturbed patient is harsher than the most heartless boss. Their despondency wrings tremendous imaginings, and they could sink irretrievably into self-pity if "their" doctor didn't care even that much about them. Neurotics blow everything out of proportion. He once found one who complained embarrassingly loud about the few minutes in the snack bar in front of seven empty coffee cups and an ashtray full of butts.

Whenever the train pulls into the station littered with the detritus of the city, he finds it impossible to shake a dominance of contempt. Not he for the city, but the city for him. It frowns and utters deprecations in the crowded and blaring atmosphere. It did not want him and would laugh if it squished him like a grape, enjoying the pop and ooze, and doing its best to make him turn mole during the ozone alerts.

His office was in the business loop, three blocks from the station and reachable by a sequence of underground parking lots. It was his habit to take the lowest level, where the blowers rumbled the impression of silence and solitude. Such an attitude did have its price. He once took the last, empty rail car early one morning after several hours of court on a full day. A schizophrenic he had pronounced cured, had brutally murdered a haberdasher in the way he had seen on a television program. Preoccupied with the trial and consequences, he took no notice of a hollow-eyed character until a moment before a terrific blow. They said he was made of very firm stuff to have pulled through. His insurance paid for most of the cost. But once out, he figured a severe drain of his clientele who, during his lengthy hospital stay, realigned themselves with available doctors. It took months to straighten out his credit accounts, and the quarrel he had with a policeman who refused to believe his temporary license was valid cost him an additional workday in a court appearance.

There was a spat with Myrtle the day he started in on Joe, but he won by raising his voice to her accusations and suspicions between h and Cathy. His friendship with Joe then took on an auspicious importance that continued to outshout her objections, sending her to the chocolates she always rushed to when despondent or on edge…which was all the time. Myrtle was fat. Cathy was even fatter.

That first night was a testament to his skill and professionalism. It was textbook perfect, personally removed and incise, garnering clues and new paths to pursue from beginning to end and lured coherent speech from the patient who hinted at an awareness of the real world. Had Dr. Winkler been a surgeon instead of a psychiatrist, in a formal operating room instead of a bedroom, and with tiers of glassed-off students watching, he would certainly have been a soundly applauded individual. As it was, when the hour granted per patient was up, the applause came from within. He talked awhile with Cathy, who assured the problem was being rectified, set before him heaping repasts as tribute. He ate while talking of strategies, being stingy with the convoluted words of his profession, until he eyed her admiration. He sprinkled more sentences with elongated and stilted diction. Everything was fine when he got home to clean the fan above the stove and drink port wine, watching a who-done-it on T.V. He fell asleep in his chair in the middle of a droning talk show. Myrtle sometimes called him to bed but refrained that night. She was having hot flashes.

In his briefcase the next morning, smothered inside the pages typed by his competent secretary were two books. One was a taunt Hemingway tale, that, as a psychiatrist, he found pertinent and interesting, although read it once before. The other was a book of stories about the Rocky Mountains, impounded from Joe.

Fighting the city-bound push, he managed to secure a train seat. And as he did, he had to justify his not relinquishing it to any of several ladies who glowered from their feminine prerogative. There was research to be done for a friend, vital research enough to make him defend his stand with a countenance that, in short, said, "go away".

The creased and frequently read book of stories was opened. Another world beckoned and taunted him to enter, to sit back and listen as an ebb fire crackled the fofarrow yarns. Written in the dialect of the speaker, the professional could see the sleep-heavy men pass the pipe, smell the perfumed smoke of burning hardwood, and was able to relax as he hadn't since he could remember. He was, as an observer, a keen audience to the Spanish silver miners on the San Juan ridges playing their stories in the fire's light. The sage of New Mexican deserts formed before him as tale after hair-raising tale unfolded in masterful narration. The snake that devoured the cliff dwellers slithered around the faggots and, lunging, snapped a listener up in panic then dissolved into a squaw trudging under the weight of an enemy warrior she was carrying to safety who, in his gratitude, saved her tribe in many an exploit. The journal of Spanish officers and friars that abandoned the leader of a murderous expedition was tensing with hardships and hints of the just desserts of the man when the smoke hissed and enveloped the men and the scene.

The train slowed to a stop astride a platform that materialized in front of the window. The doctor joined and kept pace with the porters' pushing racks meant for destinations further down the tracks.

A veil he alone saw protected him from the glum scenes spreading from the sign, "to the trains. Spurning the low-level catacombs, he went up the escalator to the tiled lobby populated by racks, counters, and plastic chairs with televisions bolted to the arms—all being looked at, utilized, lounged in, or bypassed by endless movement. Sunlight, patched in blue, led him out and to look up. A cloud assumed the humped shape of the rescuing squaw. A gadding soldier of fortune on the brink of his fate followed her, as did the soldiers of the lost party, columned up in not-so-perfect ranks and rows. This was not like him. To toy with his senses was a vile act for one needing a removed attitude, a clinical mind. What fighter there inside came out to ward off and force him to pretend the imaginings were just that and not seen. His intellect concerned itself with the upcoming affairs of the day. But the uneasiness did not quit.

He looked at his secretary from an unavoidable different viewpoint. She was more than an efficient worker, there to earn money for more college. Her svelte lines were attractive, like both the Spaniard's kidnapped daughters; her voice was melodious, like the reassuring squaw. Everything about her sparked with a beauty out of place in a business environment. Somehow, his voice changed during his customary good morning. Her response, her replacing the usual: "have a nice day, Dr. Winkler" with an effervescent and compassionate hello, balked him so bad he could not recover. He smiled an unabashed smile and swore she puckered her lips in a blown kiss. He must have imagined it.

The day advanced as no day had advanced since his college graduation. An expectancy was in the offing. The hours until lunch were agonizingly long. And the lunch hour miraculously found him asking his secretary out. A yes was immediate.

On the way down the sidewalk, instinctively navigating around obstacles and avoiding pedestrians without touching, he learned about her, how she came to the office and why, and what her plans were. It was surprising. The stuffy airs displayed at work were a façade. Her real self was erudite and spunky, with a brass and sass and a movement of life that admitted she had to fabricate a business mind and plastic attitude in order to get through the day. An avid outdoorsman, she fondly recalled the month's long hike she and her girlfriend went on in the Pacific Northwest, her mountain climbing, the soccer team she was on in school, and the poetry composed when in a cave on an Aegian isle.

The restaurant was crowded with many veteran patrons like him. There was no hope of not being subjected to several indiscretions jokes certain to be dragged home as gossip. He didn't care. He wasn't doing anything wrong and found her conversation legions beyond theirs. They never did realize he wasn't as avid a sport fan as they. That he talked about it at all was attributed to their dwelling upon it and he not wanting to be a social recluse. Sure, there was shop talk; his colleagues were crows chattering about this client or that. Those two were his only choices, all day, every day in and day out. It was a capsulated world exposed by the girl who had a journalist's talent to understand and combine the myriads of other capsulated worlds into a coherent whole. He raptly listened, too interested to say much up to the unwanted hour when both had to return to their occupational conformities.

His craving to return to the book was dampened by knowing the pages would open after he left her. Relief from the two opposites was found in his work. Nothing disturbed him all afternoon once at it.

When the last client had been reassured, the finishing touches applied to a report, and the office readied for the janitor, he repaired to the elevator. A hopeful glance at the receptionist's desk took him aback. SHE was still there, waiting. Together they talked and walked to the station, oblivious to the city. The parting was the shaking of hands and a, "I wish things were different," look on his face and a, "don't feel so low. What we've got is fine enough," on hers.

She monopolized his thoughts until added as the heroine in the doings of the Blackfeet, Utes, Snake, and Crows.

More disposed to get to Joe's than listen to Myrtle's after-dinner discourse about what a selfish person their son was, he excused himself and left without piling the dishes in the sink.

The hour normally allotted elapsed into two and moved close to three. More than a doctor's inquisitiveness was exhibited. He asked questions not related to the cure.

Joe was not drawn three hours closer to sanity. Cathy was sobbing and entreating powers beyond his for a remedy because the end of their savings was nigh. He could not put his arms around her, but led her to his place and, milky with diplomacy, got Myrtle to promise her an in, in the laundry chain where Myrtle managed a unit. Tears still streamed until assuaged by the news her children could be put in a day care center, the cost of which could be written off federal income taxes. The women then hurtled into that kind of talk singularly female, but the doctor did not hear. He was busy elsewhere, not observing, but in the circle about the fire, eating up the tales the mountain men were telling about themselves, and laughing at Jim Bridger's interpretation of Shakespeare.

What little realization there was of getting ready for work the following morning occurred through a crisis in his life. Waiting and keeping his distance from the twin commuter tracks, a charge of incredulity could not be withheld. Of a sudden he had no idea what or why he was there. Last night's stories were about events that distinguished the years for the tellers. But him! What did he have? Years of todays were represented in a moment of revulsion. Yesterday seemed the day he completed his schooling and, with Myrtle, embarked upon a promising career. He had not felt the flow of time. But there was no repudiating the years; the yardstick being his son, his grown son clerking in the parts department of a rail car manufacturer.

An evening's worth of reading was crammed into the ride to work. The pioneers were gaining hold and the mountain men losing their grip on the land when he emerged from the subterranean chasm and into the light not as blinding as conceivable possible. Stone-faced walls surrounded him, dark river gorges everywhere spewed torrents into a central river. The granite and marble were the same on all sides as the injun fighter, used to judging his whereabouts by the distinctiveness of each canyon entered, found no points of distinction in these canyons and got lost. A uniformly dressed professional, dazed and foundering in a morning rush, stands out and can expect to be besieged by questioners. A policeman set him off in the proper direction.

The strong smell and sight of familiarity brought him out to perform the old conventions according to old covenants.

His secretary noticed the thud to his steps, saw the glassy look not seeing what was there, and came out from behind her desk. Her steadying touch, once recognized, stabilized him. She certainly was acting in a curious manner. The others there, the professionals huddled around their pre-appointment coffee, the punctual clients and patients, saw nothing that warranted such blatant affections. They had seen a doctor enter. They knew how a doctor should enter; hence, the doctor came in according to how they visualized the act. If he should utter Pig-Latin or Mex-Tex as he went past, they would hear and know it as doctor talk.

Luckily the patients that day were the same old reliables and could be appeased by mumbling the same imprecations that had exorcised them before. He was better by, and, to no small extent, because of the promise of lunch. The talk then was one-sided and spiced with colloquialisms and gestulations, not keeping to his character. It was obvious he didn't have the background to prompt credulity, but being sincere, was intently listened to by the girl. Mistakes were caught in some of what he said but not announced. She was no tenderfoot to the land or tales he was wild-eyed over. A suggestion was made, and the idea both leaving before Christmas for a week in the untameable center of the continent sent him tingling with anticipation. Any concomitant guilt feeling that it might be a no-no, was purged by the realization of a dream and a dream guide as well.

A better psychiatrist returned to improve his practice. Joe, by supplying him with the details of his fantasy, was fast on the road to recovery. Dr. Winkler had him convinced not to worry, told him his escapes were just the thing needed to revitalize a deadened spirit, where it could work demon fast for promotion. By not pushing it, saying lapses can and would recur, and guaranteeing he was not like an alcoholic where one more drink was fatal, Joe was up and at his job— much to the relief of Cathy.

All the books, articles, and magazines taken from Joe's reach for his own good were now marked and frayed, with recently underlined sentences and marginal remarks, not on the shelves but scattered across Dr. Winkler's library, the tongues of many markers sticking out. Pictures from Western magazines papered the wall.

The trip—the first time he would see what was west of St. Louis—was the upcoming event that made him purposely skip the annual alumni party and not answer the thirty-year high school reunion request demanding to know his status in the pecking order. No, he didn't do those because he was aware only of the promise and excitement of real adventure.

Undertones of derision abrading his respectability did not faze him. Everybody knew what he was about but was ignorant of the inspiration allied with the future deed. They demeaned him as base and vulgar. But they didn't matter, and the only people in his world were the patients interested just in themselves, who were daily losing to the pioneers slapping hands with trappers in for the season at Fort Bridger. By his side those days was his constant companion, turning heads and sparking the eyes of many a weathered face. And with continued cold receptions and reprimands all the way, he went into the nether world of better times and better places.

From observer to acquaintance, he was now an old chum whose shrewd bargaining and ready wit won him a reputation with those who swapped goods and regards. Fandango was added to the fofarrow when he introduced his Quaker witchcraft past to the web of late fire yarns. It was a fine time with these folks who still wore their bark.

But, watching the trains come in and wind away toward Deseret to the southwest, he longed to join them at the next departure. What indecision there was crumbles upon the smiling, "so go ahead" of his partner, the western queen. The skills of smithing and wheel right picked up during his stay, along with a willingness to help those in need, were responsible for his tardiness. Winter came without warning and the trains were in for the cold. "The miners aren't," was all she had to say. It was settled. They were to leave before Christmas, letting those behind to quaff their own holiday cheer.

That wasn't the way it worked. In the line of men were the Brents, St. Vain, Roubedeaux, the Autobeas—the southern Colorado men who changed course immediately to the badlands upon the rumor of gold.

Ready to take on any assignment, he was too eager scouting suspected camp smoke and got lost. Worse, no game worth shooting was anywhere and his browsing like a rabbit did not quite an incessant hunger. Indirectly, he plodded toward real smoke when ripe with the smell of cooking fires, too wasted to care when all signs pointed toward hostility. But his grit prevailed and when he ended up smoking the pipe with the chief food and friends were his. When he left he did with a fealty almost of family... a knot he had no idea how taunt until finding them withering in a famine. No amount of help was too much so when the famine broke, he was right with them, recapturing the stolen horses, which led to the hard times.

He stayed to care for them until they regained their footing and was doing their reconnaissance when what looked like an entire tribe rose from nothing to barrel upon him and a fellow scout. So keen was his horsemanship that the horse was the one who faltered, spilling him. Scampering up, not ten steps were taken when a lariat had his feet out from under and dragging him to a shadowy figure. Curses befitting the situation were heard—complete in their eastern twang. It was Myrtle!, taking him back to work and responsibility. Ropes immobilized his hands and feet and, like a bundle, he was carried home.

No time period could be discerned. The location did not vary; he did not, could not, move from a tiny, white canyon with a rectangular sun beaming white light. Periodic grey shades, drifting between the third and fourth dimensions, would come in, speak in metallic tones, do this and that, then leave him alone to doubt their having been there at all. One shade, however, did come in that was clear in every dimension. Nowhere in his secretary's talk was there the slightest ring of professional impersonality. There was meat to her phrases, and a communicated reason for the visit.

They said he was getting better and allowed him to join the patients recuperating in the ward. Nobody doubted he would win through the non-communicative barrier made since the time of his hospitalization. Each day was a climb up a mysterious ladder. The doctors glowed at his rapid recovery. And the day of his release was imminent when his secretary, steeled in resolve, her hair up in an ugly sister bun, bustled in, made demands left and right while brandishing important documents, and ended up escorting a very rational and respectable man with his things through the electric doors.

No roads led back to the city, to the skyscraper where he worked, or to the suburbs where he lived as her car, stocked with clothes for both of them, homed west into the amethyst and blue streaked above a vanished sun.

By awakening to the heat and gold of day magnified through the window, he realized that his having slept. Hardly aware of the car humming up miles of incline, his attention turned to the orange walls and empty road. The sights were restricted but monotonous in a solitary, charming way, conditioning the viewer for what was slowly approaching. Satisfaction and well-being...swell being considering his abductor...aroused him with sultry movement.

The scene shifted its sights and grandeur. A curve was followed on the road. A wall gave way, and an expanse spread before him in servings of quiet strength. Tock mounds heaped here and there seemed very close but were miles apart. The flat between them never never-ending, knowing the geological slow and steady, which demanded all things to take it easy. Slowly did the yellow carpet rise before the reaching spires that grew and grew and encompassed the car and its passengers. Imposing formations that could not end were composed of building blocks which sped by, both there to have the man, that precision of human emotions, staring with unutterable emotion. When on the highest thoroughfare, on the apron of the summits that kept a dignified spacing, the girl turned onto and up a pass. The accelerator to the floor, the car crawled to the top, passing over many, many switchbacks. Trees and greenery sank below the white crowns that tipped a polite hello. On top of the pass, with both out of the car, hand in hand, they viewed and respected and were moved by what was understood as an absolute.

The shadow of a sharp-edged storm wafted in review over a lower slope. A circle of sierras rippled in the distance. And the girl pressed the man's hand, affirming his comprehension of the vast sanity and appreciation in the clear eyes of imagination which shapes man and men.

A WORLD CHAMPIONSHIP

It was Plaza night, the good time celebration finishing off the week-long, three-countywide, snake hunt. The obvious winner, Ansel Head, whose rattler measured eighty inches in length, seven in breadth, had been hard pressed to maintain his modesty ever since snagging and slaying it. No one imagined a larger kill, and, in the week, none were half the size.

A regard for tradition kept everyone from admitting they already knew it had been stuffed and handsomely mounted, ready to replace the smaller snake from the competition four years ago, before Zielinski's tavern burned to its cement foundation. Intimates gleaned that Mr. Head was hard at his speech from the circumspect hints offered by Mrs. Head. Others had been kept waiting in front of Kieth Javonovich's meat counter until he appeared smelling of sawdust, of chemicals, and rubbing his hands clean of varnish with a spanking white cloth. (He never used a rag.) The customers had the courtesy and insight not to ask what he was doing. They knew his skill at taxidermy and mounting, three-fourths of the bucks and boars' heads at Zielinski's had been his work, and the moose's head, whose flat antlers overlapped into the face of both adjacent bucks', was once the talk of the town. He was now working on a sequel. His son's mélange of refurnished antlers above the bar promised a continuation of the dynasty.

The dining room, located to the left of the front door, rapidly filled up and spilled over into the adjacent, less formal snack area. Extra tables and chairs had to be brought in from the pallor with its oaken bar. Amongst this throng was Colonel Ream, the feed man, a veritable fixture of the place. Seated next to him and his wife was Major Blucher, a poultry raiser and one-time state legislator who copped the envy of Judge Maximillian, the hard moving but unsuccessful candidate for the county commission nine years running. An old campaign poster with a much younger picture of himself is still tacked to the telephone pole outside. Many others would be up still had it not been for a covey of neighbor boys and their obsession with drawing mustaches and beards. Fate and the town council permitting, he planned to keep the survivors up until that day when sympathies turned around and for his propositions.

Jim Pavlovich, his uncle, and their families arrived, received the cordials from Mr. Zielinski, and then found a table next to the wooden gate separating the snack area from the small change counter. More streamed in, funneled by the news of the record and on old world penchant for seeing for themselves. Those bent on observing exactly who the new arrivals were soon grew weary and directed their attentions to local conversations. The ebbing interest principle, an unnoticed arrival of several men, not just from Bayville but other communities, several from Austin, and one from Conroe.

Ansel Head arrived sociably late; his family, escorted by Javonovich, triumphed through the bar, through the gate, and down the steps to the dining room. Applause purled in front, buttressed the sides, and subsided in their wake. No one could refrain from it; the secret was out. All this admitted by Mr. Head as he self-consciously took his seat, face flushed around a tenuous simper.

It was a clapping crowd. They clapped Mr. Zielinski as he heralded the evening's festivities. They clapped with the introduction of the four who would play the Polkas after the speeches, greeting each and all, requiring of them a quick wave. They clapped when the runners-up were announced. Even those in the far corner of the snack area, by the pictures of the little league Zielinski sponsored and the smoldering ashes of the fire, and unable to see, clapped.

It was all a forewarning to a riotous applause when the winner was announced; the younger generation pounding their fists mainly for the effect prior to the "oohs" and "ahhs" that replaced the noise when the embroidered rug was removed from in front of the snake. Advancing to the stage, Mr. Head gestured Mr. Javonovich up. On stage, he was on one side, Mr. Head on the other side of the mount; a picture bulb flashed, then another, aimed specifically at Mr. Head and his success.

One of the onlookers asked where it would go, taking the half-hidden place of its predecessor just did not seem right. Many suggestions went up for discussion, mumbled and led nowhere until, in jest, the major propounded its replacement of the curved rifle suspended above the bar. Most agreed as the argument passed through the crowd. It was settled, thus portraying how fleeting emotions are. Had someone made that suggestion a year before, he would have been an instant outcast. Gone was the rifle's owner, but not his influence. His Yankee manners and prosperity had long been a sore spot until that day when he went hunting with the weapon inadvertently left propped against the old furnace the night before.

The servers waited impatiently for the end of the laborious speeches before the rush from table to table, which turned the audience's attention to the platters of chicken.

Those quickest to finish did not interrupt those with more refined habits and entertained themselves by glancing about the room. A stirring revelation was made.

Everybody knew that Javonovich was an excellent butcher and a flawless artisan, but only the men considered those attributes small indeed compared to his command of the rocks (dominoes). He consistently beats the major, a superb player and once considered, by not a few, as the best there was. It was Janovovich who pursued the craft on the cement foundation after the fire. But ho! There was J. B. Baylor, brandishing Conroe colors, and Bill Moles from Austin's City Lounge with its garish furnishings. Moles was dressed just as fancy, and this irked those now cued to his presence. In him they could see the shag carpet, the adornment of the rich city, pallor, that was all wrong and anathema to the real player. It's like crabgrass in the outfield, a football stadium in a quarry. They even allow women inside. Whereas, Zielinski's pallor is all that is proper, a sanctuary for the best game in the world; its wooden furnishings, clinging beer smell, all male atmosphere when the play was on, is just the thing for the old time purist. The word, in transit, reached Javonovich, busy mincing his chicken with a surgeon's care, alerting and compelling him to quit eating and tend to the propagation of the signal. More intruders were spotted. There was I.W. Stuart, paying no attention to much beyond the meal; Jim Cardwell, equally insolent, known as Big Jim more for his loquaciousness than size; and, most important, Champ Thurmond, too slick not to sense his preeminent disclosure. It's he who contends that the small shanty behind Bud Evert's combination filling station and icehouse in Putnam, Texas, is the center of the World's best, THE championship, matches. Every Saturday afternoon, he and his bunch congregate and settle the title with him as a perpetual winner. Since the days Thurmond beat his father, decades before, and established his prowess, exactly what should accompany his name was in doubt, contested by those of Zielinski's way before deciding to build a pallor that would be the bastion of their school.

Ill words had rent all cordiality upon construction and the vaunting that their establishment now hosted the World's Championship every Saturday night. A match was arranged in the once neutral El Eunice Grill in San Antonio.

Nothing came of it, and by proving nothing, it solidified the resolve of both camps.

Before his pallor, Zielinski himself was the champion, then Major Blucher, and finally, ultimately, Javonovich. It was he who took on Dr. LaRouch, M.D., from Beaumont, Texas, a man of renown skill, and thumped him 14-1, so hurting his ego that he strayed away to settle somewhere in California. As his fame spread, other pretenders came to Bayville. All but one left, ingloriously defeated, and that one later lived to regret winning 6 games out of the series of 15 that entitled him to a rematch...which he lost 15-0. Last word had him in the Gulf on an offshore drilling rig, far away from the main tide of humanity.

Shrewd as well as gifted, he insisted, whenever he played the major, upon a series of 30 games—just enough to counter any run of luck. For anyone else, the 15-game limit was mere habit.

After claiming his title from his father, Thurmond moved increasingly toward constructing his pallor but never did. Zielinski, a hard-spoken man who had the title thrust upon him by those who opposed Thurmond because known players, no matter what their ability, whether self-conceited or by others, went down to him as a matter of course. Had he had a killer instinct, he might easily have become a legend. Many had told him just that, but he didn't care; it wasn't his nature to compete, at least, as fiercely as what otherwise would be demanded...this he had known and, better for it, knew his true place as an impresario. Picking

Bayville as good as any town, he bent to the task of formalizing his school…a clean school without all the tactics he abhorred in the other and seen in every pallor ever frequented since taking up the game. It was his dream to oversee matches, devoid of psychological tactics or many of the other gimmicks that made up for talent. Cheaters eventually wore welts on their wrists, placed there by the willow riding crop used by an ancestor when defending his country from Fredrick the Great. It is marred, not by the dead horse that fell on it, or countless hides slapped, but by the time it came down on the massive hands of Ken Wheeler, a man Zielinski spent two months watching before he was certain hide double fives that guaranteed the securing of many farmers' weekly earnings.

It was no holds barred in the other camp---that's why the dichotomy. I.W. was accused of fingering a slightly abraded set of ivory rocks in the San Antonio match. And there was evidence of signal passing after another set was brought out, J.B. Taylor fighting innumerable sneezes, Thurmond's pockets jingling with loose change, and he not above insulting Pavlovich's play, calling it amateurish, unimaginative.

The plates were finished and picked up; the tables were pulled to the corners as the merrymakers prepared. But the music was shallow and short on vivacity, the lilt and swing produced by whole efforts replaced by reliance on mechanical ability that was not art; the musicians were ardent supporters of Zielinski's school and enemies of the spurious camp they were now so keenly aware of. The women sensed the lackluster performance but did not know why.

Custom and dogma, the explicit rules of a man's game, had banned them to far precincts whenever a match was in the offing—that resulting from a part of man's nature no female could be expected to understand, no different there, in the country, than in the cities with their rich bars enabling businessmen to get away, renew emotional ties that linked modern man to his hunting band forbearers.

Being women, daily associated with men's abuses and gluts, they instinctively allied this passion for sequestered gaming with palpable debaucheries: communing with low girls, spitting, dispersing man-jokes, doing all the things not allowed in decent homes, and using language that would foul any boy's gestating English.

Few participated in the prancing and spinning, and those only by the incessant urgings, arm tugging, and pulling "comons" by their wives. Whenever one couple whose husbands hailed from opposing camps came close, they repelled as fast as two like charges, this occurring so often that each group gravitated to a separate corner of the room. Murmuring was heard inside the music. Eyes strayed, pretensions abounded until, in their minds, two races had been separated from what, at first, looked like a homogenous whole.

This continued, and the walls were rows deep with objecting women and adamant men. The dance floor was all but empty before Zielinski, not one to hold his mend quiet, put an end to the obvious sham at revelry.

"What's yer purpose here?" he demanded of Bill Moles, staring intensely, hands firmly pressed on his hips, lips pursed tight, in accusation.

"Same as the rest" replied Moles with an ease that fooled nobody. "Ta sees if the snake was real."

"Mine too," exposited Thurmond in support of the other. The others in his camp hummed in agreement.

There was a general pause, long enough for both sides to realize the enormity of opposing allegiances.

"Well, you dun seen it," continued Zielinski in a harshness that broached complete enmity.

Distraught, Mrs. Thurmond gripped her husband's arm. But it had the wrong effect.

"You want us to git?"

"Right."

"No matter, I'd seen it…seen all you got to offer here."

"And whatchya mean by that?"

"Exactly what it sounds like."

"Them're big words, kin you back 'm."

"Able to back them for twenty-odd years."

In the language of central Texan diplomacy, Thurmond had just removed his gloves and slapped a gentleman's blow. The next move was entirely Zielinski's.

"But will you?" said he immediately.

Reputations and honor were now refuted, half a century of rivalry about to be fought, and all chilled to the fact, en masse, on intrinsic order, the men turned to the women, gave them their car keys, and begged them off, post haste. Most demurred and asked what this grotesque silliness was all about. It's not often they get away from the kids and the numerous chores; they were looking forward to this night. Mrs. Blucher had spent as much time on the confections as Mr. Pavolovich had on the mount. There was no commiseration, and a stolid front of men against uncertain women, without a definitive rally point, placed no outcome in doubt. They lost; the most domineering of the bunch going last, but going just the same, one or two issuing invectives and threats over the shoulder. J.B. Taylor, from Conroe, was advised by his wife to catch the bus back if he ever wanted to go home. It was not acknowledged. The time when he would have to consider the means of returning was far away. A mountain had to be climbed before considering the descent.

When gone, both factions hurried to the task of setting up the bar area. Tables were put back where they belonged, the battleship linoleum tops scratched by diners who wielded knives into the chicken were covered by fold-out pads. Chairs were transported in by the score. There was a dilemma: who would play who? The judge was up for anybody, Thurmond included. Others hurried to the challenge. It was hallowed. Javonovich, by right, was the only man who should be afforded the chance. The rest, reluctant to be mere sweaters (spectators), their abhorrence fired, piled into the disciples of Bud Evert's combination filling station and icehouse school and raked up opponents. It was easy work, too easy, and a players' meeting was called to winnow the number of contestants in agreement to the number of sets available, two sets per couple being established practice. Yet, being a royal occasion, Zielinski broke out the royal equipment, further culling the numbers able to play. None of those cut-outs complained.

In the early days of his operation, he had two sets of ivory dominoes for each of the five tables. That was expensive; the linoleum abrading them; they chipped, so he switched to celluloid when celluloid became available. But, for the real thing, he conspired with A.J. "Junior" Bangle and bought his hand-wrought mesquite for a trifle of their cost at Neiman-Marcus in Dallas or Houston. Other reasons to hold those in abeyance were the spilled beer, the cigarette ash, which required sanding to repair. The judge was the most efficient at keeping his hands from showing the signs of labor. He managed the Co-Op, did not work, and maintained a deft touch. Many say that's why he was well-nigh unbeatable until Zielinski began pitching whole sets out upon the marring of one piece. An enounced slump could not account for twenty-five years of indifferent play.

Experts branded Zielinski's a losing den because of the heavier sounds made during the shuffling before the draw, speaking of celluloid rather than light impinging of ivory. Lack of funds, comparable to lack of status, was one reason used to object to his right to dominate the game. The other school with proponents in Waco, Conroe, Fort Worth, and

Houston (across from the stockyards), used ivory as a matter of course. That it carried little weight with Zielinski daunted them not, and they ignored his obtrusive comment: "Yeah, 'n there ain't two in the whole bunch that don't cheat, "bellowed sometimes by getting to the point and explaining that quantity outweighed quality because no quality could stand up perfectly to constant use "unless them moon men figer somethin' new in plastics".

His is a commanding respect for the game; everyone knew that, and ingratiated themselves to this knowledge, not the man. No one challenged his title of court historian, and a good time could be claimed if several games were won, new coins lined the old pockets, and, even in the days before the tavern, a story was spun by Elston Zielinski. The gamblers, the hustlers of the cotton towns of west Texas, oil towns west and east, breathed again, huddled over oak rimmed tables clouded by smoke, drinking local beer, listening and exchanging stories of even earlier days. Countless legends would have passed on had it not been for him.

Except for the two World Champions, it was still undecided who would play whom. The eight grimly huddled, surrounded by the close thunder of the sweaters. Picking straws was advanced, but upon investigation, there were no straws to pick. From the crowd, a hand reached out, unscrewed a large jar, and removed four sticks of beef jerky. Stripped into pieces, they did for straws. It was fair. Joining the champions were, in no order: I. Stewart vs. the judge,

Moles against Colonel Reed. J.B. Taylor opposite Ansel Head, and Big Jim Cardwell facing Major Blucher, five against five, but unevenly matched after discerning eyes fell upon exactly who happened there to check the story of the big snake. What was there was the best and the brightest, reputations all, and not a one whose fingertips were not as sensitive as any lapidary. No quarrymen these. Moles, for instance, migrated to Austin ten years ago, after making a living for a quarter of a century fleecing pigeons from the cotton sections. Putting on a pair of overalls, slinging a cotton sack over his shoulder, he'd march to a gin, sit down, and take all comers. But he could be beaten, a hustler, his schooling was carried by amateurs, as he shied from those just as good or better. Gaming took precedence over skill. The colonel wasn't that worried. Ansel Head was. J.B. Taylor was a well-studied and personage came! Losing an aggregate of one hundred dollars a week to the man, and let the area be particularly insular, very haughty, then he'd stuff his pockets with fifty, sometimes one hundred dollars a day picking the pickers. College-educated lawyers were lucky to pull down half that, and many a frazzled country doctor went without what he mimed as an official occupation and listed as an indigent on the registers, considered necessities. And loathing the easy marks, the train of pigeons, forced to find steady employment, and played most of his games against Thurmond, losing constantly but gaining a wealth of knowledge, accruing new skills, better tactics each time around. And Thurmond was invincible! Jovanovich was seated, but refused to show it, forcing himself to remain quiet although knowing full well that this man had memorized over a million combinations for every seven-card hand. A city auditor, Jefferson Davis Point, once calculated he had played 14,789 games. There was not one game when he could not write down who was going to win, and by how much, after the first draw...that being against a pro, not a hit or miss amateur, more than one having seen success against him until he refused to play any.

"Now don't you get flustered," admonished Colonel Reed, recalling that Javonovich's hectic pace and quick manners were his only flaws. His aggressive games were imposing against the canaille, but his lack of patience was a sore spot if countered by a procrastinator with just the right words to plant the seed.

"Here, lemme get you a beer...want some feet?" asked one of the sweaters listening to and understanding the colonel's argument.

So, the sweater ordered a Texas beer and forked one corn-pickled pig's foot from one of the many jars on the counter.

By then, the ten had fully settled in, the champions' table in the center and most dominant was surrounded by most of the spectators, many of whom were already ensconcing the players in currents of smoke. Pop tops, then the fiz added to the general atmosphere as all prepared for the long siege.

Right behind the colonel was Robert E Winkowski, direct descendant of the first settlers, a man light with his drinks and wallet, and a very liberal bettor who has yet to learn not to wager at the drop of a hat. To this day, he wonders why they laugh upon mentioning the bet made with Zielinski. How proud he was after wrangling the odds to one thousand to one on ten dollars that he couldn't jump Ray's creek at its widest, forty feet. Coming ashore after splashing nine feet out, he was asked how in the world he could make such a stupid bet. "Couldn't resist the odds," was his honest rejoinder. Things like that were his way. So was jumping off his chair and, with it, cudgeling the judge after he made a poor move that lost him a match, Winkowski gambled heavily on. The scar still shows. Little wonder the colonel was a little nervous as Winkowski made haste to place his bets on a clean sweep.

If the odds were against the home school en toto, divided up, it was another story. The major was a decided favorite in his match. Known as a politician long before officially earning the title, he was incapable of flustering. A bear could walk in with his wife, and he wouldn't notice. But a slight nervousness on the part of his opponent sent his killer instinct a tingle. He was heir apparent to Javonovich and given five years his name would be equated with that world checkers champion in Terra Haute, Indiana. His game was likened to a chameleon, able to change with any opponent. If he was slow then the major was fast, if fast then he was slow. If the challenger was silent, he chattered like a blackbird, or remained aloof, poker faced, even disinterested to any who thought intimidation the way. For twelve years the judge played and lost no matter how hard he tried...that being the principal reason for his crusty outlook on life. He knew he couldn't be so much better, their mechanical abilities were identical, and the scientific method excised from one of his son's philosophy texts should have given him an advantage. It never occurred to him that the major knew since the day he interpreted the news relayed by his daughter, a friend of the judge's daughter, that the judge was planning to be a world-famous thinker. All he had to do whenever playing him was not to give one thought to his next move, if he didn't know then the judge couldn't possibly know. He once toyed with the idea of revealing the fact in his will.

The major's beer was set to his left. He watched Big Jim handle his. He drank it from the can. The major called for a mug then enjoined the self-appointed servant to chill it. Big Jim was a rather sloppy drinker. The major was a paragon of manners, sipping it like a businessman's martini. The other used his sleeve to wipe his face. The major ordered a napkin.

Javonovich called for air. The sweaters backed up, but it did little good. Looking around he noticed a crowd twice the size at the start. The deer heads, normally conspicuous, could not be seen. Only the rabbit's head with glued on horns above the judge near the cash register was visible as the new throng milled about. They were the old men, what was left of the second generation that had for years settled uncomfortably in and found Zielinski's that last place where they could pretend to be boss once more. And they had hot heeled with the news.

All had some skill, usually minimal, but enough for a partner in an unimportant doubles match. These old folks allowed the major to pay for their games. He tolerated their misdirected but honest plays and bewildering tactics for a good reason-loyalty. Possessed with infinite patience, never did he berate their play, thereby winning them to his side when deep into an important match against a foe who had been cool to their entreaties or aloof to their presence. The returns are paid handsomely. So well that the other, whose concentration had been pestered by their snide innuendos, incessant coughing, or heavy breathing, started playing the game. A mover, the major did them one better. Half the winnings went in his pockets and half for drinks for them…that was his announced rule that turned them ever more toward him and the bettering of his luck.

Now they stood solemnly about, totally his, honoring in silence or about Big Jim, breathing through their noses, gazing their faces, twitching, and mumbling peas and carrots for all that was decipherable of the jargon.

By far, the biggest crowd was huddled around Jovanovich, watching as he drained his beer into his slanted mug, faithfully keeping the head as small as possible while the other, city bred and honoring no locale or custom, poured his dead on, misjudging the rise of the foam, enabling it to overflow, course down the sides and empty onto the table, delaying the start of the game until a wet rag passed over the adhering slime.

Designs started to form on the tables, each table its universe, with its personalities, number of sweaters, and importance assigned to the outcome.

Not five minutes into his match, I.S. Stuart went out. The judge, sitting under the gaze of the horned rabbit, had lost and, in exposing what was left in his hand, I.S. wondrously asked how much twelve and seven make. "Bless me, I've just made nineteen…that's right, isn't it? Twelve and seven make nineteen?"

The judge waffled it so and marked nineteen down in the column under the name of Stuart.

"Down goes the old man and last goose, "I.S. candidly remarked. The judge took a big swig from his beer.

Big Jim might be a sorry social drinker, but he was a fastidious player, or appeared so, and the major pulled taut the slack, calculating when the other pondered his move, but in no way showing it. He winked to the crowd, sipped his beer, remarked about the snake, the weather and was just into an old joke when Big Jim made his move, his hand barely removed from the piece when the major's hand was already on the table setting his own in place before settling back to finish the long story.

Those few around J.B. and Mr. Head were so because the rows were too deep behind those of more interest. No import was dealt with or considered. If Mr. Head won, all well and good; if he didn't, then there were four other matches. But there was no reason to lament their second-class seats. Good dominoes were played, intermingled with flashes of brilliant psychology. J.B. was a plodder, an excellent player without personal mannerisms, machine, smooth, wheeling, and deliberate. Not one to shun Zielinski's, many of the sweaters had played him, learned his ways, and, apparently, so had Mr. Head, who, uncharacteristically, was wholly flexible, looking at ease, moving briskly after a torpid series that went decidingly in his favor. So it remained, minus the promise of the earlier action, as J.B. continued along in his predictable way, picking up one count, losing another---constantly passing judgment on every moment before accelerating the pace that left his opponent and the know-it-all sweaters out and dazzled at his consistent success so by the time Mr. Head realized the only defense was his offence J.B. had retreated into the plodding armor easily beating the haphazard play of his opponent and the throaty advice of the spectators.

The row created turned heads at other tables. Had it been another man, even Javonovich, the uproar would be half of what it was. More than a fear of declining prestige was verbalized...it was a united affection for Mr. Head that added the clang to the chatter. No one wanted to see Mr. Head lose, not again. His entire life had been a series of misadventures, always starting well, but finishing abruptly in unhappiness. When young, he had ventured into Texas from New York, where his parents had just settled. The reasons he gave for leaving were vague but being eleventh out of thirteen children and immersed in the Chez section that refused to learn English, or the new ways might have had something to do with it.

When he arrived, he did so at the height of the influenza epidemic, when all the baseball farm teams in Texas wore masks as they played. The only job he could get was hauling freight wagons of empty pine boxes until he, too, was struck. It was mild and, recovering, turned his attention to ranching-only a hand-but he was learning while saving and getting in the good graces of the owners until buying some land, raising cattle, getting married, and settling his own before that one day when a blizzard froze the entire stock, and that not a week before the completion of the barn. What was left was lost to city lawyers who paid a neglected tax unknown to Mr. Head, leaving him no choice but to go to Odessa, to sustain the family left behind, throwing twenty-pound sledgehammers twelve hours each day for one dollar. The grind allowed him only the nights spent in the ten-man tents to forget the frustration. Cast among the rest and not to be denied by any possibility, he wholeheartedly took up the games of dominoes and poker, favoring the former more than the latter. There, too, he met Zielinski, down on his luck, gruff, and still burning about selling his farm in the Sacramento Valley for an oil lease that went bust.

Zielinski beat everybody, those claiming titles as easily as anyone else, boring him to a point of no amount of winnings could temper…hitting upon the idea of building his tavern with the newly gotten gain.

Mr. Head remained mired, making money but not enough, and was quickly losing his eyesight in the dim circumference of a lantern's light. Having become as close as any human could to Zielinski, he followed him to Bayville.

Unbeknownst to him, J.B. Taylor was educated in a similar school, only rougher. Eyes permanently squinted from long hours in bad light had awarded him the name of hawk. He tasted winning then, not just in dominoes, but pool and poker as well. A prince, the man was…never whining when he lost, always sharing those winnings, and through it all, he, as others, brandished a pistol. His only misplay came not in dominoes but in poker. There, he won several wells and just as quickly lost them to a laborer named H.L. Hunt.

But in this crowd, he went virtually unknown, unpopular because he was playing an underdog.

It was partway into that drubbing, with Mr. Head just starting to regain lost control, when, out of chagrin, one of the sweaters quit watching and looked about the room. A transitory something diverted his attention to the window. With no reason not to, he kept looking, expecting nothing. But there it was again, even quicker to pass from sight as it certainly saw him. By the window, he pressed close to the side, not having long to wait before a head stupidly rose from the bottom pane, eyes madly conveying back and forth, up and down, then dilating, horror struck in front of the sweater's toothy grin. The woman immediately vanished from sight, but had delayed long enough in her fright to be recognized. It was Cathy Wosniak, Colonel Reed's married daughter, born to die in a house. Worse, to imitate her father, she played Forty-two and its derivative: Nello. The shade came down with a resounding bang, startling those too occupied to notice his actions, instantly labeling him a villain before he had the chance to defend the act with the one word, women, he was hailed as a concerned citizen. Further explanation about who she and her proclivities had brought him the honor of an outstanding man of action. If there was any unity in the place, it could be found in the mutual abhorrence of those two offshoots of dominoes.

"Baby games," sniffed Javonovich.

"Taint fit for a man," agreed Zielinski. "Might as well play old maid or chess."

Notwithstanding a soul, a recital of the merits of dominoes over all other games was raised.

"Forty-twos a game any married couple kin play," Zielinski continued. "And what's more, they do" was the remark issued by the major that started the bullying of those sitting round and making the judge that much more envious because he wished his tongue was the one that made it.

He had further cause to moan. I.S. had ignored the commotion and put the time gained to good use. The judge pretentiously gulped his beer, but, as always, his trembling hands gave him away.

"Back home in Nederland," off handedly stated I.S. "there ain't a single pallor to be seen. Been thinkin 'bout startin' one up, give lessons…beginner lessons."

The judge delved into the rocks and shuffled while remarking, "can't brand calves 'till their caught" in a serious way.

The psychology played around Big Jim had no effect. He was unflappable, and still cautious in his game of defense. Two games and the start of a third could be had in the time his first game was over, with him the loser. A promise of a good gain elevated the spirits of those sweaters forbearing enough to have stuck it out. The jocular major did not share their assumption, he knew better, one by one, J.B. meticulously turned them over: three, three, and a blank, four, nothing of consequence…game that needed 250 to win. The downtrodden mutterings heard only from they who expected much but received nothing was not exhibited by the major who rushed into the tale of a man who was allowed to shoot a softhearted farmer's old mare and pretended to fire out of malice for the sake of his friend whereupon his friend, thinking the murder real shot the stallion, reasoning that since both committed a crime neither would peach.

Colonel Reed had his own problems. His tally now was twenty-six to twenty-four, not bad considering the reputation of his opponent. Nevertheless, he could not manage against a fierce sense of impending doom. With Moles in front, toying cavalierly with his psychic, letting him stay close before disgracing him in the eyes of the sweaters, and Winkowski, working on his fourth beer and smelling profusely, behind, he felt trapped, incapable of finding momentary relief from the pressure by sliding back without being asked some inane question or not smacked by Winkowski's stink. Little wonder he lost the third and the fourth game, and that by committing a mistake even he could not believe. He was goaded into and made fun of after by Moles's comment, "I'd love to get with you someday and figger out why you played it that way".

Winkowski popped a beer open almost in his ear. He felt the spray.

J.B. Taylor quit the safety of absolute defense and came out to parry with Ansel Head, only Ansel Head was too baffled, by far more concerned with saving his own than accepting the dare. It took a while, but he calmed down neither playing absurdly offensive or defensive, and just sustaining a happy median when J.B. lifted his chin and stared cat-like in its intensity and hair trigger control over unguessed powers, that wanted to know where he got the gall to play him.

Big Jim continued to win the mental war over the colonel. He, like the major, had and was employing one of his protean plays. Big Jim may have been slow, but Moles was impossible. Painfully he would grip a selected piece, carry it part way up, stop, wait, ponder in a subtle way that drew his entire body back against his chair, only to shake his head, and return the rock to its exact point of departure. Another piece was selected, also carried halfway up, also stopped, but in stopping his eyes narrowed into a frozen face, the ends of his lips turned far down, further than the saddest clown. At last, the piece was played, relinquished when his index finger parted from the left corner.

Mr. Head had steadied down, and became used to the stare, and was seriously considering asking Winkowski to fetch a pair of sunglasses. He warmed to it. It was a good play, such an act would flout the other, and direct the attention of the spectators to how silly he was. That he should do it needed no debate. Whether he would be entirely another matter. Time passed, clearly revealing an all too timid soul. Excuses did no good. He knew he couldn't say it and gave up.

He always was a timorous sort, often guising the fact in joviality and cheery smile. To the outsider, particularly an urbanite, he was not to be trusted. Everyone who labors in the cluttered world of man discovers that the most invidious competitors, adept office politicians, yes men are those who prance happily about, issuing good cheers as ingenuine as pyrite.

Bayville is not a world cluttered or replete with strange faces. Those he saw he knew, and they knew him and recognized him as a stalwart of the community despite his past. After a year or so of consistent losing Zielinski himself pulled him aside and forthwith lectured a half day on the absolute necessity of ridding himself of that bad habit.

"Yer gotta be mean iffya wanta play...laughing when yer lose...If I ever see ya do that agin I'm gonna shag you out 'n lock the doors."

From that day he lost the need to manufacture disingenuous and painful airs, shed most of his timidity while finding himself good at something.

Thurmond, dead even with Javonovich, had been much like Mr. Head when young, but there was no chance for him, when things really mattered to turn out the same way. Circumstances were just too favorable. He too found reawakening upon the discovery of the game, but he was thirteen not thirty-three, the day he found the meaning of self-sufficiency.

Since he could remember his father had been a man more recognized than the fathers of his friends. Not until he was ten did, he finds out why, once he did, he became sullen; it's hard having a famous father. His age kept him away from the Evert establishment. And for three years he was a melancholy youth, all the world beyond his powers…his life over before adolescence, when on that magic day, he was invited inside and asked to join a doubles match. The long dullness vanished as an instantaneous red success boiled magnificently in his veins, radiating from the happiest traveler into adulthood there ever was. His life was set, all he cared about was the game, beating his dad before his twentieth birthday, then racing off into virgin adventures. Only once did he stagger in reign, although contended, decades long. That occurred when love rendered her influence in the guise of a beauty ignorant of the strength of his first love. As is always the case, he set one mistress aside for the other thinking things will work out, glossing the new one with qualities she did not possess. It was Amarillo fats, world champion poker player, that fished him out of the bar life, cleared his mind to the point where he was able to file and win a divorce. He picked up where he left off.

Ansel Head began drumming his fingers on the tabletop. No look could be seen in down turned face.

The situation was in doubt at both the main tables. The crowd devoted to the major, was shifting back and forth, one even pretending to be drunk, complete with peccadilloes and totally obnoxious. It didn't seem to help.

Moles whose low but piercing voice announced the score after losing a game caused that crowd to hopefully turn their heads-reacting perfectly to the bait and raising one mass groan after he allowed the overall score.

"My sakes…already? I didn't think, it, again" ejaculated Stuart after winning another quick game from the judge, who according to plan was supposed to retreat into an immediate caution, but just as quickly won the next and countered with: "Mercy, that's the quickest game I've ever heard of" that naturalized any erstwhile ground gained.

The crowd maintained the same number only by émigrés matching immigrants. Twelve new faces could be recognized by eleven o'clock. The bunch at Roy's Feed Corporation and the Co-Op were there more as curiosity seekers than loyal attendants. They had little knowledge of just what's what at Zielinski's and, besides, had their own hangouts. It being their habit to eat and drink at every function by the time they left many of the refrigerated wines were gone, dozens of empty beer cans strewn across the bar, and all the pickled eggs, polish sausage, pickled summer sausage were gone, leaving only the corn pickled pigs feet, pork hocks, and jerky for what was developing into an all-night affair.

A flickering light passed through the worn gaps in the blinds, landing just above the copper foot rail. The old Nutrina Feeds sign was acting up. It as with all things was not just ignored but not noticed, so restricted was their concentration.

Each contestant was fast approaching his limit, closing every minute onto his true self. Had it not been for a wealth of luck, the judge would have long since been subdued. Drowsiness combined with that favorable turn had a stimulating effect that made him talk on and on, safe from retort, no matter how much he bragged, gilded the lily.

"I'll have you know! I once everybody in this place one night" was one of those blowings. "Folks said I couldn't do it, proved what their full of."

And so, it continued, hours on end, his past pounded into what appeared a hapless, chained, listener until the inevitable change of fortune, and I.S. quickly regaining lost ground and then some before remarking, "You musta been right good bat back then, rusty now? Gimme twenty."

Ansel Head, out of desperation, matched Taylor's stare with one of his own, and by matching the others slowness was lagging far behind the major and Big Jim.

Champ Thurmond was beginning to speak, pretending to have lost track of the down and accused Javonovich of claiming a down out of turn. Taken aback but still a gentleman, he made no reply other combining the help of the sweaters to reaffirm his honesty.

Came morning and those sweaters not around the champions, the major, or Ansel Head were playing pool, sleeping in their chairs, or continuing the drunks.

Probability had evened all luck out. The colonel had lost but was spared from Winkowski's wrath because his obligation to duty was stronger than any group loyalty. As for the bet, he just called it off. Not one taker argued. The judge met an ignominious fate and slunk quietly out, so disenchanted and broken that he snatched and tore up his campaign poster.

Misgivings now abounded, the bet takers not trusting their wisdom in most cases as the major was faltering as bad as Javonovich, a man beaded with perspiration and reeking of beer almost as much as several of the onlookers-those who would refuse to believe they had downed over twenty cans. Big Jim, as always, remained imperturbable, not once varying his game or in any way acknowledging a sweater's chide remark. Tight-lipped he had started and shut mouth he remained. Absent were the offhand comments voiced in other matches that, for a while, established color alongside his name. And they were sharp! Cutting to the quick with unforgiving thrust, known to more than one losing opponent. Sometimes blatant, most times disturbing like late in the game when all, but the other's rocks had been played or in his hand casually remarking what was in his rival's hand, maybe miscalling the guess allowing the other to play just what he wanted him to play to prove the error.

The major, and his fans, laughed at him, cast bewildering looks, gasped in amazement, and sighed at his lackluster ways, but he did not react. He had no emotion.

A hesitant light overcame the flicker through the shades and impaled to and through one large blue cloud. Zielinski had since cleared the bar of drinks and secured several hours sleep. Onlookers still watching staked territories out where they could find support and have some kind of view. Rights to these spots were respected as few were energetic enough to give challenge. If excitement stirred across the way, then they stretched their neck. If sight could not be gained, well, they did their best.

Premonitions and bad consciences were slowly being suffered. Not once in the history of Zielinski's pallor, before or after the fire, had the doors not been locked at twelve on Sunday night. With work everyone's religion, the custom never passed up for debate. Now it and the sect weren't even considered as tottering wakefulness deadened them to the real world as much as the soundest sleep. Even Javonovich, the example of old-world gilt and go known to have met the rising Monday morning sun with the abashed curse: "…And I ain't done a thing all weeks!" was lost in a universe of choking fumes, fuzzy teeth, dizzy heads, light arms, squint eyes, and a devil's desire to keep on.

The ray of light grew in strength, itching the shingles in sallow light rapidly dividing into grey then green before the yellow red of a budding day. The interior brightened. The blue cloud dimmed. A noise was heard from outside. It was a woman, a very angry woman advancing rapidly down the street. Not a half minute passed before continuous and belligerent raps were heard on the door. Nobody answered or replied to the comments made. Ansel Head didn't stir, and no one stirred to find out why he didn't although no man was ever more tied to apron strings as he was to that fuming puppeteer outside.

In little time she was joined by several others and they by an uninformed curiosity seeker or two. It was a strange sight, these women howling in larger congregations protesting an uncommon strike.

The strikers were not left alone; the phone rang continuously with no chance of ending until picked up. This Zielinski did and was in the process of offsetting it back down when the female voice bawled Champ Thurmond's name loud enough for those about the bar to hear. Significantly biased, Zielinski did not hang up but called the champ to the phone. Necks stretched and eyes watched as he clumsily rose, twice having to grip the table's edge before bracing himself. A welling although unaccountable, impulse ordered Javonovich to pull the table toward him in aiding Thurmond in his escape. Too proud to pay attention to the snickers and sly remarks Champ went directly to the phone. There, for the first time all night, he displayed a definite uncomfortableness and lacked control even in extenuation. To prevent the rest from hearing an obvious rage he pressed the receiver tight to his ear. Twice in five minutes he mastered an apology that didn't sound such. But the conversation continued, and he ran short of double meanings.

The tired eyes of the sweaters turned from him, the object of central importance, to each other. There was unity in their gaze and introspection working inside each soul. They pretended not to notice as he hung up the phone or gloomily returned to his seat. The phone rang again, this time for J.B. Taylor. Again, the female voice, the vituperations, reinforced by past irresponsibility, measured against her idea of what a good husband and father would do.

There was no activity in the room the only noise that from the outside and faint mumblings from the phone. The place was awash in sympathy. An obscene remark hurled inside fired latent feelings, confronting hoary stirrings long asleep into loud wakefulness.

Maggie Meyers, the oldest, biggest gossip in the county, pounded on the door demanding her no-account husband, come home to his chores. Mrs. Zielinski agreed.

Faces turned toward her husband, who, in answer, took the stump. "You may not have fess up to it, but I 'ave 'nd I better say it fer the good of every gent in the room. Thar's more than a world championship at stake here…what we do now means the fate of the whole game. Give in here 'n we're a laughingstock. Stay 'n we'll make a point nobody'll ever forget. What'll be gents? Go or stay?"

There was a pause for thought.

"Stay," said one.

"Stay! Shouted two more in unison, leading the rest in composit roarings yelled in cadence with pounding fists and kicking boots. "Stay! Stay! Stay!" continued the cry that resurrected positive calls to action.

Piloting them, more than Zielinski, was Big Jim at last free to express real, pent-up emotions by highlighting the game's proud past, of its rough origins, tough times, and fine future. Taking wind of these dialectics, Mr. Meyer obtained a spare set and, holding it high, challenged any comer to a match. It was immediately accepted. Others got their own sets until every ser, each table was in use.

J.B. slammed down the receiver and rushed back to his table pulling the chair up with a force that wedged him tight. The night long work that drained the color from his face was undone. What now showed was the vigorous red of rebellion. His moves were like the rest-snappy, the quick, and precise motions of spirits knowing a mutual responsibility.

And so it went. The morning, the afternoon, the evening coming and going as the group, enlarged by eager recruits, continued on in spite of those outside.

The outside crowd also grew, but considerably more flexible, with knots of people coming and going little wishing to remain. Cars could be heard passing by honking their horns. Policemen from nearby Taylor coming in official capacity left Zielinski's after muttering mere lip service to the necessity of so and so to return to the city's public works-their jawboning fooling none of the ladies.

A brick was hurled through the window. A woman was taken into custody but soon released as the policeman caught sight of a gang of ragamuffins fleeing from another act of vandalism.

Food and luxuries were imported from the back door until it too was blocked, trapping those inside.

By night, both sides knew exactly where they stood. What larder there was in the pallor was rationed off without cost. The many wines were held back in wait for the celebration all stoutheartedly worked for. A new night was entered.

By now meaningless, if score was taken. The major twice defeated Big Jim, Ansel Head fell before J.B. Taylor, and the world champions still even.

Men slept atop the pool tables, on the floors, anywhere they curl up.

A new day came threatening fewer antagonists. Only the most stalwart ladies and vandals not yet bored by the game were about. Many suspected a ruse. But no, with the advance of morning, the barricades vanished while the air relinquished the sauna of humanity to those of native repose.

Under the scrutiny of all Zielinski ventured out, retarded in his initial movement only, increasing his pace and ease upon each step. No vile utterances hailed him from afar. He disappeared around the corner, not to reappear until ten minutes later swaggering victoriously up the far end of the street, championing a broad smile; "We done it boys, they're gone," said he before they had time to positively surmise it so.

Once more the pallor vibrated with celebrants, this time higher pitched in the roarings of success. A rush commenced on the wine case. Chilled bottles passed round willy nilly. Hands slapped shoulders, laughter rose and rose as onetime foes combined in a joint revelry.

With the last barrier broken, real feelings were allowed expression.

"You know," began the colonel to Zielinski, "I've always hated that rabbit's head your wife put up there."

"Know…you're right," replied Zielinski before hopping atop the small change counter to pluck it down.

The young man jump turned the major's wheels into an idea.

"Know we came here to dance a coupla nights ago…never got to, savy?"

They savied and cleared up. The four musicians, slow in finding their instruments began playing. The music and stompings rang forcefully onto the street, lasting continuous hours, scored heavily upon the ears of those who remembered the day of the fire.

THE COURSE OF ALL MATTERS

In the mass of new employees, one man's boyish looks were indistinguishable from youths as young as they looked. They, not he, were the accustomed stock of summer personnel at Yellowstone since Chief Joseph rode through leading his Nez Perce into legend. College kids between semesters, those who postponed college for touring and shy of means, hands from Minnesota turkey farms, they joined many who envisioned endless parties and many more thirsting to put new packs to the ruggedest test to make up the congregation. Uniting them also was their surprise at the diversity and likenesses of lives and locations of an America spanned before every eye.

By concurring with every opinion, a Californian untravelled east of Utah uncovered his closeness to a Georgian whose sightseeing once stopped at Alabama. Two girls who had not seen each other since high school were astonished that they were residing in the same part of Chicago without having any idea.

To taste something different was what attracted the kids and what brought the man. And though they did cackle too much trivia, he didn't mind, until the inevitable round of biographies. Awkwardly, he divulged enough to set him apart. There was no way to explain the years away to such innocents.

The constitution he packed was individually hewed and a detriment in a society of labelers. Being the odd man out foisted upon him an attitude that developed into martyrdom. The present situation kept his distinction from being his solitude. Society's fringes condone degrees of eccentricity.

When all forms were filled and clothing handed out, the group dispersed into smaller groups bunched about those with cars. By the man's side were a guy and a girl assigned to places on a roundabout way to his.

"Nice chick," the guy whispered.

Ambivalent toward pretty girls, the response lacked enthusiasm. Pretty girls, though, sure to quicken breath, had accounted for too much grief. Unapproachable courtesy was the customary act not diverted from for his comely rider. Her being unexpectedly replaced caused no regret.

The new girl, regardless of how long she looked at her, wasn't much. No barrier of beauty could keep the man from being more himself. With any hope of attachment impossible, the ride maintained the good note started upon.

The other rider sitting in the back did not join with the banter except to detail minutia about himself. He was a tolerated cipher. The man found a receptive audience to his opinions and observations, shaping the flow of the conversation. That he impressed her was obvious. It was commonplace, once he felt like talking, which wasn't often. He was too acerbic toward a society that had no place for his talents to ever bask in amenities.

She reciprocated by brushing the tops of topics he missed. Proof of her won intellectual baggage was let known by claiming attendance at a medical school. Hardly looking the type or age, with an old woman's fatty arms below a child's pudgy face, his history of misjudgments demanded he believe.

As the wound into the heart of the park, it grew difficult to sightsee and manage a budding intimacy. While the prating of the inconsequential passenger at last ended when dropped off at a tourist's village, as incongruous in the wilderness as he was in an intelligible conversation.

His departure was celebrated by a lunch that the man superciliously asked the girl to. Two dollars represented two-thirds of an hour throwing crates of chickens onto trucks, but he had lost twenty the day before lost twenty to a speed trap and survived. Finances would not interfere. Over a year had elapsed since any girl had sat across any table from him.

Her etiquette was almost flawless. Good breeding showed despite a roving eye. Abashedly, her inattention stung. Attention was a treat to the man. Girl-like, he cornered his eyes, finding out the waitresses' uniforms were under observation, not boys.

"Haven't been in a dress for years," was her comment, followed by a more rueful: "They're all so alike," that conjured unappealing images to the man as well. Months of underpaid, repetitive work hurried him to a sacrosanct vow. He had come west to shed frustration. Great vistas, he hoped, would release a spirit too long confined. More pandering bare subsistence for a zombie's obedience would then be the catalyst for getting all there was to get in the time available. What refreshment awaited a plan numb and dumb during work, alive and vital and at the slightest call to adventure afterwards!

Accepting the shackles as they were, he was unchained to vent freely, representing nobody but himself. No gloomy prospect adhered to hold down a vivacity launched at a listener who braced fascinated. To a tourist trap in a thermal area adjacent to Lake Yellowstone, their relationship drifted to more and more. Why did he let it be? He'd never see her again.

When he let her off, a macho wave of ado did. Her flapping dejectedly softened nothing. It was the land, not people, he cared for. Emotions he would unbend for no one. That way, he wouldn't get stung.

Along the thoroughfare cut from a continuous forest, elk with spring's fuzzy antlers grazed oblivious to swarming tourists taking their pictures. Getting through the narrows was hazardous. Glances at the beasts were his allowance, and what made him jump at an impulse.

Spitting the rhetoric of a college coach, the man stopped for a thumb, standing where the road was uncluttered. Old do-not-dos were influential. A sordid class of cop-outs, hitchhikers were not as no qualms kept him from assailing the vagabond with all sorts of questions.

In the argot of the region, a world apart forged into being. Montana pipe crews, from worm to jagman, how bartenders are the men to see when needing jobs, where a name and social security number completed the hiring fell away from the traveler with great ease. That reputations are the resumes handed to the jagman at the next project was refreshing. Reminiscent of the frantic frontier.

The rider himself was recently bailed from a D.W.I. by a boss who liked his work. With two hundred dollars, between jobs, seeing friends in Jackson, Wyoming, the fellow confided in luck with a surety the man envied. His backpack switching in perspective from wall to wall when he let off a Jackson Hole was romantically apt.

Getting his affairs ordered at the marina where he was to work preceded the backtracking to the thermal area, where he was informed were his quarters. An employee's compound tucked in the woods, painted brown and home for a flock of sparrows, was no barracks as remembered from the army. As a base of operations, it would do. Mountains rising on or below every horizon were a wall keeping the outside remote. "On the outside," a popular phrase in the army and school, hardly referred to any longing to be out. As much as time was once wanted over with, it was now treasured.

Compassing the situation set him about like a boy on the loose from his mother. Looking through a window, there in the cafeteria, was the girl polishing chair legs.

As the only person known, she sprang back to significance. He waved, flaccidly, and did not knock. Leaving was excused by insisting luck didn't turn right. He did the best he could.

The insularity of the society made detachment impossible. A new face in the cafeteria was an event. Chatty introductions directed the talk of his first and subsequently scheduled meals until all were known. Remembering names was not the problem as with other jobs. Each worker wore a name tag. The ease with which the kitchen crew was antithetical to the busy dishwasher. She scarcely broke from her labor, in no way showing that her having spotted him to spring a surprise. Hand in hand, he let the pull lean him close. Never had he affected someone so. It was almost worth being embarrassed. Almost. Her short-cut hair, fat, bunched smock, and ugly sores mocked affection. He could have none with her packaged so terribly. Fate was just salting his aloneness.

An artificiality ironed his smile to shape promises he would not keep. Let loose, a last look was had at a table decorated by fine females. Not one paid him the least mind.

An inactive period of some while preceded the gathering of volleyball players. By the time the man joined, both sides were overmatched. An Amazon in sports shorts regaled her position by waving him away. In reprisal for a grade school comedown muscling onto the other side was done with a verve that did not diminish. He did not run, he hopped, and lunged, spiking, slamming, and issuing cleverly done put downs out of sheer fun. By the unrestrictive good time did the years of overwork stood up in all their sterility. He dominated the show, being so avid that some thought him overreacting for popularity. One who took his volleyball seriously was piqued at his sacrilegious antics. A runt reeking of pretense showboated for the slap-handed approval of the Amazon. When another berated his hogging the ball, Pam-the girl-rushed to his defense. Her lauding him turned many off. It became a webby melodrama, with bruised egos, irritants, and desperate shows of coolness... all the slough the man wanted away from.

Came the night, and he, with Pam, joined a group talking under a porch light. All they were in college, sacrificing for degrees as worthless as his turned out to be. Though he didn't tell them. Despoilers ruin pleasant moments. But as these kids continued, how enmeshed they were in a misconceived world became all too evident. Expectations for them still held in a future they would disbelieve anyway. In time, the man suffered silently through enough and left. Other than for necessity's sake, he would have no more to do with such waifs.

His roommates were shades of the same color. A minute to know them sufficed. While getting the chance to sneak into unfinished letters home hardened suspicions. After three weeks there, his bunkmate had not ventured beyond the boardwalks and asphalt tourist trails. "Beautiful" and "nice" were the most forceful adjectives commissioned from a sentimental vacuum.

But there were those he could fasten his interests upon. More than a few, although two had the lead. Both students were as dissimilar as imaginable. A blonde Californian who ran track burned to keep his running up and stretch his vision from too much L.A. The other approached the outdoors from an opposite direction. Unathletic and with a stutter, the ungainly fellow admirably passed off a minority's disparaging remarks by abiding only by his passion for the wilderness. As a source of information on trails and topography, he was unmatched. Hyping a climbing school and rough water raft trip and leading the way to a geyser-warmed river evermore made him confident.

Nor was the Californian the only runner. Several girls ran, albeit far from the harrier's caliber, for the same sake of exercise as he. There were more of them than boys regularly scheduling a run. Three were pretty. Slopped up in running garb did not detract from roving male eyes or slack the man's puerile want to show off. Years at it had matured a strong distance pace, no week shut up in a car could weaken. Sprinting the last quarter mile that first run, unshotted the bucks and left the girls minutes behind. Figuring just how he would review stragglers-paramount the last few yards-was decided for him by Pam, who awaited at the finish with much fuss. She mothed about mothering him while the three he had impressed huffed half steps into the girl's dorm. It was typical. Unraveling the sense things made was senseless. An uncomfortable evening juggling his revulsion and Pam's feelings ensued unto separating for bed.

Breakfast reiterated her idea of possession. Being up since five didn't waver her flight to his ability, personalizing the service by another exhibition, hanging on each morning's grubby sentence as if golden. Unfortunately, the early hours extracted their due from what she had. "See you at lunch," she said upon his departure.

As inauspiciously as the day began, its progression would have been startling had the man quit enjoying noticing. A water and dunking fight erupted on the docks that abated only after all hands were at least wet, if not drenched. The manager didn't care, open as he was to such, seeing how he had thrown his architecture over to live as he saw fit. Much name-jiving iced a pleasant way to lunch, long enough to squeeze a five-mile run into.

Standing sturdy afterwards, no torpid afternoon was in store. Bikers, hailing, as it turned out, from San Diego and Oregon and, on the other hand, Illinois, were ruddy and garrulous with open road optimism. Many were middle-aged, from the middle class, and waggish with stories transfixing the man and nearby eavesdroppers.

Patiently waiting for their finish, another worker, a retiree operating the campground's Laundromat, got his free cup of coffee while getting into stories of his own. Timid until feeling the make of the new employee, affinity was simple upon uncovering a very real coincidence. The retiree had been the commissioner who had officiated the man's Eagle Scout ceremony when the man was a boy. The interface readied the expansion of common experiences into reminiscences, introducing a Michigan that the man didn't remember. Lithuanians plying their craftsmanship to furniture, famous for its craftsmanship, as overseen by the foreman emeritus, were but one of many nationalities come to life from the retiree's fifty-odd years of experience. More sketches amply testify to dramas worthy of any stage. No old man's tales here. His years in the Upper Peninsula were made for stories. And did they come, concerning the factory or not? Camp tales. Bear charges. Scout survival trials and accounts of trout spawns came off mental records for the edification of both.

Of course, waiting customers had to be served. The old man understood and went, knowing many days for furthering the subject, not knowing what seed was implanted by an offhand comment.

As the employee performed mechanically for the tourists, his thoughts wandered about fish spawning upstream. The process was an old as Dick and Jane. He had seen films, studied migratory inducements, and even written about them. But had he ever seen it? Had any idea what it was really like? Heard the white rush of quick water? Plucked a fish up? No, on all accounts no. He had never done any of those or knew of any who had.

Exploring the stream a mile from the compound was a must, inciting and anticipation not had since a little boy's Christmas Eve.

Supper talk centered about a dance EVERYBODY was going to Pam, veritably pleaded he come. He declined. And when he marched out of the courtyard, from a gaggle of unmounted riders came a halting female voice asking for the pleasure of his company. Images of countless lost opportunities flashed back to strain his resolve. The welter of overused excuses called up to stay association included a new deterrent. His social incompetence didn't matter. A "no thanks" was emphatic.

The broken tree clogged stream, purling lakeward, was another world of discovery come true. Trout clouded the easier reaches in their mystical torture to regenerate an ancient rite. The magic of life, seduced by its essence, was extolled in the slapping and thrashing of Cutthroat crossing shallows, by the marsh through which the lower stream flowed, and a frame of reference, the inclusion of a feeding moose rendered timeless. Watching the beast lumber sleepily in an unmarred setting was prehistory recreated. From behind, a mule deer scampered flawlessly across tangled trees. All things ashore reinforced perfectly a blend of dusk colors on the lake, slightly disturbed by ducks landing in the background.

Darkness settled opaquely to make the lapping shoreline a fortuitous guide that should have topped the experience, but didn't. Steam gently rose from the thermal area to present a whole new wonder. The empty boardwalk, shrouded in warmth, was an avenue through another dimension. So many facets, rivulets of sulfur water somehow visible with colored algae, isolating mists, and bubbling pools came together as the boards squeaked underfoot to distinguish the undefinable day crowds perpetually missed.

Fiddle music rang once in the compound. Introversion pulled none of its usual strings to detain his entering the lounge to promptly learn the spoons. "Ole Joe Brown" was then spiced with an extra that the man delighted in so much that a blister formed to hurt.

Returning revelers were disturbing. As cliques formed, the musicians set their instruments for after-party beers. Most everybody, it seemed, had gone, including the man's two close friends who had enjoyed themselves immensely.

Each car skidded to a stop, unloaded as if on fire. Funneling into the lounge, postmortems crystallized for one bunch the idea that they hadn't had enough. Their disco dancing left behind a remainder that squatted in a circle playing cards and drinking games. Neither obliged an invitation, accommodating the man's distance as a rebuke, and tightened amongst themselves. Pam would have likely gotten him involved. If she were around, which she wasn't.

The night waned past the early hours considered by the youths as the shank of an evening. The gamers petered out, napping before going to bed. The swingers returned drunk, screaming about the hell they wished they had raised. While stealthily pairs commanded the later hours when most were suspected to be fast asleep.

It was they who accentuated the sting. With reading in the showers out, the only alternative was in the lounge, where his presence didn't help lovers love. Alice couldn't have shrunk further than he wanted, wonderously pretending he was alone with his book.

Precursing typical mornings after, the whole crew of tourist caterers staggered numbly to their nine-hour shifts. Nobody from the previous night was exempt. And nobody thought much of what had reduced them to their present states. Least so the man to whom last night had no significance when a new day offered its hours to remedy sores. He would go to the next dance.

There was no need to beg. A friendly co-worker insisted he come with him that same night, and any other night his van was in operation as a shuttle bus.

A tape deck entertained the passengers packed in the vehicle at the dance. None were overtly enthused, and that was good. The placidness of the group verily assured the man he could perform as they did.

He wished. While they twisted to upbeat country, he reenacted the doings of his last dance a decade ago. In the bleachers, terrified, the shadows hopefully hid him. Marooned there, a self-stylist didn't help by denouncing those deadbeats on the sidelines. It was torture, watching gorgeous girls go to uninhibited guys he considered morons.

The van loaded up with him, reluctantly coming after having his name called. Notoriety is the ultimate hurt to a misfit.

Dourness stood him out in the group, come alive. For obscurity's sake, he sang, softly, to the music they sang to. The girl's foot tapped. His foot tapped. A favorite song furnished refuge. Partway through, a foot suggestively pressed his. As a signal, his imagination wheeled free...too freely; a fact borne out after a worthless wait for a follow-up once unloaded.

Cornered by solitude, he wrapped himself in himself and faced the question begged for too long. Why was he, well, a cripple seared to the pith. As a creature removed, how could fellow creatures understand what he had no understanding of? A Job's punishment doubly damned because of no possible solution.

Work, despite its faults, was a common ground uniting misfits and the perfectly adjusted. Everybody does the same thing, wearing a similar mask of decorum.

Over with, deciding which untraveled trail he would travel was cut short by Pam's effusing their going to a square dance. Her presence assured he wouldn't be ignored; he assented.

And he was glad he did. What was once the domain of army sergeants and comparable peasants wasn't fifth rate at all. Learning the steps, at the instructor's pace, was rigorous but worth the sweat when the dancers got dancing. The misplaced foot replaced by a squeezing hand, inattention by attention, indifference by constant concern, unattractiveness didn't matter. Pam's beefy frame went tripplingly across the floor, lighter than those unencumbered. Nor did her energy diminish, recharged as it was with him, even for another, smaller dance in the lounge.

For weeks afterward, he let her into his world whenever her cook's schedule allowed. It was a marriage between passion and self-interest that had its highs and lows. When times were gray, she was there with consolation. Given her blunt lamprey leechness, her juxtaposing her day off to match his, annoyance was understandable. He couldn't add a shorter hike to the ten-hour one around the Tetons because he promised to take her home from the climbing school. She attended because he had.

He never let her know when she ticked him. She suffered enough slurs for her conduct. The token Jesus fanatic publicly called her an abscess. Clods, of course, ridiculed her person. Girls gossiped behind her back after some aberrant stunt, of which there was approximately one a day. She too wasn't acceptable; as a result of her exaggerations, unabashed tomboyishness, found no comfortable clique except in the fantasy home wrapped around him. He was all she had. About the whiff formed a veil of secrecy, curiosity impelled only him to do anything about.

Why she galumphed as if Miss Popularity with the opposite case was intriguing.

The turnover of personnel was rapid. Disgruntled employees left their jobs without breaking in newcomers to the workforce or circumstances. Pam enjoyed a moratorium getting to know the new girls over fountain shakes. Away from home, homesickness entrusted to her a revealing lot. A bond of empathy formed whereby Pam found herself also unburdening more than a complicated restraint previously allowed. To which her friends reacted with one thousandth of the shock which wracked her after accidentally telling the man her real age once Prince Charming willfully sat on the next stool. Just twenty, out went the medical school. An uncomfortable pause was politely skipped over. But changing the subject did no good. Gamely, she withdrew, badly suppressing emotions so he wouldn't add Camille to a list of names she was sure were all bad.

Her friends were aggrieved that she should be hurt so. It was silly to the man. Words, he cared more about the spoiling of a late evening. Never had he refrained from dumping bosh upon any stranger's innocence. Others were licensed to do the same.

Gleaning the whole of television make believe, with her advancing toward him from nowhere at high midnight, no convict ever went as stoically to his disserts as she in the courtyard. Self-flagellation led every work. No excuse was remotely alluded to. She was miserable and pathetic with such introverted hate.

Diplomacy was a must. The wrong reaction might leave scars. Who knew the soap she had swallowed?

Being unobserved in this scenario was the saving factor. Between them, that's where he wanted it to remain.

That's where it didn't remain. At breakfast, lunch, and supper the next day, he was hounded by her girlfriends as only teenagers could for a reason for her display. They picked and picked and, from chagrin, got the answer. Sympathy loosening their knowledge of Pam's past dissolved most of her mystery. Pam, it was slowly constructed; she was not in school at all but was a cannery worker. Shunted from foster home to foster home since childhood, in so many years, a dozen guardians had passed responsibility for her on. Her natural parents? One had to be Indian. No need to bother which. Not after all the years, as a ward of the state, dumped into a social system that ground her personality in a way these girls had just an inkling.

Further details were superfluous. Interstices, the man filled in for himself as he regarded somebody else from an untried viewpoint. Pam became more than a curiosity. Her being fascinating unlocked the man's mail so he could put himself in her shoes. Life had been much more bitter to her than to him. Ugliness set her apart more than his shyness ever could. A tough fiber had to have been woven to survive. Cat calls, anonymity, hard work, what minor irritants they surely were compared to having nobody who much cared. A speck of protoplasm must have been her self-assessment. How could she have lived? He, with his parents, whose concern he had taken as a matter of course, had strained and twisted without fear of breaking, and who unequivocally cared, was more than Pam could hope.

A little girl warped and wrapped all wrong was what he saw in the bigness that had reached out in her girlish way.

Being involved with somebody so much wasn't flattering. It was captivating, once really thought about, obligatory in the only satisfactory way.

Transformations, not known for outward displays, withheld much of its pomp here, too. He greeted Pam in no unusual way when next seeing her. As expected, she had weathered the problem. Derangement had nothing to do with it. Just loneliness. And that was partly removed by a light grip held long enough to convince. The rest, which came on when he invited her to the stream, led to more of the same.

On trail or off by the lake, her past was untouched in favor of sharing the offerings of a blessed place. Appreciation went hand in hand with the understanding of a world laid out obliging no code of ethics. Amoral and unpredictable, what is, is and no more, accommodating everything, even him, even her.

THE DECISION

"That'll be one strawberry shake. Is that all?" asked the waitress.

"Yes, I don't think I want anything else, thanks," replied Dennis Mulburn as he pushed his chair in closer to the table and fingered the twice-read menu. Showing no emotion, he sat quietly inside the roadway diner. On stage, the supporting cast filled nearly all the booths and counter stools. The chattering of many different conversations contributed to a proper mood, a sullen, introspective mood.

Memory of incidents came and went in tempo with the coming and going of customers. Thoughts of lofty aspirations in recently bypassed youth, of how real they were, of how untrue they became, made him sad, gave him a leaden feeling in his stomach.

He was unnoticed, anonymous to all but his waitress. This was what he wanted; it was unusual and therefore a welcome break. His name was often in the sports section, more than once on top of the page, in bold black letters. He was a prize fighter, heavyweight division, "An up-and-coming talent that could win on his tremendous will alone."

Leading up to the last fight, he could never work alone in the gym, always hounded by reporters and those who had gained interest in having someone of note in their neighborhood. Once outside, he was public property. Honking horns and well-meant shouts punctuated all roadwork, his name dutifully spoken in exaltation whenever he walked the streets until the only refuge was home and a candy store owned by Mr. Gibbs (a man who had watched him grow up and whose confidence in all matters made for true companionship).

The waitress came by with the shake, placed it and the check in front of him, making Dennis turn out of himself long enough to offer a polite, "Thank you."

His huge right hand, calloused on each knuckle from long hours of training, had been hardened by a mixture of rock salt, vinegar, and white wine. His fingers were massive, half again as thick as the ordinary man's. Of similar proportion, his face was equally imposing – an illustration that matched the rest of his features hidden by his seated position. They were classic, as perfect as the Olympic wrestlers recounted by millennia of sculptors. His posture was squared, his table manners impeccable.

Thoughts raced there and back as he took a bite from the whipped cream. His career had gone afoul, his desire a flicker of what it used to be. His star was still rising, but he desired to fight no more. Why? He didn't know.

He took another bite.

He had become interested when, as a junior in high school, a friend had come to class wearing a seven-jeweled watch and explained he got it for one fight held to raise money for a local charity. Interest waxed greater when he learned that its value was more than he earned in a week in the lumber yard after school, most of which went into the family coffers. He too decided to enter.

Wiping his face, he looked down at his wrist. The watch, the memory of how he felt when receiving it, flashed back and over him.

Held every third night, four competitors in each class met in three-round bouts with the winners advancing to the finals, where a fourteen-jeweled watch awaited the victor. Those two matches ignited something that couldn't be explained. His first opponent, lanky and slow, had jabbed with a right. Instincts that had forced him to duck gave him enough time to take stock of the situation, so he could throw a right to the body, and then a right to the head. It was simple, yet masterful, enough to confuse, defeat the other, and receive the loudest praise two hundred voices could raise.

The victory was addictive. Part of the thrill was outwitting the opponent, as he did in the final bout that night. The other part was the self-discipline needed for stamina. The satisfaction of knowing you are in the best shape possible in the effort to push oneself beyond the all-constraining limits. Brain and brawn, discipline and art – it had all the qualities he respected.

He boxed as an amateur until the steady promise of fame and fortune forced him into the status of a professional. By law, he could box only once every five days. With one thousand professionals in a city possessing seven boxing clubs, each staging six to eight bouts a week, he found himself lucky to fight once every three weeks.

The winner's purse was fifty to one hundred dollars, with thirty percent going to the manager. No adventure, his world became one of indebtedness only partly assuaged after a bout. Little expenses, such as a dollar a week for the use of the gym and showers, a dollar fifty for gauze, seventy-five cents for tape, and two dollars for omega oil and rubbing alcohol, if he couldn't afford three dollars for a rubdown, all proved of vital consideration. What hurt the most, what was tantamount to whether he could remain alive in the newly chosen profession, was the cost of food. Needing more than the normal caloric intake, his meals had to be larger and well-balanced. Sparring for three to ten dollars a crack paid for some of this, odd jobs paid the balance. The former taught him the skill involved as he carefully noted each style, each trick. The latter taught him better than before the necessity of rising to become one of the best or to suffer the loss of pride and self-worth in the boredom of mechanical labor.

The grimy, low-class environment around each gym, the stale, foul smell inside repelled all but those whose scowl was so representative of their makeup that ugliness went unnoticed, stench and blood a part of their lives. They could see no other way of carrying on. It did not attract him, never did, never would. He saw that immediately, but so great was the command to prove himself to the world that he looked beyond it, ignored it, as he fought with a might and main to secure the treasure of the cold art of mind over matter. No weakling, he developed into a hungry boxer who saw ways to beat any defense, counter any offense.

He fought to outwit his foe, always enjoyed the better physically conditioned body, and knew that he had to make his blows powerful to gain the other's respect. In his fifth preliminary fight, he proved this and more to himself when, blinded by the sincere hatred of losing, he lost two pints of blood and would have fought on until bleeding to death had the referee not called a technical knockout. In his half-conscious grief, he won the admiration of the crowd and a certain promoter in particular. By judging the fight as setting in proof of a genuine fighter with a keen running streak of cruelty, he missed the plain truth that what he saw was a boxer with an unnatural ability to take punishment and insulted when knocked to the floor. Dennis was hungry, not desperate. If forced out of the business, he always had a house and family to turn to. He had not the advantage of being, not moneyless, but hopeless. He would never get low enough to consider such tactics as striking an opponent's bicep a paralyzing blow when countering a jab or breaking him down by illegal conveyances that first brought only a warning before the default as: pushing his foe's head back when in a corner, or spinning him around, dizzying him before the blow. Never would he think of intimidating him by arriving late, not looking him in his eyes, acting indifferent to the entire affair. He fought with tensed, worried, all-out efforts that exposed all his desires. He was straight, not a blood-lusted killer who bared his teeth.

He quit school; he had to, so much of his time was needed as both the promoter and manager of his gym took him under their wings. "He's going to be a good fighter someday," was the comment so often made in front of him and others that he found trouble hiding his thrill at having a storybook future.

Work piled atop work as he compared himself to the past greats and present superstars. He read all he could, learned their techniques, understood the mechanics of the "solar plexus punch", and learned that an uppercut reaches its maximum effect right after it is started. He took care to size up an opponent, see his ways by backing into corners when fresh in the early rounds, calculating how he would do this or that to counter observed methods if cornered and dazed in later rounds. He insisted upon top-quality sparring partners who box outright in the manner of future competitors. So ambitious was he that his creed, "If I can't outbox'm, I'll outwork'm" became the fast-growing roots that made his name for promise, a byword for grit and excellence.

He took another bite. Looking down at the table, then up again at the strawberry shake, he knew now what he did not know then. His roots had grown not in soil, but in sand, not into the nutritious earth, but into a substance of vanishing nutrients that resided atop bedrock.

Along with steady improvement that was making all praise valid, he acquired the added sobriquet of being a "good boy". Prepared to fight anyone, he may have been frightened, thought himself not at the proper stage for such a challenge, but never made verbal that fear. An illness once removed a main feature contestant. Telephoned only three hours before the bout he was asked to stand in, readily agreed, and was at the club with an hour to spare. Not gifted with the steady nerves that allowed his opponent to rest before the fight, reporters found him vomiting in a bucket. He won the fight.

Remembering the "soak-offs" (those who stood little chance of beating him, fighting only for the loser's money and used to promote the name of Dennis Mulburn), he thought of Primo Carnero, a long past world's champion whose name appears obscurely in yellowed magazines and books on boxing of interest only to aficionados. Advanced by dishonest promoters, managers, and agreeing opponents (out of their own free will or otherwise), the poor six-foot-six-inch two-hundred-fifty-pound fourth-rate boxer won bouts until his backers squandered all their money, and he was penniless.

If it were only that easy, to blame outright thieves for one's misfortune, but children's stories no longer made the fact bearable. The answer went deeper. The fact that he knew that an innocent giant had been sucked by leeches until he could bleed no more than thrown aside like so much rubbish set him apart from those he fought. They knew only the great names, never read, if only to improve their style. Joe Gan's great punch, a right after blocking a lead, the body hook of Battling Nelson, became lost underneath a mountain of printed words. The five-year obsession of Tunney to beat Dempsey was no more than charred paper to those who considered their zeal to win a quality unique to their own.

His research allowed him to realize the value of the press, of how "newspaper finishes" were the final judge of a bout, and how promoters could prompt a legion of reporters to make or break a reputation. Dempsey was the draft dodger, no good, who beat Carpentier, the war hero. Only later did he become the most exalted of sports heroes, one above the rest in all other fields, after the famous long count. All but Dennis ever saw beyond the moment where the hottest item is the greatest of all time. It was his sin and downfall.

The slow realization of this came as he progressed upwards and met more people involved in the business. A wall began to take shape, separating him from the prattle of the crowds.

The crowds cried out in one voice when secure, none would be heard individually. If their favorite won, he was praised to the ceiling. If he lost, unfairness was claimed. If he was overwhelmed, the insurrection of a few pitter-patters for the victor made more pronounced the overwhelming silence.

Audiences who live for sports invest their heroes with more meaning than they invest in family. They become family and regard them personally. It is their life. It makes their lives easier to bear. Watching fights, they care little for the names of those who fight in the preliminaries, seek only the punishing action, and are crueler than the cruelest of opponents. As eager for the bout as the boxer, they do not have to suffer the punishment, think little of it as the fight progresses, are constantly demanding action, hard, cruel action that keeps them returning, that is the life's lifeblood of the sport itself.

Still, he worked harder than the rest. Giving up all those things that make life so dear and valuable to others, he allowed himself no social life, no honest friendships – all to be a winner. This was the world in which he lived, the world he promised to leave when his career was over. Girls were a menace to him, were too weak, and would take too much of his time. Often, he had fought the "party boys," those who spent each evening on a date or inside a bar. Strong in the first three rounds, they were weighted targets by the eighth, easy pickings by the twelfth.

No girl understood. When asked what he did with his time, a shy shrugging of the shoulders would always precede the self-conscious answer of training or working out. Upturned lips were always the response, but so many women were available that odds were favorable. He could not last and ended up meeting one who accepted him as he was: kind, curious, and considerate, only immensely selfish with his time.

Not as purged of the memory as he thought, no hurried barricade could stop the impending wave. He quit eating, sat back, and stared forward.

She was all he had ever wished for. Comely, her disposition was composed when under stress, magnificent when happy. Life to her was a dream come true; together, it was exquisite. She telephoned the gym twice each night, once to say, "Hello, and I love you", and the other to say, "Good night". One evening a week was pushed aside to take her out. No longer alone, his soul melded into hers to tentatively surrender that which was formerly held safe behind a sweaty glove, inside a grimy gym. It was the missing piece of his incomplete spirit. It was too good to last. It didn't.

Once again, he trusted his growth to inutritious soil. When he was away fighting a planned program of three bouts in six weeks in three cities, she met another, older man of no promise and lesser worth. He knew the game, had no other ambitions that required his time, said the proper words, promised the proper things, and won her over. Like a precious stone ripped from the unwilling earth, so was his torture when she backed away from his caresses, told him she loved another more.

All plans crumbled to nothing. A siren, she had enticed his heart out of its fortress, made it float ethereally on the dreams and wishes she fondled, held dearly then, after a suggestion from another, slashed at as if it were a loathsome monster, not ever looking as it limped back to the fortress leaving a bloodied trail in its wake. Then and only then did he ever feel that which a fighter, not a boxer, ever felt.

The numbness of shock set in, unmovable and irreplaceable: he felt himself destitute. He needed friends in abundance, but he had no friends, only those interested in his career, so they could profit by it. For him, they lent a business ear. Stripped of humanity, he wanted to devour his enemy. No illegal tactic would stand in his way.

His sparring partners noticed it; those who watched noticed it. Plans were drawn up. A fight was arranged between their charge and a former world champion, needing only one more solid victory before challenging the present title holder.

II

At thirty-five, the former champion was old and knew it. Mistreated by years of fifteen-round battles, he had never lost sight of the dream once his. In love with the lost goal and the sport that revered it, he now found both unfaithful mistresses, taunting him, playing with his soul so that he could never stop loving, stop being hurt. Only Dennis Mulburn stood in his way.

Of all the training camps Dennis had gone to, he remembered this one above all. Nestled among sheltering hills that allowed no chance entrance, it allowed an uninterrupted schedule that was a replica of the most demanding of the best who fought. It was a chapter from the life of a monk, fifteen weeks devoted to one thing: beating another man.

Breakfast of oatmeal, ten miles of cross-country running each morning, was succeeded by a lunch of meat and bread. After lunch, he would be rubbed down and allowed to rest before an early afternoon spent throwing the medicine ball, punching the bag (smaller and more slender than normal, it was more difficult to hit), swinging Indian clubs, and throwing a football. When finished, he would receive another rubdown, then spar. After a supper of cold meat and stale bread, he studied techniques, talked over strategy, played some chess, or shot a few baskets until it was time to sleep. Standing between him and the outside world were his manager and trainer. Like eunuchs, they screened all who wished to visit, granted or withheld permission to listen to the radio.

Monomania propelled him through the day, seven days a week. Always did he see the face of his opponent. It leered at him atop the next rise, ducking left and right as he punched the bag, altering the features of his sparring partners. Ever laughing, he made fun of his recent loss, was the indifference of nature sneered at his petty dreams.

Two weeks before the fight, he was allowed no mail, received no calls, and met no new acquaintances. With a week to go, he did not ride in cars, wasn't allowed to read the write-ups or shake hands lest he lose his hypnotic concentration. He was ready, felt he had the strength to give his all in every round. No other life than the ring that was his universe could be remembered

The crowd favored the former champion who, in his prime, had symbolized the rugged individualist – the most noble personality of man. Suffering sore, making human errors alongside displays of brilliance, always believing in the promise of the future when collared by present defeat, he had won their imagination, and represented the high praise of mental strength. When he won, the celebrating throng felt they had won, victors over the antagonist who was no less than an enemy of mankind. Many possess comparable traits and were never thought of – they didn't win. He did, and in the process became a hero.

As time dragged, he and his legions into older age, wins became fewer, and comebacks struck with lesser impact. His admirers became sullen, hoping for the near miracle that never came off. His tactics changed; no longer a charger, he became a tactician, trading youth and speed for age and experience. A representative of the past, his name was mentioned after such phrases as: "Remember when…" or "I saw him fight…" Dennis Mulburn was a newcomer, an unknown evil that blocked their vicarious time machine to younger, happier, stronger days.

The ring was between the pitcher's mound and second base in the baseball stadium. The temperature was one hundred degrees, one hundred five under the lights. The crowd, unnerved by the slow commute and sweaty crowds, made their discomfort audible by raising tumultuous cheers at the entrance of the one-time champion. Little was left for Dennis.

In his misery, Dennis intimidated him, didn't look him in the eyes, acted as if he couldn't care less, and refused to touch gloves before the first round. It was the conflict between a human shell and one with an excess of humanity, but with a terrible fear of losing a lofty position. One had nothing to lose, the other everything.

Starting springy and eager, no sign of the age difference was visible. Mixing up his punches, Dennis led with a left feint followed immediately by a short-left hook. A right feint...a right hook – miss, then a left hook that connected. The many expressions Dennis memorized from tapes provided just the right tell to anticipate a right he could harmlessly evade with a quick duck. Dennis countered with a hard left that preceded a series of close-in chops. They clinched. They broke. At long range, Dennis tried a left hook that scored, reeling the foe backward against the ropes. A moment's pause allowed the younger fighter to spin him around and hit him with an accelerating uppercut. The former champion fell to his knees. Warned, the violator nodded his head to show he understood. Now a villain, the crowd booed each success, cheered every failure. The action began to slow. Dennis let his opponent draw him into each corner, was careful to watch for more mannerisms, and saw that he slapped his left hand on his thigh before striking with the left. On his part, the older fighter was led to believe that he was in command, that he cornered the youth because of superior skill, not knowing Dennis wanted to work in close. It was his best position.

The second round was like the first. Hard fighting eased by respites of clinches, accentuated by myriads of blows heavily thrown left and right, hooks, jabs, and chops to the body and head. They parted at the bell, somewhat dizzy under the heat, even on points. The next two were similar, with the youth one point ahead because of a left feint followed by a right into an unguarded chest.

Midway in the fifth, Dennis slipped, fell to the floor, and stayed there for the nine counts. The crowd yelled its approval. Mistaking a blocked right for solid contact, the former champion, visibly exhausted, had his confidence restored. Unwarranted but there, it momentarily propelled him beyond true capability. He opened a cut over Dennis' eye, thought the time was right for the telling blow, and came at him at a half crouch, characteristic of his younger days. Beginning the assault in tempo with the rising pitch of the crowd, the bell cut off the action. The minute respite removed confidence, made his draining stamina obvious, as he had to be helped up.

It was in the sixth that the turning point occurred. Experienced, the former champion cursed a foolish move, realizing he again had assaulted too close to the bell, before he could do any damage. It left him weak, so weak, he knew his next assault had to be all out, and with plenty of time in the round to finish what he had started.

A minute was spent half jockeying, half bullying the youth to the ropes where, in close so the younger fighter couldn't punch back, he pushed his head under Dennis' chin, used his opponent's body as leverage so he could punch rapidly to the stomach and kidneys. As they parted, he saw that which he had been waiting for – a sizeable opening caused by stunned reactions. The moment presented itself. The advantage was taken. A titanic right that brought the youth down, almost caused him to follow, saving himself by grabbing onto the ropes. The crowd again roared its approval, again heard the nine count. Upon his will alone, Dennis was helpless. Empty, glazed eyes did not see his opponent. His arms hang limp. His step was flat.

But the champ couldn't take advantage, at least to the extent needed to succeed. He didn't have it in him. He knew he didn't have it in him. He tried, but he was too spent. He had no reserves to throw into punches. The youth did, and though his punches looked less potent, they stung more.

Dennis blocked a short right to the jaw, stopped a left hook to the midsection, and finished the round obviously in charge. From then on, the overbearing heat, the long weeks of training, the strength of youth, and a numbness in his stomach proved sufficient. Then a strange thing happened. From villain, he became the hero as his ostensibly weaker-looking blows were more powerful.

In the eighth, he noticed a subtle change and saw his foe's style change. The ostensibly powerful but weak blows now looked as weak as they were. And it was obvious he had become afraid. This fear was seen only in Dennis, whose rapt attention to such subtleties had proved paramount. As had happened before, animal instincts pumped enough adrenaline to overcome any vestigial compassion. The strong were to hold sway over the weak; that was the way of the world, the way Dennis thoroughly surrendered himself to.

He played with his foe, circled about him to look for an opening for his left, found one, and planted it – staggering the other, making the crowd roar its new allegiance. He had become in the flesh what the other could only recall.

The older man staggered. Moving at quarter speed, blinded by fatigue, he made little pretense to defend himself. Five to six tries were needed before one punch landed. No longer did his punches have any snap. He had to force them out. Only experience rescued him, pacing himself with such devices as leading the action to his corner just before the bell, resting during the clinches, and letting the other do the maneuvering. The last out depended upon outlasting his stronger foe, hoping that he would miscalculate his strength and fall prey to the heat.

Continuing with force of will, Dennis Mulburn was visibly shaking when given the decision. A loser on points, his boldness gave him the victory. He was all the old fighter he once was before being incapacitated by age. From one who always took chances, he became one who would not be sensational, never start a punch unless sure it would land. Having evolved into that type of athlete who was just cautious enough to achieve modest success, he would fail to take the do-or-die gamble, trading skill for daring. From the people's champion, he did not become one of the small-hearted and forever afraid who will always fail at times of crisis, but one of the more unfortunates who had sufficient courage but betrayed himself by relying too much on caution. In close decisions, he refused to even imitate boldness and lost.

Shouting in a louder voice than that given at the entrance of the old champion, the crowd stood up to welcome their new hero. Their fickleness sickened Dennis, causing him to converse deliberately with reporters. When all information had been given and he was sufficiently rested, he left by the back door. Immediately surrounded by waiting autograph seekers and well-wishers who offered to pay cab fare, a path was cleared by two policemen that not only made his route easier but also allowed him to see the former champion enter his ten-year-old Pontiac entirely alone.

All sports are ninety-five percent torture and five percent thrill. The drama, only seen and recognized by himself, wobbled him. Bridges fall not from hurricane winds but by breezes that match its natural rhythm – this cannot be reversed or thrown out by forced will. At his peak, the new hero began the slide downward.

The magic numbing quality that helped garner him fame was gone forever. Matched against the top-ranked fighters that now stood in his way to the championship, he met them unprepared. No way should he have fought them. They were not thirty-five but twenty-six to thirty and at the peak of their careers.

A better boxer for his experience, he did prove his worth, losing two on very close decisions and winning two. Time had soothed the pain of romantic loss. Events obscured events, leaving general impressions.

He was now at the "ragged edge" of his career. Boxing well and making proud those who predicted fine things, his course hung by a precarious thread. As he began to suck on the straw, he knew that the next fight would be the deciding one, and probably the last one. For over a year, he had to force himself to train, to spar, to see his opponent's face, look at his eyes, learn his nuances. It did not come naturally. A lack of drive was added to the mistake of believing boxing an art. To rest is to lose; he was going to lose.

III

Looking for solace, he had sought out Mr. Gibbs, the one who he knew would patiently wait for just such a confession. It was a hot summer's evening when Dennis spotted him closing his shop. Walking in measured steps that tried not to advertise his presence advertised his presence. "Hello, Dennis," said Mr. Gibbs, without looking up from the lock he was trying to open. "What troubles you?"

"Oh, nothing much."

"Now you wouldn't have come half sneaking up on me like you used to when you were a kid if there wasn't."

"Well… truth is, there is something."

"Tell you what, either I unlock the door and we talk inside, or go to the Bahamas and talk there."

"No need to go to the Bahamas," said Dennis, once again struck by Mister Gibb's description of the travel office four stores down from his candy shop.

As he watched the old bachelor fumble with the lock and shuffle inside, he was overcome with the respect that had fascinated him as a kid a lifetime ago. Over the years, that fascination had morphed into veneration. The more life Dennis lived, the wiser the old guy became.

"You don't have to tell me what's wrong. I always knew. Want a soda?"

"Sure."

"Dennis, I'll put it on the line. You have talent, not a one-way talent like most, but a broad talent. You can do anything you put your mind to. You want to know why? You're curious; most aren't, not the way you are. Can't compartmentalize. Don't have enough character to put things in perspective, let alone organize one's life by it. You're special. You've always been special. Your curiosity gave you the character to organize life into perspective, allowing you to favor one thing for as long as you choose. Now I bet you are choosing to withdraw from it, not consciously, but from feelings, a second sense developed from all you did, training your brain."

"How can you tell all that?"

"Like I said, I have seen many people, seen what happened to them. Those that failed did so because they hadn't trained their brains, never disciplined themselves, never had the curiosity of the world to get out of themselves. Their world went as far as they could see."

"So, what are you saying?"

"I am saying you just need to act on what you know to be true. You came here to hear me say that"

"Maybe."

"You always did."

Dennis remembered the times he sought Mr. Gibbs. Being honest, most of the time it was to corroborate his decisions. To take the jobs he applied for, to avoid girls that worried him, to sell possessions to finance training, and to throw himself into training.

"Now you know that it is time. You know very well that having the world by the tail does not mean everything is wonderful."

"Yeah, maybe."

"You know the inevitable can't be avoided. It is tough for everyone. Nobody wants to admit their body isn't what it used to be. Remember Jesse Owens said the mind might be right, but the body just doesn't respond. And his times could have won a bronze medal thirty years after the Berlin Olympics.

" 've got a mind. Not using it punishes you. But that didn't bother you as long as your body continued to perform. What did Benjamin Franklin say? The ring is now too small a world for it. I may not have done much or gone far, but I've seen fifty years' worth of people from behind this counter. Never turned away from a story or a problem. Didn't always agree with 'em, made a few mad, but still respected me. Learned more than if I had traveled the world. People are people. Those that fall into trouble are messed up; don't know what they want, have no self-respect, blame others for what they know to be their fault 'cause they don't think high enough of themselves to try.

"You've always had self-respect, always tried, never blamed others. That's what made you a boxer; can make you anything you want. Remember Tommy Sanderson?"

"Yeah, what became of him?"

"Ten to twenty for armed robbery, the only thing they ever caught him on. He is a lot like you 'cept don't think much of himself, forced himself to do what he didn't want to do, and almost wished he'd get caught. So did Bob Bruno, Chuck Mathiers, and the rest. No self-respect. You have it because of your curiosity. You know your place. Want to learn all you can about the world."

"That seems a lot for just a kid who came in here long ago."

"I see a lot of people."

"But everyone is different."

"You'd be surprised. The fact you'd devote yourself to something fit. What it was easy to surmise, given your circumstances."

"Circumstances?"

"Advantaged kids go to Wall Street. Gyms, not bank buildings attract your group. It is what you were familiar with."

"Was that bad?"

"Is it bad Kenyans win marathons? Canadians play hockey, Brazilians play soccer, Jewish kids become doctors and lawyers. It's ."

"So we are all predestined?"

"All go as far as their abilities take them."

"There were many guys more talented them, bigger, stronger."

"But not wiser. Only you have not given, don't put it on your shoulders. You accept it for what it is: some good, some bad. Get out of boxing. Life for you shouldn't be confined to fifteen feet surrounded by ropes."

"Think you're right."

"Like I always told you…or maybe you don't want a candy store owner to flap at you anymore. You ever hear of Robert Colbert?"

"Sure! He knocked out Jack Johnson, Harry Wills, and more. Maybe the best fighter in history. Never really was that popular 'cause the rest were afraid to fight him."

"What would you say if I told you he was still alive and living not more than a block from here?"

"I wouldn't believe it."

"Well, he is. He and me been good friends for twenty years. Eats at the Bahamas every day."

"You mean that guy, that small chunky one. He never spoke a word about fighting ever!"

"He's the one. Like to meet him?"

"Yeah," answered Dennis in self-reprimand that withheld any exclamation so long he had written off the man as one of no particular distinction, unworthy of deep questions.

The route that was taken was on the same sidewalk that was the main avenue of his boyhood world. So often used, it had long since become unnoticed. Unchanged sights unlocked many memories. He did not think himself a fighter, but more a boy who wanted to see a great hero and decide whether to start on the long, hard road.

The tenement house was without distinction, one of like thousands whose removal would stir no interest beyond the passing remark of he who could not see above the crowded buildings or around the corner. Once inside, they had to walk slowly to let their eyes get accustomed to the unlit interior. Dried odors hung in a currentless suspension, creating the smell peculiar to that building (one of the two or three unthought of distinctions that give celebrity to each structure, each person). Before reaching the top, they passed by a door on the left trying to muffle a loud argument and a door on the right that allowed through the excitement of a football game. No further sounds were heard as they stopped in front of a door marked ROBERT COLBERT. Mr. Gibbs knocked. The sound of mattress springs releasing a heavy load, the noise of the floor grudgingly giving way to each step, thankfully creaking back into place, was of quick duration before the door opened, not to the expected length of an inside chain lock, but to a sudden completeness.

"Hello Jim!"

"Hello Bob, brought a friend. You've met, but think you might get to know each other better."

The room was small, poorly lit by a single light bulb hanging from the ceiling. The furniture was scant, non-decorative, but neatly kept. A stack of newspapers matched the height of the bedpost. Two pictures hung over the bed: one of the South Seas, the other of San Francisco at sunset. The room was the cheapest available in the building. For derelicts and passers-by, it was not meant to be vested with a caring settlement that did not hide but removed entirely the expected atmosphere of paranoia and self-pity. More than removed, it had been thrown out immediately after detection, not by fighting effort, but by a sweeping wave of lifetime duration.

"Have a seat," said Mr. Colbert, pointing to two plain chairs, himself sitting on the bed.

"How's your cold, Jim?"

"Better. Been taking good care of myself."

"Are you really Robert Colbert?" asked Dennis.

"Yep, been called that ever since I can remember."

"We've met a lot, only I was just a kid."

"Yep, I know you. Been interested in your doings. Watching your fights."

"I never see you at a fight. Watch 'em on T.V.?"

"Nope, don't own one. Don't have enough money to buy one. Just have enough to eat."

"How come…" he began to ask before being struck by the realization of the life this man had led and how he had been cheated by avaricious managers and promoters. The newspaper's label of "The Fatuous Fighter" came back in waves of advancing revulsion. "How come you live like this? What do you do with your time?"

"Rest a lot, read mail, keep up with the newspapers."

Dennis glanced down at a few opened letters atop the bed, the ones that were being read when they had knocked. The only legible postmark was dated thirty years before.

Everything was at different poles. The barren days, the isolation, a past trust in mankind that fetched only the rotted and ruined, the loss of the sense of time, should have broken him, made him little more than a shell awaiting the release of death. Such was not the case. A fighter not in the blood lust sense, his lack of education, ignorance of worldly standards, had constructed an unassailable protection that allowed a beam to radiate from eyes half hidden by wrinkled skin. When the beam hit, its heated fullness made Dennis ashamed of any self-pity – so great was the impact.

Simplicity, the title of "Fatuous Fighter", was overruled, cast out by the winds of dignity. His roots were wide, wide enough to enable them to survive in any soil and realize a harvest that no melancholy could destroy. His was the joy of living that made vain and pompous all exclaimed outward trappings of life, transcended far beyond any bondage. His ebullient glance equaled that displayed by Cassius Clay after he triumphed over Sonny Liston – a moment's exaltation muffled underneath proud works that dared any challenger. He had that rare gift to feel the height of one's life all the time. It was dignity born from what the saddened world lacks – the thrill of accomplishment. Eyes of dignity can live happily; eyes of intelligence can't.

A three-way conversation ensued. Sprinkled by lighted jokes devoid of any hate, praising the inherent good quality of man, emerged in the spirit of competition, an attachment of fellowship ensued. No phony laugh was promoted to cover anything unhappy. There was no need. The talk rolled smoothly into detailed accounts of matches, boxes, and life.

"Jack Johnson, now there was a character. Most of what I remember of him is that smile. Not to be mean or to heckle, it was just his way. Had it when he trained, and he trained hard, 'n had it in the ring. Planned and careful, he was as good as the best of any time. Always remember that. No one is the greatest. Statistics don't tell the story. Every time is different; you can't compare the top dogs of two different times. Take me. I was the best for four years, period."

"I fought three or four hundred fights from San Frisco to Sydney. Have no favorite, only remember the good feelin' 'fore 'em 'n dat fine drained feelin' afterwards. Win or lose, it was still good. Always loved to fight. Fought pro since I was sixteen. Family was too poor to send me to school, and I wanted to help 'em. Worked in the neighbor's field when I was ten; found an old bag, filled it with stray 'n used to punch it way past dark 'till my mother drug me from it. Fought a champion they had in a circus. Beat him. People liked that. I was hooked. Became a champ myself. Paid a hundred to anyone I couldn't knock down in four rounds. Since then, I went into every fight with my heart set on fightin' as best I could, not just winnin'. Always gave my best. Always proud of myself. If I lost, I tried to figure out what I had done wrong. Sometimes I fought people too good for me, sometimes I didn't feel right for fightin', other times I fought bad."

"What do you think of the crowds?"

"Loved dem all. I'm folk. They're folk. Got along with all of dem. Some did get outta hand. Can't blame 'em really. Too pumped up. Sometimes you'd think they're more scared than you. One crowd does come to mind, not 'cause dey were noisy, but of what happened afterwards."

"It was in Bangkok in the middle of a monsoon. Been reainin' for three days. Everybody sure it would rain a week more. Decided to keep the fight on schedule. People came from all over. Important Thai officials and top folks from other countries dressed themselves in native costumes 'n other colorful clothes. Many traveled through the rain on foot or by bicycle. Trains charged those with fight tickets half fare. Never saw that in the States. Felt kind of spooky when all dem people went to the national temple to pray 'n offer presents to Buddha, asking him to make sure I lost, like what I was going to do was against God or something."

"Really was rainin' the day of the fight. Everybody got stuck in the muddy streets. The ring was so slippery that we decided to fight barefoot. Forgot his name, but at the time, he was the best fighter in the whole Southeast. People's favorite. Knocked me around good, down a couple of times. I out-hit him, mostly jabs that don't hurt much, but scored more often. He as good 'cause he wasn't afraid to fight, mix 'em up, trade punches, 'n take chances. Anyway, when I was given the decision everyone started to boo, almost drowned out the sound of the rain. Then he, wish I could remember his name, said something I'll never forget. Best thing I ever heard; made me glad to be a human, a boxer, 'n alive to hear it. It was translated somethin' like this: 'I'm proud to be the first Thai fighter to try for the world title. To represent my country for a noble goal is more than one man should ever hope for. Did I do? I fought as well as I could 'n am personally satisfied that the decision was a fair one. If I'm not sorry, my countrymen, then why are you?' The crowd quieted right down. Some apologized to me afterwards."

"I was world champion then, 'n believe me it's a full-time job. When they say 'world' they mean it. Crowds jammed 'round me in Manila, Singapore, in Melbourne – everywhere I went, even on a walk. Visited a leper colony. They knew about me. I never felt sorry for myself and seeing them made the notion a fact. Felt like I was the luckiest man on earth. Promised to give 'em a thousand dollars from each purse."

"As champion you have to watch what you say 'n do. Once said I don't particularly care for shrimp, which I don't. Got at least a hundred letters from restaurant people 'n shrimpers from all over the world. All that power scared me."

"But don't think it was all note and no worry. When I was a kid, I saw how much other kids worshiped those with big names in sports, kinda lived for dem 'cause their life wasn't much. Remembered dem 'n always wanted to give 'em somethin' when I 'came champ, but never could. Never had any money. Expenses 'n taxes took a lot. People always promising sure-fire schemes that my handlers always bought into turned sour, leaving me with little, nothin' when I turned forty. Had to hold down three jobs for five years to pay back what the government folks said I owed them. Made good only one check to that leper colony."

"Was on the road most of the time I fought. Saw little of my family. Always woke up in different places. Had to rub my eyes 'n throw water in my face 'fore I realized where I was 'n what I was to do dat day. Kinda like being reborn each morning."

"What hurt the most was how my friends took to me. Afraid dey were botherin' me. Came standoffish. Answered questions quickly. Didn't write out stories like they used to. I want to be liked by everyone, not just for me, but for the sake of boxing. Was lonesome there for a while."

From there, the conversation drifted, covering a myriad of topics in its eight-hour course. One, in particular, made

Dennis force back tears that embraced the source of human goodness when the half blind old man said about an article that appeared in a cheap sensational tabloid: 'Read where kids were starving in Mexico City. Pleaded with the paper to give me more facts. Told me they were eatin' out of garbage pails. Gave me an address to send money. Hocked most of my furniture. Tain't right for kids to be eatin' that way, kids dat don't get no chance in this world."

That was a year ago. Thanks to Dennis Mulburn, promising fighter, Robert Colbert, former World Champion, had been removed from obscurity by several well-placed letters. Persuaded to leave the tenement almost by force by those who thought him long since dead and ecstatic to see living boxing history, he once again enjoyed great numbers of friends. Proper food, lodging, and companionship allowed his simple joy of life to affect many others.

Dennis began to suck at the bottom of the drink then looked at the check. Having the same qualities as Robert Colbert, he thought of his other characteristics that shrouded the little thrills of daily life, pierced deep into the reason of life – curiosity. He could never be like Colbert. He knew too much. He could not go on with boxing: he ruined his chances the first time he opened a book. A penetrating phrase came to him as he began to twirl the straw, making small circles in what remained of the shake. "The simple truths of youth become the complicated falsehoods of our middle years. It's the price all must pay for being alive.

Everyone can tolerate a body that begins to sag and wrinkle, but finds it hard to accept the decay of ideals. Life is a dream that never comes true."

The shake was finished, and the check was paid at the counter. He walked to the door, hesitated, then entered the outside world.

STATUS

Caught in a sudden storm, Billy ran to Bud's newsstand. Bud wouldn't mind. He had let Billy snuggle inside the unsold five-star finals ever since the police had removed him from the museum's steps. The smelly ink of the morning edition had always chased him out before customers arrived.

Billy huddled into a corner. His ears throbbed with the thunder and the rain pelting the roof. His closed eyes could not block out the lightning. The strong smell of ozone obscured an unexpected smell of paint. He did not notice the newsstand's new paint job.

The humidity that followed the storm was unbearable. Sleep was impossible inside the newsstand. In a few hours, Billy had sweated through his clothes. He was damp and clammy. Arising sooner than usual, he made the day longer by starting it earlier.

It was too early to panhandle. He felt too sticky to rummage in greasy garbage cans. He wanted to take it easy, for once, see how the city comes alive.

What he found was puzzling. I noticed him. More than that, it was paying its respects. A greeting came from the same milkman who made a career out of chasing him away from his truck. A window washer bade him good day. The janitress who had daily lectured to him about the work when he lived on the stairs said she was glad he was doing so well. His bewildered expression deterred no well-wisher. The working class was turning its cobalt rumps around to look at him.

Imagine Billy's surprise when the later rising, lavender rumped class yanked him from the shadows, he fled to praise him. For just existing, they wouldn't leave him alone. They were blind to his glad rags and wine-wrecked face. Executive types bashfully recommended their country clubs to him. Very prominent men, those whose pictures had made the financial pages he had slept on, asked about his opinion of the market. By mid-morning, he had as much control of his life as a general or a diplomat.

He was shunted here and there, from one plush suite to another. A retinue of attendants saw to his every comfort and anxiously hung on everything he said. The attorneys of his new friends appeared in droves to answer the questions posed by a herd of reporters.

Billy was stupefied. The long, sumptuous lunch and even longer dinner, followed by wine, left him satisfied, for the first time in his life, stuffed. Although the nutritious food soon nauseated him, he still appreciated it. He appreciated everything, but was talked out of thinking a thank-you was mandatory.

"Glad to do it, sir. Our honor entirely," said a company president.

"Let us know if you want anything else. You've got a blank check with us," said a chief executive.

Good churchgoing as a youngster was the only explanation Billy could think of for his abrupt turn of luck.

Adjusting to luxury was as hard for him as adjusting to destitution would be for a tycoon. Bundles of fat Sunday papers would have been more comfortable than the buoyant bed he tried to sleep on. Both the bath he took and the pajamas he wore were irritating. The lotions he had slapped on stank. The bedroom was disturbingly big. The hum of the air conditioner kept him up. Strange smells kept him up. He was not particularly happy.

Come morning, he was. He was able to get up at his leisure, without being bombarded by bundles. He could lounge around and ravage the delicious edibles, immaculately dressed, cobalt-rumped butlers brought in.

"Yous guys can beat it now," he heard himself say after finishing breakfast. The butlers beamed as they removed the china and must have drawn lots for who would bring in the paper, for that particular one beamed most of all.

There, Billy was on the front page, smiling above a caption attesting to what he had read verbatim from a paper handed him moments before the picture was snapped. He wasn't particularly shocked to read in the accompanying article that he was a leading candidate in the upcoming primaries. "The party didn't know what it wanted until he appeared on the scene. He'd give voice to the unuttered wishes of the nation," concluded the accompanying article.

As much as Billy would have liked to, he couldn't luxuriate in bed. He felt obligated to measure up to what was written about him. His feet touching the floor precipitated a to-do that ended with him dressed, fed, and deposited behind a mound of paperwork in an elaborate study.

The clanging of telephones, slamming of files, whirring of machines, and chattering of secretaries combined in an orchestration that reminded Billy of his beloved streets. He was comfortable with the commotion. It made fooling everybody he could read the documents easier.

If only his subordinates would be satisfied with a quick glance as they were with his unintelligible signature. He had to ensure his lips didn't move as he read. The customers who had bought Bud's Forbes and Times never mover their lips.

The janitress would have been amazed to see how hard he worked, to see him work at all. If he had been paying attention, he, too, would have been amazed. He shouldered his share of the burden for everybody else's sake.

In came a camera crew. A microphone was shoved in his face. Cameras whirred. Questions about his plans and opinions came one upon the other, without time for Billy to ponder his answers, without time for him to realize he was appearing on the inside of millions of television sets. Without being aware of it, he was one of the two-dimensional gods he had worshipped. It was all so hectic and overwhelming. It was hard to believe he was so important.

It got easier. As days piled upon days, he didn't have to play the role everybody gave him. He came to favor cigars rather than keeping up with the paperwork. His signature was no longer an indication that the document had been read. A press secretary kept cameramen at bay until his make-up man made him handsome. He didn't watch his diction. He didn't have to. People heard him without listening to him. He could do no wrong, do nothing unremarkable. Life was fun once he understood his prerogatives.

He had a freedom he didn't know existed. Idiosyncrasies people had lectured to him about, people now adored. His every with was some subordinate's command. His every mood was publicized. His fame spread into the gossip columns. The affair he was reported to be having with a starlet he hadn't heard of couldn't have pleased his P.R. man more.

He took to really reading some of the papers he signed. He didn't care if his lips moved. He mumbled and demanded definitions to troublesome words. Nobody could hurry him whenever he plowed, word by word, through any document that had attracted him.

He'd often keep his staff late. Not keeping appointments didn't faze him. He did whatever pleased him. His years at living without an income had schooled him well in the art of making the best of what was available.

The huge amounts of money he had control of didn't scare him. Seven-digit figures were too big for him to comprehend. He rubber-stamped giant appropriations while taking forever on trifles. A proposal about replacing paper coffee cups with individually purchased mugs was still on his desk long after weightier matters had come and gone.

"This here's where we gonna show da party we know the value of a buck," he said in an emergency staff meeting he called. Pencils scratched across notepads, recording the minutes and doing mathematical calculations. Janitors were kept busy all night cleaning ashtrays and waste cans. Reporters were kept busy the next day interviewing the party elite who had been flown in.

"Like the afterglow of a thousand sunsets" was one journalist's description of the rumps that entered the committee room.

Days of consultation and debate ended with the redrafting of the party's bylaws to include the measure hailed as a sign of their future leader's fiscal sagacity. By labeling him a monetary conservative, leading news magazines corralled his elusive personality into a type of people could deal with.

Opponents had a target to shoot at. As the primaries drew near, they predicted what he would do to ruin the economy. Editorial writers the nation over made good use of the controversies he aroused.

His face stared at readers from every major magazine's cover. No rational political expert gainsayed his nomination in the convention. If not for the sake of tradition, the convention would not have been held. The groundswell raised after his first ballot nomination was recorded on a seismograph some jokester brought in.

The array of weaponry pollsters' use should have included a Richter scale. Landslides were predicted in the chigger latitudes, and where the oceans lap ashore. Only in the cornfields was his election slightly in doubt. Voters there were historically leery of the upper crust. A lavender butt and a farmer's tan was the combination husbandman looked for. They habitually disdained the veneration the one-in-million, purple-rumped, accept as their due.

Billy's campaign headed toward the country's heartland at just the right moment. The great crusade he thought the campaign would be hadn't been a great crusade at all. It had been depressing. Neither the regal treatment and epicurean delights he had grown used to, nor the power he yielded, compensated for what he had to do as a politician. Saying and acting one way for one region while saying something else, acting differently for another region grated on him. He had lost track of who he was. He was a phony, and a phony who can't justify his phoniness to achieve his ends is in trouble.

He was in trouble. He had been pushed into wanting the presidency. If so, many people weren't dependent upon him, he'd have given up. Wanting only the best for himself, when his caravan emerged from the smog of the West Coast, Billy finally decided to look out for Billy.

His entourage knew something was up when he forewent champagne for bagged muscatel. "I'll show dem what's for," he vowed as he broke into the cornfields.

His first few whistle stops set the tone of the whole campaign. The sparse crowd that turned out to hear: "I's here ta see dat them big shots don't run you over," wasn't sparse when he said at the second stop: "I'm not a lik better 'n yous," and was huge at the third stop where his concluding remark: "Wes in dis together," made them roar.

Objections from his P.R. people were futile. Billy did what he pleased, making fun out of the "tomfoolishnesses" he had encountered. Reporters didn't have to dig for interesting copy, not when he' tell VP's he'd play golf with all the utensils surrounding his plates at banquets.

He hadn't just slept on Bud's papers. Billy had made good use of the flashlight he possessed. He was able to poke fun at officialdom because he knew so much about it. Opinions he had privately ironed out at last gained voice.

"No need to apologize, you didn't say anything," he said to a governor who had apologized for a long speech.

Like that, he became a humorist. He was like no candidate the nation had known. People turned toward him to have a good chuckle. His organizers repackaged him. His policies were played down in favor of his gift for social criticism. People suddenly wanted a wit, not a statesman, in office.

"He'll make a terrible president, but what a candidate!" was the refrain heard in his camp.

The opposing party went to the twentieth ballot before nominating a compromise candidate. No faction wanted responsibility for championing a certain loser. Not since the inception of the country would there be a more popular president than Billy.

...

It was an unusually hot summer, one that had weathermen spicing their presentations by comparing present temperatures to record temperatures. The mid continent wilted. Billy and his entourage wilted. Air conditioners couldn't cool the crowds that packed the auditoriums where he spoke. Not that the discomfort detracted from the entertainment. Billy made people forget it. That he thought he could count upon.

The repercussions of the one time the temperature, and not he, heated the crowd were far-reaching.

In a typical city, in a typical assembly hall, in front of a typical audience, he began a typical presentation. Not until he was well on his way was anything realized amiss. People started to care about their discomfort more than they cared about what was said. Epigrams that had floored other audiences didn't floor this audience. They went right by them. The building smelled like a locker room. Ink ran all over the reporters' soaked notebooks. Billy was lathered up, and wobbling. His speech became incoherent. He babbled, rolled his eyes, and, with a splat, toppled over. An outline of his body was in the pool of sweat he was pulled from. A bombardment of flash bulbs lit him up head to foot. Newspapers had a choice of a hundred pictures to embellish their pieces about the incident.

They chose one. It was the most embarrassing. It sold papers and upstaged the articles it was supposed to augment. Few read about the mercenaries who had been paid to manipulate the thermostats. Fewer still cared. But the photo! Reprints soon outnumbered the originals that had gone through the wire service. For their Billy was, his once deeply purple rump faded almost to lavender.

Diminished crowds didn't appreciate him as the larger crowds had before the incident. Columnists wrote about the corrosion of his animal magnetism. Despite listening to more and more intriguing material, people were not responsive. They applauded out of courtesy. Cat calls about his right to criticize his betters were commonplace. His idiosyncrasies started to pique people. The word "vulgar" frequently appeared in editorials. "The Great Vulgarian" was the epithet that shadowed him wherever he went. Husbandman thought as little of him when the cornfields were behind him as when the cornfields were in front of him.

The funds his party planned to raise for a swing across the East didn't materialize. They tried bond issues, raffles, and taking out loans. But people wouldn't buy bonds or tickets. The litany of "no's" from loan officers drove Billy's campaign manager crazy. Money coerced from party regulars kept the campaign alive. By putting their fortunes into the coffers, bigwigs invested their all in the effort.

Yet the East also sidestepped him. Rumors of a third party were in the air. Crowd after crowd turned orations into shouting matches, some going as far as running Billy off the stage or forcing him to hide behind the lectern. Fires burned his effigy. The longer he remained in the acidic, hot-summer, urban air, the more abuse he had to put up with.

Billy blamed his decline on not having attended church as an adult. Those who had latched their lives on his coattails blamed Billy. He was a national disgrace, a figure to revile, someone songsters warbled about, decrying the end to a public scandal. The country that had hauled him atop a pedestal wanted him to crawl to Calvary.

His people deserted him for the third party. Some went so far as to skip to the opposition party. Bigwigs sued to retrieve their money and their reputations. Personages Billy had sniped at won the sympathies of the same people who had enjoyed the snipes. Intellectuals and common people alike scraped the burning issues of the day to pool their energies to get Billy out of the scene.

Ground swells of the national scandal shook the international money market. The national currency suffered severe devaluation. The nation had lost face and, with it, the confidence of the worldwide business community. The problem had exploded to touch every person inhabiting the planet.

In an unprecedented move, the legislature reassembled with the elections almost upon it. Committees and subcommittees stayed in session, day and night, hearing evidence that investigative newsmen had aroused the entire citizenry over. Big money, big government, and big business conspired to indict Billy on whatever illegalities they could think of. Accountants studied his books with an eye for putting together a case against him. Manning the latest in electronics, secret service agents were ordered, if the situation deteriorated beyond hope, to frame someone to dispose of him.

...

Billy wasn't helpless throughout all this. He had a second sense where danger was concerned. He had always had it, or else he wouldn't have made it to his middle years intact. He was wise. He knew how to look at a gift horse. Everything the Salvation Army had given him had been a bribe. Ward bosses had paid him for his vote. Nobody had ever done anything for him without attaching some strings. That he expected. Deep down, he also knew he was predestined to be a panhandler. That was his assigned niche. He blamed nobody but himself for the scorn he was subjected to. He should never have had the least bit of faith in good fortune. By sneaking back to where he came from, he disappeared from the face of the planet.

For insurance, he would hide in the cracks and crannies until dark, when the sordid appear like cockroaches. A week of nightly vigils had to come and go before he felt safe to emerge in the light of day. Even then, he tiptoed around, shying away from people, afraid they'd recognize him. Gradually, he realized people looked through him as they had before his adventure. He quit tip-toeing and was even brazen enough to begin greeting people again.

"You remember me?" he asked a bustling businesswoman he recognized as a former camp follower.

"I wouldn't dirty myself by associating with people like you," was the quick retort.

He wasn't altogether inconspicuous. The janitress renewed her old disapproval of his sloth, and the milkman glowered at him whenever he came too close to his truck. He was again the same Billy who had given substance to his area of operation. His life was back to normal.

He had forgotten about his experience until one morning when he was rousted from sleep by Bud throwing extra fat bundles into the stand. Splashed across the front of the election specials, in vivid color, was the winner, his purple rump not quite as deep as the purple paint inside the newsstand's once drab interior.

THEY HONOR THE NIGHT

Motes of red and white lights shone bright and commanding in the darkness of a moonless night. Outlining neither shapes nor presaging any noise, those behind regimentally followed those in front, guided by the thin green ray emitted from an unseen box in the center of the landing zone. The target beam, its either degree inclination shining between the sixteen-degree amber trajectory and five-degree red grade, challenged them, calling them down to the dare. High up, the set of floating lights dove down low, canted upwards over the treetops that populated the draw in front of the meadow. The two search lights, one pointing forward at an angle, the other straight down, washed the land, passing over the dips and rolls like wave motion under a cork; its beam flushed unsuspecting animals from what was once perfect camouflage. Online, they now roared through the meadow in narrow vistas of wind and noise that called attention to a discernible bug-like shape.

The whirl dispersed dandelion seeds, drowned the sound of nature's crickets as the rays pointed the way to a row of ground lights in front of the box. There they slowed, sketched the helicopter's metal outline against the opaque background, righted themselves parallel to the ground, and crept forward, showering the tall weeks with mighty winds, waiting for the signal of the ear-muffed officer standing just behind the box. With one battery-operated light stick in each hand, he spread them full length. The helicopter hovered. He positioned them in front of his face, not six inches apart, and waved the craft in. It moved closer. Moving his hands to the side in continuous sweeping motions, the ship moved left, away from the box and guide, hovered for an instant, canted forward, then took off on the runway of air, the ensuing rush making four nearby spectators secure their hats by continuous pressure of one hand. Attending full concentration on the vanished craft and vanishing on board lights, they did not notice the returned quiet of straightened grass or soft speeches of hidden insects.

Two pilots: a captain and a first lieutenant; a warrant officer, a CW2; and a visitor, a second lieutenant from a nearby field training exercise encampment, stood at the edge of a dirt roadway that opened into the helipad cut that afternoon by enlisted men armed with swing blades.

To their left, another invasion of flooded lights roared up the slope, the heavy wind chops predicting the onrush of a second helicopter. The landing pattern was without flaw until ushered in front of the box, where, in a troubled attempt, the HUEY slipped into an unsteady hover. The guide hurried, labored to make each signal more exact. The craft failed to respond correctly, its tail drifting dangerously close to a barbed wire fence of a lost boundary not yet run over by maneuvering vehicles. The guide pointed to the left skid with his left hand and made sweeping motions to his left with his right—signaling that the tail was in danger of striking an object. The pilot, a young warrant officer just out of flight school, realized the unseen danger and corrected–overcorrected and spun the craft about until facing the opposite direction. Slowly, with great trouble, did he rectify his mistake, move to the right, away from the box and guide, and take off, nose pointing downward, tail forward, providing the necessary configuration for thrust.

The wind, the longer chops of sliced air, the lost outline replaced by the red and white blur, happened in quickening speed. The night once again became slow and clear, and quiet.

Only two helicopters, the first had made its final pass, flying instead to the post hospital to take some medications to a civilian hospital eighty miles away.

Wearing "nomacks", the first lieutenant unzipped his lower right trouser pocket, fumbled through a poorly folded zoned map of the military reservation, and pulled out a half-empty pack of cigarettes and matches. Lighting a match, the shine identified three similar faces: gaunt, sinewy, and browned by the sun, with narrow slits for eyes. Belonging to the 103rd medical detachment, supplying air ambulance support for the division either in garrison or in the field, theirs was a particular branch of the Medical Service Corps, an envious branch for the officer who dreamed of romances and services to his fellow beyond a desk piled high with papers inside a hospital or daily inspections for a garrisoned ambulance platoon. They were the elite, knew, understood, and cherished every aspect, the whole along with any part of its meaning.

"Always happens that way," he said after the cigarette was half finished. "Always some little thing somebody overdoes or forgets. Never fails."

"That's the truth," said the captain.

"I'm not about to argue," replied the warrant officer.

The one left out, dressed in ordinary soldier's fatigues with only a shined yellow bar on his hat, blackened rank, and insignia on his collar to tell of his officer rank, the second lieutenant, fated to remain on the ground or ride as a passenger, felt himself wanting in.

Making small motions, he was certain they awaited his questions.

"Have you flown in Vietnam?" he asked the captain.

"Yes," he said with heavy, unlit eyes. "You want war stories?"

"No, not really... just want to learn somethin'," rejoined the lieutenant somewhat cowed, definitely respectful.

"Well, I kin't remember one incident from 'ginnin' to end even though its been ma life goin' on five years. Have to have somethin' remind me of one. Maybe a certain person's first name, maybe a 'ticular noise... 'r smell, anything kin do it. I'll tell you one thing I don't forget. That's the first time I ever air evacuated anyone. The time I thought it was the most dangerous 'n tragic thing I ever did see. Only lader did I find it routine. Had it occurred further on, there would 'ave been no way in the world I would 'ave 'membered it."

"What happened?"

"Got the call 'bout three 'r four on a hot sticky afternoon. Wanted to leave my hootch like I wanted a shot in the head, knew when I opened the door it'd be like stepping into an oven. Was a torture to walk to the ship."

"Found it a priority."

"What's that?" the lieutenant solicited not a little ashamed of his own ignorance.

"Had only two hours before being reclassified to urgent or four to die."

"From stappin' in ta landin' everything I done was mechanical. Weren't any butterflies like the older pilots said y'd get."

"Not a word was spoken after we landen on a fluorescent strip in a tight clearin' near the D.M.Z. Medics carried the doped up casualty to the ship 'n loaded him aboard. Left leg shot away, only red and a bone. Couldn't or wanted ta imagine the pain he felt or would feel once the morphine wore away. Thought I would pass out, but didn't, and the flight back went as smooth as could be. Only after I landed 'n plopped m'self in front of the officer's club bar did I collect enough thoughts ta ask myself why I was there. How 'n ta world could I 'ave been there? Captain of my high school football 'n baseball teams. President of the letterman's club. It wasn't natural. Like those medics, I got use to it. Never affected me like that again. Saw a lot worse since, open chest wounds, you name it, I saw it. Now I don't think of high school anymore 'n hardly any a college.

"Is that the same with you?" the second directed to the first lieutenant.

"Yep, same with everybody I'll bet."

"Just like flight school," interjected the warrant officer. "First time out your scared of everything: 'n even though the instructor is right there you think he might not fix your mistake till too late. Need a lot of coordination and are afraid you don't have it. Only later do you realize that anyone in their prime could have done it."

"Providing they dun foul up," interrupted the first lieutenant.

"Right, so long as you keep up 'cause once behind, and your given a small number of flying time to be at a certain stage. With a waitin' list an arm long you got no second chance.

"Slowing, hovering, and take-offs were the toughest and most folks flunked them. Not that they're so difficult but your hands and feet have to be coordinated just so. Have to think about them at first and it's a pain. Only later does it 'come easy as walking and you don't even remember doing it. Don't get me wrong, all through school 'nd after you're afraid of losing proper torque and spinning out. Saw a captain do just that during our first solo flights. He was a sharp one, anti-torqued perfectly and auto-rotated down, figured out how to cure it right off. If he'd done anything else he'd have crashed for sure. They let him pass; they let all captains pass, but none below. We have ta earn it. Believe me, I felt I won the right to buy a thousand wings when I stepped aboard another ship after the example of that captain. Main trouble was that we never had more than five hours in a HUEY; trained in two different kinds of ships. Never thought I'd make it, but did, and have a thousand hours between me then and me now."

"Not till you get a few hundred hours under your belt do you begin to feel confident, "included the first lieutenant. "The twenty-five hours out of flight school don't mean much more than a spit in a furnace… can't forget it though, only a few thing stick witcha, 'n that's one. Remember it as good as my time in Nam."

"Was fresh from the states 'nd a year of flying civilian emergencies: EMCIV. Would get calls to fly to traffic accidents, transport docs and nurses to where they were needed, and a thousand 'n one other things, pretty much like that. In Nam I was assigned to the eighty-third med. Loved it. All I was, was a pilot with one ship, some equipment, 'nd two other cre members to take care of, nothing else, no platoon or section to keep track of or buildings to inventory nd sign."

"Super bunch of guys. Everyone liked to party. A bunch of drunks is what we were. Some stayed that way the whole time. But, no matter what we did, we weren't as bad as the 339 air assault company. Most were warrant officers who could get anybody gold leaf for a song."

A questioning squint formed on the younger lieutenant's face.

"Just like any American cigarette pack 'cept joints inside."

"Everything legal there. Only the army made the rules. Anyone with the littlest initiative could get a vile of smack for a tenth of the state-side costs. Had a shakedown once nd found a full vile inside a hollowed-out bar of soap. Became suspicious when I felt an uneven displacement of weight. The crack had been washed smooth.

"The 339th partied us into a hole, especially after a successful mission. To show off, they wore red neckerchiefs like the artillery. Would walk into a bar and just dare anyone to start a fight. It didn't take much 'n in no time, every bar near the post was off limits. To belong to the 'air devils', a select club of theirs, every new warrant had to fly a loach (light observation helicopter) under Huang Bridge. I'd give it a four-foot clearance, but they had no wrecks.

"We were young, a lot younger than me, 'nd were just interested in getting the job done, nothing else. I stood by the rest of the officers nd did it the way it should be done. Some of them thought it daredevil to jump into the ship 'nd take off, not even checking. I never did that; checked it even after the crew chief finished, no matter how good he is. Never let another pilot check. The feeling was mutual. Even gave it a spot check after a call, no sense in having more casualties, 'specially with me as one of them. That's one reason that the unit never grew, even though it got two replacements a week.

"By order of the base commander, a full bird colonel, we carried a configuration of three liter racks 'nd had room for four ambulatory patients. First echelon maintenance was pulled every day; second echelon pulled quarterly, semiannually, and annually. Third echelon was never necessary—thank goodness, 'cause I became used to that ship 'nd it would have felt awkward had they put in a new motor or blades.

"Seemed like an average of five calls every three hours came in for 'engineer icebox', the detachment's call sign. That gave us: 'engineer icebox one five', an average of two, closer to three a day when really getting down. I liked it that way. If not, the colonel loved to pull surprise inspections, 'n I'll tell you it's a pain to stand at attention in the condition we usually were in, 'n he's nit-picky to the max.

"Between flights we got with enterprising mama sons…wrinkled 'nd spitting the bittle berry that blackened their teeth.

"My first call came at five A.M. of the second morning I was there. Was given only a six-digit coordinate, told that the casualties were tactical urgent—those with minor injuries but would jeopardize the mission of, let's say, a combat patrol, 'nd that was all! Didn't say what direction enemy fire, if any, was coming from, whether they needed a hoist, the wind direction, anything.

"Could not forget that moaning if I tried for a hundred years. It was foggy 'n we couldn't see much outside the cockpit. Maybe that was the reason we were getting interference on our frequency: 1751. At the time, we thought it was being jammed. Tried another thing it was 1748; but they weren't there. It did not occur to us to call it off. Knew they were close to one of our firebases, could home in on their lights 'nd get positive location through smoke.

"To make matters worse, my co-pilot: Jim Cochran, crew chief: Bob Bailey, 'n my medic had just walked into Nam on their first tour. The medic was straight out of Fort Sam Houston 'nd, get this, had never worked on anybody in his life. So new that he had taken aboard an entire 1500 chest, two full blandet sets, a splint set, 'nd would have lugged in an orthopedic set had another medic told him it wasn't necessary. He also had never flown before.

"The mist made the air heavy 'nd the flying easier than if it was light; but it was dark, completely dark outside. The glow of my instruments made it more so. With no more than a hundred hours under my belt I began to get my initial taste of what I heard about but always dismissed—vertigo. Honest to hell, when I made what the instruments told me was a left turn, my senses said it was right. Would have sworn to it. It was as if I turned to the right now. Kind a panicked. The instruments were straight, but the panel bent, just like on a right turn. I didn't feel sick or queasy or anything. I'm sure it wasn't that. Don't know what acted on me. Straightened out and fought like mad to ignore my feelings, trust the gadgets, but it was tough. Jim once told me he saw a Cobra charge out of a low overcast, straight into the ground. Blew into a fireball…official report had the pilot losing his bearing 'n not believing his panel. Did my best to hide it, but the way Jim kept glancing over, I'm sure he knew. Just too polite to make mention of it.

"Made it to the firebase just when it was clearin'. Went northwest two miles, lowered, then turned my searchlights on. Met small arms fire ahead and I split, straight back to the firebase 'nd hovered. My radio starts working. What do I get? Important information, an eight-digit coordinate, and the number of patients? No. A lieutenant colonel ordered me back. Wanted to tell him where to get off. But he was insistent 'n I wanted to make the army a career even then, so I remained contrite, formal, then went out. His little tirade broke all medevac and radio procedures. Even mentioned his name, his unit, while flapping at me as if he just caught me sleeping on guard. When I got up enough courage to turn the radio back on, I called in some gun ships which was in complete agreement with S.O.P., and waited. Five minutes was necessary for them to be aloft, twenty to clear the area.

"Was still afraid of some arms fire so came in the opposite direction—the direction they should have told me in the first place. Found the site a bunch of trees, perfectly canopied rain-forest. They neglected to tell us that. Over the radio cam: 'engineer icebox one five, this is wasp bobsled seven six, over.' I said I read them lima charley. They said: 'Icebox one five this is bobsled seven six. Popped yellow smoke.' That's a stroke for you! Four spottings of yellow smoke were immediately seen from four different locations. Told them to try it again but not to tell me what color, I'd identify 'n they'd concur. They did and I did. Luckily, I had a hoist aboard, 'nd told 'em I was going to lower it. They said they expected as much. With my lights on, it looked like dropping a sinker into a pond.

"Sure as anything, the guy on the bottom grabbed hold before it touched ground. About a ton of static electricity shot through—presto—another casualty. As we sat, perfect targets just above the treetops, firing started again. In their rush, they set all three on the hoist, one per fold-out seat. The hoist can handle six hundred pounds, but nobody dares trust it, especially when you look at the thin nylon rope. Had the devil of a time getting them through the trees. Just before they reached the level with the door, one tried to jump over. Told him to stay put, but he was a marine 'nd half out of his mind—two are synonymous, so don't know which made him worse off. Tried anyway. Missed 'n knocked his head against the floor and started to slip before dragging him inside. The other two rode the hoist. Total injuries were: one broken leg, one sprained ankle, 'n one suffering from electric shock—fair enough because they did jeopardize the mission. Remember that. If you ever call an injury in make sure it's classified right. Call in an urgent 'n he's not there, might be a real urgent that will pay because we couldn't get to him.

"That's one example of how the little things pop up, wreck a mission, wipe out a crew. Learned something because of it, though. Learned not to say I've received the message before getting' every drop of information. We were lucky. We had a hoist. Don't have enough fingers to count the times other ships went off only to radio back for us. But I'll tell you something, 'nd I'm sure it'll be no shock to you, demanding that they give it 'n them giving it are two unrelated animals. Don't think there's a marine that can remember enough information to get you within a degree of where he is. Grunts always leave out something: wind, weather, terrain, liter or ambulatory, always something: 'nd then there is, of course, Charlie.

"Some rumdumb in my detachment ordered a ship off without authenticating the call." Explained the warrant officer. "The ship came down not five miles from the base."

"Keep my S.O.I. on my dog tag chain and, after that, so did the rest of the pilots. The guy who ordered the ship off got burned, bad.

"That lieutenant colonel got his on both counts," returned the lieutenant. "I wrote a note to the commanding general, went right by his battalion commanders. He called in several of his battalion commanders and chided them for misuse of radio 'n medevac procedures. I was not alone in my complaint, but the colonel had it in for me."

He put his cigarette out by rubbing the burning tip on the soles of his boots; field stripped it by shaking out the unburned tobacco and by putting the unburned paper and filter in a pocket.

"Next week got another call, not the next to be sure, had a batch in between. Again, the little things almost did us a job. They stated the number of patients all right – six, three urgent and three routine, but not which kind: walking or liter. If we had known then what we were to find out, we could have called the evac. The hospital's emergency room and I.C.U. and give them more specific information than just three urgent patients on the way.

"No enemy fire, no need for a hoist, gave us the eight-digit coordinates, weather clear, wind north by northeast, five knots. Once airborne, it took us twelve minutes to get there, all set to take aboard six casualties. What did we find? For one thing, they had the landing zone set up on a dirt road. That was just wonderful, and to show our appreciation, we started to spray dust and dirt, and rocks over everything, including the patients. Seeing through the main window proved impossible, so I guided the ship in by looking through the chin windows. Ignored the ground guide. Didn't know how to give signals; crossed arms to hover and went through a dance I've yet to figure out… shook every signal off, but he didn't understand, and the liter bearers came running up. No choice but to land on the road.

"It wasn't as bad as it could've been. Don't know how many times we landed during a small arms fire 'n waited like ducks in a shooting gallery while the litter bearers, up from their hideaways, resigned themselves to the exposure 'nd ran toward us.

"Got six casualties all right, six-liter patients: one requirin' heart massage, two with severe burns needing IV's, two with IV's already, 'nd one with a sucking chest wound. The three-marked routine was once, but has since changed. All had been in or on a reconnaissance vehicle that struck a mine.

"Where could we put them? Had racks for only three, one atop the other. To add to the mess, a liter bearer racing round the other side ran smack into our protete stick. They were built onto the nose back then. By breaking it 'nd 'coming the seventh patient, we lost the ability to know our speed or direction 'n would lose the ship's service till fixed.

"'Nother rifleman turned liter bearer ran to the side all right but couldn't figure what to do from there. Tried to put his end of the liter on the ship, trouble was, he was in the way. Then tried to set one hand grip on board 'nd push with the other, almost spilled the patient. He tried everything, even jumping aboard 'nd hauling it in that way which wasn't so bad if he hadn't stepped smack atop a burn casualty or nearly broke an IV. Oh, he was a gem! Lucky thing we weren't being shot at. Our medic finally got free enough to order him 'n the other liter bearer to sit the liter on the ground, move to the side, pick it up 'n slide it inside. Don't ever order me again private, 'was the parting comment of that spec. four.

"Normally we'd stick a patient with an IV on the bottom rack cause of gravity but that guy needin' a heart massage, he had to go on the bottom for leverage pushing down on his sternum. Put the one needin' 'n IV on the second rack 'nd the one with the sucking chest wound on top because the waste bottle should be lower than the man. Laid the other IV on the floor 'nd taped the solution to the hoist. The crew chief was given a cram course on heart patients; Jim sat next to a burn patient strapped into one of the seats. Last burn laid on the floor.

"To add to it, a major told us not to bump them. Better us than a ground ambulance, still, there is the game and I had to play it, kiss him where he wanted to be kissed 'n said I wouldn't. It did. It always does.

"A little while later Jim was replaced by a C.W.3 with three thousand hours flight time that really knew his stuff, handled the ship like a baby, and learned her idiosyncrasies right off. Was good 'nd was confident, too confident because he's not around anymore. Died in a crash just after Kissinger finished writing his name in Paris.

"They were having a fly off for who would supply the army with its planes. Hughes aircraft was one of the companies, Bell the other. Can't remember the third, a small concern 'nd licking their chops at the thought of fixin' that with a juicy government contract. A captain piloted a ship of one of the other companies up to twenty thousand feet 'nd the blade fell inwards, crashing through the windshield. Both pilots were unhurt but the crew chief had his arm severed. Got the craft down on 'n easy descent 'nd, by luck, the tanks didn't explode on impact. By then the crew chief had bled to death.

"Started to conduct an investigation right then and there: put ropes around the wreckage, but a man who had a healthy interest in the company and was buddy-buddy to the fort's chief of staff, convinced everyone involved it'd be better to have it done on a hanger. So in a private hanger, it went. When reconstructed, an investigating committee was picked by the general. Not one of them had a mechanic's background. All were officers 'nd received T.D.Y. pay equal to that if they went to a war college. For the month they were there, they lived in a high-class motel, had room service for every meal, 'n all the extras in the world. Finally came up with the cause—a pin that fits inside the rotor assembly had been rolled instead of machine cut. Its maximum stress capability was figured at ninety hours—the exact number of hours the ship had at the time of the crash.

"Word was hushed up for a while. When it did break, it was after Hughes had won the contract. Hughes has it made. Not only do they make the machines but build them in such a way that only their tools can fit the parts. Got the army both ways, which is O.K. with me. If you can make an extra buck then do it.

"There are a few of the losing company's ships still in the army inventory 'nd that C.W.3 got hold of one. He knew about the faulty pin but took off from Fort Bliss to Fort Knox anyway. Stopped at Fort Sill where they keep repair parts 'n junked aircraft, when he felt it start to go. They wouldn't give it to him at the cannibalization point, said it already had eighty hours on it 'ns wasn't reliable. He agreed. The next day it was missing 'n he was airborne. The army couldn't prove anything on him. Didn't have to. He crashed, killing all four people aboard. Sometimes I swear it's better to be new and scared than experienced 'n confident.

"Not long after I got the man, maybe a day or so, we got a call from a hot sector. A firefight had lasted most of the night. It started after a phantom went down 'nd a fire ship called in. They're out of the army inventory but were HUEY's with a long tube in front that spewed sodium compound at so many hundred pounds of pressure.

"Theory behind them was that they would smother enough flames to clear a path to the burning ship. Trouble was that they only found bodies. A ship's crew is either thrown or remains inside; if inside, they died in the explosion, if outside, they have to survive the fireball. The 'nomacks' can withstand that for a few seconds, the man is saved, provided he's not wearing synthetic underwear; only cotton doesn't melt. Being cumbrous and sitting ducks were more good reasons to scrape 'm.

"The fire ship was shot down 'nd set up a nice little landing zone—right on the side of a hill. The wounded were urgent all right two were to die on board, both by burns. Another was shot in the leg. The bullet made a nice clean hole, traveled through the leg, up the chest, 'nd out above the left nipple without doing serious damage. Weirdest thing I ever saw. A fourth was escorted to the ship ''nd quietly strapped in.

"Like I said, we were facing down an incline. The main rotor blades remained parallel to the ship just a few feet above the ground toward the rear. When four patients had been secured we heard 'nd felt a sickening thud. Why they didn't come at us from the front so we could see them is what I'd like to know. They were taught that in basic. Luckily, if you can call it that, only one was killed. The fifth casualty 'n the far liter bearer were unhurt. I didn't feel bad about it. In face, I cursed his stupidity. Only later, lying in my bunk, did I realize how calloused I become, something I promised never to be before I went into the army.

"Everything seemed to be going fine when we got aloft. Our plans were changed because of that body bag. After we unloaded the casualties we figured on going to his unit: first of the second infantry and hand his remains to the battalion's S1 for burial. I didn't remember that guy on the seat. The medic did 'n went back to check. His hand was on the seatbelt when the guy bit him, hard 'n deep, drew blood and almost cut the carotid artery. Undid his strap, pushed the medic out of his way, 'nd jumped into the bay, tipping over an IV of ringers lactate attached to one of the burn patients. Before doing anything else, the crew chief grabbed hold of him, started fighting and found himself wrestling with a madman. Shouting something like: 'Death, all I want, all that matters,' he pulled open the door 'n threw himself out, complete with a hundred fifty pound crew chief who had no thought of letting go.

"I don't trust a lot of the army's equipment, but I'll trust their safety straps. Buckled around the crew chief's waist and attached to the wall, not a single connection came undone when yanked by the jerk of two falling bodies. There they were, suspended like a fish on a stringer high above the rain forest.

"The C.W.3 began to haul them in. This time the nut was as weak as a kitten. Didn't really want to fall. With a leading part in that little drama, it was all I could do to keep the ship at a fifty degree cant to compensate for the weight, all the while bein' lowered to the ground. One thing done wrong, one misjudgment on my part, a wind change and that would have been all she wrote. But it didn't 'n when they were hauled aboard, the psycho received a closed fist for a reward. When he woke up, no Houdini could have broken from those bonds.

"'Bout the same thin' 'ccured back in the states after ma tour 'n Nam," expounded the captain. "Had a stick a jumpers on board, special forces, all 'c' licensed 'r better in civilian life. Flying over the canal zone in 'n adventure trainin' exercise. The jump master had me lower to 2200 fee, just 'nough for a hop 'n pop. But they were rigged to static lines believing: 'n who am I to argue, that they could not stabilize themselves soon enough fer safety. Had on a main, a reserve, a M-16 with ammunition, inflatable water wings, 'n enough stuff ta last 'em a week in the jungle. Throwing out a roll of cray paper, the jump master told me to fly half a mile upwind. On the far point of the windline he gave the commands: 'Ta the door, ready, boogie, 'n to one, two, three, then, with a broken voice, shouted somethin' ta me. Couldn't turn around and ask 'n the intercom wasn't workin', so I got the work from my co-pilot. Told me that the third man's chute had caught on the skids.

"The jump master climbed down the skids to have a better look. The man signaled he was conscious by touching the top of his helmet with his free hand then began to open his cape wells, screaming that he was trying to cut away. The reply was right to the point: 'You do and I'll shoot!' At the time I thought he said it to scare him. Later I realized that if he did we would be left trailing a full canopy just eager to get into the tail rotor 'n crash us. The man re-snapped 'n allowed the jump master to grab him. All the while I had been lowering the craft, now at a thousand feet. For that, the man yelled, climbed back onto the skids, into the ship 'n hollered: 'We're too low to open! Go up! Can't open here! His chute ain't secure, he kin fall any moment! Go up!' Got it up to two thousand feet when the canopy slipped a little, tearing a five foot hole in a goyer. Back down. He locked his legs about the other's waist, grabbed his head then, in a modified bear hug, held on while he pulled out a knife from a sheath on his reserve 'n cut the static lines. Down they went, shapeless black dots underneath a tattered ensign.

"One dot emerged then disappeared beneath a nylon cloud. The other slowed, his open reserve playing peek-a-boo with the longer length shattered main. Both knew how to land in the trees 'n came out just fine.

"Always happens that way," replied the warrant officer. "Only defense is to learn, not make the same mistake twice and hope your first boo boo isn't your last."

"I'm sure your right," said the second lieutenant before wishing all three a good night and walked back to his camp and an evening cup of coffee.

DOGOODING

A casual observer of Jackson, Wyoming wouldn't perceive the intense competition rampant among its businesses. The western flair to everything was a necessary façade, very often too expensive for otherwise conventional tourism. Severe restrictions on advertisements left survival dependent upon rigorous management. Those who mistook the location as a promised land of scenery and success invariably joined like-minded concerns from Boulder, Colorado, in bankruptcy court. Turnover was rapid. And nothing turned over faster than the enterprises that tried but couldn't make it at 141 Crab Tree Corners. The undistinguished building was distinguished as an albatross to whoever set up shop inside. Until a firm established itself as the strongest contender the jinx had yet met. Smilingly sanctioned by the federal government, the American Red Cross got its shingle hung before laissez-faire could do another gambler in.

Establishing her command was a veteran street corner cadet who never relinquished her Salvation Army zeal for saving souls. Accompanying her were two young ladies whose dissimilarities weren't noticeable on government time. No one on the team was mistaken about their job. From the moment tradesmen presented them suitable offices, the entire community was introduced to available services, and the three during open houses, teas, suppers, picnics, and meetings announced over the radio. After hours were times for more familiarity, the chief and the serious, piano-legged, case worker socializing with the best ladies, the platinum blonde socializing in the Cowboy Bar.

So long as the beauty did her work, nothing much mattered. She was a good person, had to be or would have flunked her interview. And dedicated. While her colleague and superior attracted housewives and street people with difficult problems, she would diligently bend to the mountains of paperwork rather than entertain the virile set that stopped by. Males learned to assume gentlemanly manners or get out. The most patient would wait until the end of the day for her hot side to emerge from the cold. Others, less patient, once her reputation was established, volunteered for free duties that the chief couldn't thank them enough for. She glowed and glowed, even wrote a letter to the editor about the industriousness of maligned youth. Devotion to cause keeping the lady's bags heavy kept her subordinates late and took a lot out of the volunteers, making them husband their energy and time because it was true the blonde appreciated unselfishness, very much.

Although available, the other woman had habits that ensured her reaching the top echelon of her profession. Acts that might not dissuade a sailor did dissuade possible paramours. Intercepting just lit cigarettes with air freshener when in her car was the kind of spontaneity most could do without. Propriety replaced the missionary zeal of her boss in effecting the same outward show.

Given enough time and anything new merges with the established. The seasonality of Jackson accelerates the process. 141 Crab Tree Corners was a fixture in two months, with nothing to undermine the fine job being done there.

Though the running of their trade veered not from what was taught several social changes ago, the locality was such a melting pot that no one attitude prevailed enough to be run afoul of. The routine had been settled into. Events had been calendared to fortify their raison d'être. Which resident would offer lip service as opposed to those willing to help more had already decided so for themselves. Like the Rotary, American Legion, and unlike the Elks, who had slaughtered their namesake, the Red Cross had conquered yet another frontier.

With the re-establishment of the spinsterish ways to two, the perpetuation of the third's full life wasn't all that envied. Time and space had never previously gotten her away from nuisances. In the city or country or way over there where there are humans, there is human nature. Out of experience came a crusty attitude about what to expect. The heckle of hecklers wasn't so bad that way.

A bar hopper, exposure increased the percentage of meeting undesirables. The obnoxious, the promisers, the deft and clumsy, her schooling was keen on anything. To get to her took above average wiles, like that of a man who once sat on the next stool, showing not an ounce of interest. As a ruse, inattention works miracles for stags on the prowl. She succumbed and earnestly asked about the paratrooper tattoo on his forearm and other things, concerning someone whose curiosity got the best of them. His shy replies were so soft and convincing and unassuming, the relationship struck was still going strong at closing time. A friendship was on the rise when, tipping his Stetson for goodbye, his raised had exposed a sheathed knife. Not in drama class was she ever better at getting away with faking her emotions.

The morning after a good one was no time for another headache. When the ex-soldier presented himself sharply the next morning, the blond plumbed deeper into her thespian background. A scene would be ruinous. But nothing could have been further from things as they turned out. Of all those who had interrupted the typing of narratives, the misfits and malcontents, only he made going back to work a bother. Nor did he confine himself to her. Gregarious and polite, the duo who usually kept busily to themselves were enthralled as far as they could go. Etiquette must have been drilled in somewhere, for at the proper time his backside was to the ladies on out the door.

He became a regular and a favorite. The times he didn't come by were fewer because of it. With his background a mystery, the need for the knife was explained away in the fractured psychological jargon learned as a prerequisite to the women's profession. So, when absent for a while, side trips were tentatively made to and from work to find out why.

In the shadow of Snow King Mountain, across the sparkle of Cache Creek, the congregation encircling a gravel pit was too loud to dismiss. To it the three went, to receive quite a start.

Keeping a circus crowd screaming was two knights having it out wearing woken helmets, with wooden swords and shields colored with personal crests, one being that of paratrooper wings.

The combatants bashed, parried, really went at each other, constrained by rules of fair play, the crowd certainly wouldn't mind dispensing with. The honor that went untrammeled made the fight tedious, and if this sport superseded football, it would have left the spectators unhappy.

At its inconclusive end, naturally, only the blonde elbowed her way to one combatant. Embarrassment was mutual upon unhelmeting. Explanations weren't mandatory but offered anyway, breathlessly and with modesty. Hard to understand, what was in his wallet said a whole lot more. A card proclaiming his membership in the Anachronists Club was on the opposite side of an army identification glossy.

Reared between two brothers who went army, she knew it belonged in federal hands if he was legitimately out. And had to restrain herself from snitching. As it was, developments favored tight lips.

During the fight, the chief went and fetched a policeman who, remembering no laws against such sports, remembered the name. The reputation associated with it took a repeater to build. Serious crimes a frequent of stir do not do. Or are in a way blessed. In his case, the most recent accuser had joined the parade of former accusers in withdrawing criminal complaints. Making friends was his talent.

That his opponent was once a former cellmate with similar offbeat hobbies was the word that got back to the blonde. By acknowledging the news with terrific concern, was she able to conceal her secret and get her chief to focus on raising a sunken soul? As for the intermediate member of the triumvirate, she would be satisfied punctiliously doing the paperwork.

An unshakable believer in original sin, her potentate quickly confronted him with accusations, hoping to stun the evil away. Nothing quaked, no fever sweated, mildly, with contrition, the man admitted his blemishes. A crescent was "ah shucked" in the dust by his shoes. Evangelist trumpeting or Jung's, James's, and Freud's recommendations weren't needed to lure the why out for appraisal. Gladly, it was volunteered.

Divorced parents, shunted between relatives, menial jobs swallowing time to learn a trade, anxiety, drink, it was classic. A sad society's child who also referred vaguely to how an eighteen-wheeler he had begged a loan for had been wrecked by a drunk he trusted. No mention was made of the military.

As case workers, progress reports were facts of life. Their exacting format very often bored holes into evenings.

Monotony was purposely deleted from the glittering job description of service to mankind. As their stay moved along, their sympathies attracted every freebooter in the tri-state region. One mendicant so much life another; it became their pleasure to do all they could for the one who didn't make demands. He was their showcase. Papers about him piled so high that the intermediate saw visions of publishing an article. A good one would walk her past those with more time in grade. Feather the cap of her boss.

With so much interest in his person, a swagger in the man's stride would be understandable. Such was not the case, the endearment of do-gooder to being done to ran past professionalism.

More than ever, his coming by was cause for mild celebration, while consternation reigned when absent. Too long an absence and to jail they would go, finding him apologetic and insisting the caught up to him misdeed was of a past severed from the present.

There came a time when the leniency of the local judge was severely taxed. Granted, each charge, when leveled, had extenuating circumstances, but enough was becoming too much. Found rummaging in a garage, the injured cat he claimed to have been helping made an excellent ruse. He was right about pinning him with saddle theft. No state court has ever clearly defined circumstantial evidence. In an argument over mineral leases, his name magically appeared and took expensive legalities to erase, much less prosecute. Through a dozen cases tangling a dozen litigants, he went, coming out, going back in unscathed, unperturbed, living as either a ward of the community or sponsored by someone with something to gain on his side.

Getting him a real job in accordance with God's will was possible only when the midseason quitters left a Yellowstone concessionaire desperate. As a dishwasher, he fared so well that a manager saw to his promotion to cook. Intermittent check-ups found him immensely happy and in a group providing the fellowship sorely needed. The knife that had no former use was used in a filleting capacity. He grew popular, was sought after, and enjoyed himself right up to that night he was whisked off the road, charged with D.W.I., and stood before a magistrate one believes impossible to exist outside the movies. Had he been five hundred yards down the road, the Red Cross and a lawyer for the concessionaire would not have had the time they did getting the sentence commuted to one at least reasonable.

While locked away, the tourist season ended, two journals rejected the article, and the blonde became a devotee of the 'Getting the Most From...." and "Human Sensuality" fad, suddenly in vogue across the country. Frustration, she was convinced, was at the heart of aberrant behavior, including knavery and reclusiveness. Unable to do anything for her boss, she had a surprise awaiting the man and her associate once the prison gates parted.

Cornering her quarry with a sensible argument was not the method the blonde employed. The associate was instead bombarded by innuendo, allusions to more stimulating lifestyles, and made to feel jealous about the fun other people had. Done right, the not entirely unattractive woman had a grain of adventure injected in her orderly life when the parolee was steered to her doorstep.

Getting him to eye the woman temptingly was probably the biggest bit of conversion of the blonde's career. Indirectness wasn't the way. Point blank, his life was accosted for the ruination of her studies was said to be inevitable. When several sessions passed and all that the twain understood was his lust for her, the blonde played her remaining hand. Either he dated the woman, or his desertion would become common knowledge.

Preceding him to the door were wisps of an expensive aftershave. Clanging together as he clasped hands behind his back was a sterling silver bracelet loose on his right, a digital, six-function watch tight on his left. Rising from armadillo-skinned, cactus-roughneck-topped, no. 16-toed cowboy boots were an indigo dyed soft-shouldered denim suit filled out by the man who couldn't afford any of it. It was the puke necklace the social scientist decorously eyed. And was the conversation saver after the easy to get out "how's it been?".

The apartment was a show window, perfect and antiseptically fit for an operation. How it was kept so was revealed by the woman's disapproval of his touching things. Why she did not snap was understandable. Facts needed to chink the holes in her article made her the perfect hostess. His insistence not to drink alone made him the perfect guest.

Starting slow, together they began to guzzle. She to mesmerize data from him; he to get mesmerized so the evening wouldn't be a total waste.

They got familiar and, familiar, were candid. Excuses for abnormality were hidden behind when the sharp were exposed for the sham they were. To her credit, the woman berated her for replacing work with living. To his credit, the man begged no forgiveness for his unsavory biography. Weakness of character, he claimed, and not separated parents or luck no worse than anyone else's deserved no sympathy. They were both afraid of life. The fear just manifested itself differently, with the higher status of the woman making her no better.

The spirit of the date stayed with the daters well into the chemical re-stabilization of their systems. The department head was thrilled at the born-again Thanksgiving. The blonde patted herself on the back. The woman never looked fresher or was more outgoing. And if a steadying force could be applied, rising from bellhop to assistant manager of the largest hotel in Jackson was inevitably in the man's future.

The said influence was dubious in many points. Sure, she'd like to be an anchor. But uplifting people had been her profession for so long that seeing it domestically took some doing. A rigid framework of status had to be toppled. Compromising the Robert Redford and Dr. Salk of her most intimate dreams was a crippling blow. Then there were doubts about her homemaking, motherhood, and companionship. What would he be like tied down? Could she separate his future from his former self? Would matrimony end or invigorate her career? To these questions came many more questions than answers. Her poor head whirled so much that the comforting of her prospective mate cured only the symptoms, not the uneasiness. A measure of solace was found in even later hours at work.

Not long after, fortune took a fairy tale turn. The jinx of 141 Crab Tree Corners was not to be denied. Unwilling to tip its king, fire was the agency used to declare a stalemate.

Sirens screamed, lights flashed, and people gathered, but with a conflagration of such size so infrequent, the fire department humiliated anyone connected with its operation. Property and irreplaceable documents, even a life, should have been lost. Town officials would certainly have had a lot of explaining to do had a blessing not materialized to reduce the calamity to misfortune. Ash, layered and sweat-soaked, half dead, the ex-serviceman was identified by his intended as the person who saved her and the key records.

From that night on, the tide of the man's life flowed in his favor. Rare is the individual who is so honored as he was. Gifts and appreciations poured in from the U.S. government down to tourists whose vacations were highlighted by the drama.

Elected mayor on the strength of his ownership of both town papers, his honor made sure the exclusives concentrated upon the hero and not the fire. Where good journalism would place pictures of the gutted building, baby and adolescent snapshots of the man appeared instead. As acting fire commissioner, the police chief counseled a patrolman on what to do with an empty gas can with a scratched cap and a bent knife found in the back alley.

Capping the excitement of a true-to-life adventure was the consummation of a true-to-life romance. The wedding of the social worker and hero was a pageant that shouldered those previous into obscurity. A fund was pooled to send the couple off in a dazzling late-model car. With the whole town their permanent friend, with a solid financial start, as the two drove away to happily ever after, the woman cuddled close to the man who proved that, with love and consideration, anybody could mend their ways.

LIFE AFTER DEATH

No one school of thought had succeeded in attracting enough subscribers to be lobbied into policy. Almost all the homesteaders in Jackson Hole had long since attested by displaying government certificates. The casual indifference of second generations was a warning to parents who were themselves getting used to their lives and location. What to do? After all the work and struggle, the flat between the Gros Ventres and Tetons was disturbingly settled. Rodents and coyotes playing their immemorial roles, the ungulates, flourishing in quiet, were as satisfied now as ever. Not so the human population. The common stamp of a pioneer was rooted deep in blood, excited by discovery, and winning through difficulties. They had tamed a land that the Indians couldn't after unrecorded hundreds of years. Now that it was done, they were bored. Get ready for winter, then persevere with cabin fever 'til spring when the cycle goes full round. The carrying capacity of the abyssally poor outwash plains held the number of hamlets servicing the good folks to three, keeping entertainment light from that quarter.

The ease could have been received as a reward. But wasn't. Physical prowess never excludes the cerebral. Lugging building materials from the lower slopes for unneeded structures was sheer busywork. The land was cleared as much as possible, with advantageous life patterns established, and what was better to do than encourage the influx of excursionists from their northern neighbor, Yellowstone Park? Dude ranchers advertising rugged adventures were a coming reality. Hardly a major stream came down from the mountains to level out unbothered by fishermen. Species of fish known, not to the region, but to eastern or western anglers, were planned to supplant the less remarkable Cutthroat Trout, Grayling, and Mountain White.

It was Jadiah Peters who followed up the soundly rejected proposition that they too petition for federal park status with the belief that outsiders would thrill to such communal diversions as dog sled races. Something could be made from what offsets the monotony between equinoxes. Skiing, those dark ages before lifts, was possible via tow ropes. As was tobogganing and sledding. Established courses could be used for locally sponsored summertime cross-country or horse races. As for the necessary capital, Jadiah balked, knowing it could only come from visitors willing to spend when such dreams were faced. Outfitters and rafters were all moonlighters, doing their share to pump activity into the Hole when away from, say, Mr. Menor, ferrying folks across the Snake. Banks close enough for involvement shouldered no relaxation of stern interest rates. Then there was the smell of the one that had been folded, ruining many relatives of local farmers.

A road as good as that following the Madison and Firehole Rivers from West Yellowstone to the lake was on paper only, along the tortuous Lewis. From the south, vacationers had to decoach at Hoback Junction, way far away. Allaying the timorous by asking for a permanent detachment of U.S. troops got nowhere. Complications were taking the shape of a Gordian knot; no Alexander was showing up to rend.

"What's needed is a wonder," Jadiah stormed out of order at a summit meeting in the village of Jackson. "Geysers, paint spots, petrified trees; hell, Injuns comed to Yellerstone from Ohio fer its obsidian. We got nuthing but what a handful don't need nothin' moran some gear for."

"It's history that makes people come and see. Dull Knife, Crazy Woman, Liddle Big Horn, and even Cassidy's Hole in the Wall are better known. If Colter was half the liar of Bridger, or literal, if, if, if a history of beaver men didn't dominate," lamented a sourdough who perked Jadiah's imagination.

"A deduction here, boys. What's all the noise ta history anyway… works! That's all, writ down in books by bookmen what get it hearsay anyway.

"Buntline never went west. His Cody twern't nuthin' like the drinkin', sometime scout, real one. But even cowboys bought the written picture of da cattle trade. Edison's movin' pictures spittin' out lie after lie. Injuns never attacked a wagon train. Hung aroun' ta barter."

Accounts of similar persuasions persisted on into what Jadiah was driving at.

"Masterson, when a sports reporter with my cousin, after refereein' the Jefferies' fight, said the whoppers spoken 'bout him made him rich. His brother Mat was twice as wild. Who knows 'bout him?... Boys. It's time for a change. And lemme say ta polish the hills for show."

"Such as?"

"Mining. Colorado's got a million tales: ghosts, bad, good luck, loose ladies, and mean men. Moran, one town got known without a strike, 'til they burnt down."

"That's too far gone."

"Nope, the farer fetched the better. No lawsuits or complications without feet ta step on. Who's to say Garnet Canyon twern't a reopened and closed Indian or Spanish mine? Lost mines, broken fortunes and men, everything."

Influenced, the village council, as individuals, pondered the concept and, in a huddle, bantered pros and cons interminably. Such insularity as they had for years been accustomed to bred the age-old smugness toward strangers. Czar Catherine, being taken by Prince Orloff, was brought up as a grandiose fraud and got away with it. So too all the rascalities of financial pantheons. The idea, considering its size, was certainly appealing; all the work that lay ahead, turning these men into boys wanting to put one over. Yarn tellers could find a fresh audience for anecdotes too often told. More and more, the longer it was considered, the closer the quorum agreed. The holdouts were the same obstacle seekers of issues past. Though their objections smacked of the usual: "let's not jump into this half-baked," their persistence did tone rising adolescence down to manly stage acting. The blue of a smoke-filled room suffused each with a hard-to-dismiss politico demeanor. A common ground was reached after the rolling of many non-existent pork barrels and trivial special favors.

As the gentleman's agreement had it, the plan was okayed in a watered form, easing a few unruly consciences. A bogus past would be advertised, but with a third of the boondoggling. Despite the minority of arbitrators being shopkeepers of some sort, the remainder were not without the same constitution. Farmers, even self-sufficient ones, are businessmen and are just as adroit in the wiles of salesmanship. Let the tourists come eager for hard rock fantasies. As customers can be persuaded to buy what they don't want, so can they be steered to other attractions. Calculating minds projected a time when the sham could be superseded by honest come-ons. Yellowstone's southern neighbor would then become an indispensable stop on numerous itineraries.

What this corroboration didn't outline was thought worthy of consideration. Early morning, inching its hours under sleepy flesh, was no time to floor anything other than adjournment. But Jadiah, cognizant of his importance, was susceptible to insights. Luck alone held them at bay when, out of the ruck, one flashed, promising to involve those taken aback in more haggling. A legend, one tender to hearts, representative of the religion of work and sacrifice, was wanting. To captivate, by another American myth, the throb that its citizens could identify as the best in themselves. What was the consternation of many? A mule, he affirmed, was the stoical beast of unsung heroics. Considering the hour and crude offer, the polish of a born raconteur needed all its glitter to put the suggestion across as better than any more glamorous. Eagles, beard, the Oz menagerie were too overworked, trite. A boy and his wonder dog. How maudlin, as were further substitutes introduced by the prejudiced. "After all," said Jadiah. Franklin wanted the turkey to be our national bird. It's more American than eagles." An oblique reference to a horse that ran as fast backwards as forward, by its inferential weakness, broke the brunt of the attack. Why Jadiah's idea wasn't way off came to vogue half to persuade recalcitrants and half out of true conversion. After all, what mule hadn't done a yeoman's service? If only the way of things had given them one endearing grace. The spiteful western continent's camel, into their yoke they went, hating every molecule residing outside their hide. Only in retrospect could the life of one be raised as exemplary. Nobody could scoff at their importance.

Since to laud the breed would be an empty gesture, picking one above the rest, stuffed in death with commuted human qualities, consumed the fat part of a second session. The first order of business being the renaming of Jackass Flats, the last dealt with the kind of monument pooled finances could erect. Between the chosen luminary, after much exasperation, was at last chosen out of convenience.

The leathered carcass of Old Sam, on a nearby refuse heap, was available.

The rearranging of Sam's background unreservedly bound the rearrangers in fun. The family who would have had it much harder without him, the families who handed meals out during his unharnessed retirement, ascribed to him adventures at a mine bedazzled with every tale imaginable to excite the gullible. A contingent wove sensational rescues about themselves and Sam and swore they'd swear their veracity if accused of leg pulling. All in all, should these tyros stand ten paces from Ned Buntline, armed with paper and pen, Belle Starr, Buffalo Bill, et all would find their match in Sam, the posthumous wonder.

For uniformity, Sam's story was printed, handed out, memorized, and burned. Tripping over particulars was prevented by an assiduity of detail remarkable, for they were more used to using their hands than their heads. Schoolboys infuriated their teachers by attending more to that than their lessons. Neither were the portals to Christ immune. Under the shadow of the Tetons or well away, both chapels were indistinguishable in conducting secular prayer. Bible stories and aphorisms were re-read for pertinent instructions.

As for the work, since nature had kept her distance, it was an anodyne for those who didn't want their calluses to go. Lumbering, chiseling, chinking finishes to cabins before their partial demolishment, hewing wooden tracks to look old, ties were purposely buried or used to board up never-opened mines. The local smelter disgorged records of smoke, making shoddy stuff shoddier. The more disused the appearance, the better. Never had the community chartered its enthusiasm in as gigantic an effort as the deception in the making.

Like beasts, they toiled, day heaping upon day, under the direction of village fathers who needed no tricks to encourage. Midsummer deadlines were tight enough. And, as it developed, a pipe dream. Too much had been bitten off to be chewed. Time taken off concealing the operation from the inquisitive or park people was time wasted. While the time needed for promotion was scarce to nonexistent. Nobody had any idea of modern techniques. A friend of a relative as distant genealogically as spatially removed was a foot in the door of a coastal paper, if he had evidence. Which required more progress and a biased cameraman sympathetic to the cause. Local shutterbugs just didn't have the skill for poignant presentation.

As for the monument, that too was found more troublesome than anticipated. Where to put it, what would the inscription be, its size and general impression—after all, a miscalculation, remembering its subject matter, would be fatal—were each a matter of contention. So much so, centralization was a must.

With the components so unrelated, a committee's jurisdiction was proving itself inept. One man's powers should go no further than his talents. Stepping off a prestigious post needed strong motives. Promises of absolute managerial say in their allotted sectors were one proviso. Better recognition in a historical pamphlet, the "Frontier Wives" was another. Being citizens of a democracy, untainted by corporate philosophy, who would direct, be the omnipotent one, was earmarked for squabbling, not to be believed.

Bolstered by the ground recent temerity had gained, Jadiah wielded his salt to affect a vivid argument. Based on his idea in the beginning, why shouldn't he be the man affirmed by a few? Then Jadiah was floating, on top of a world giving him exclusive dominion. Forget his advancement was bred by the resurrection of Sam, whose irritability got him through coyote-raked pasture years to die at the right time. Any means to such fortuitous ends were fine.

From top to bottom, the enterprise got off to a reinvigorated start. Now that leadership was defined, done so sincerely, and right. An initial inflow of Yellowstone's sight-seers was making good their hotel bookings when the waning season brought with it something to go south for. An attractive booklet vaunting Sam's heroics was displayed for sale in a shop erected in full view of a statue. Commanding a dominant place in the park, a bronzed over, more horse than mule, reared back on his hind legs above an impressive plaque.

Mule races with tempting prizes, odds, and all sorts of attractively presented ends, and concomitant with the vein responsible were huskers volunteering in droves to hype more of the same. To retribute trade, deputed with the trust of a community that had worked so hard, it aggrieved them more than anyone else when the gush fell to a dying trickle. Why fewer eyes gazed upon the sun, glimmering bronze, wasn't difficult to solve. The bite of the come-on was shallow. More about treasure was the consensus; or get Sam into the national spotlight, make him an Old Faithful.

Whereafter Jadiah, being looked at with dethroning eyes, took the urgency of the building crisis to do what he had no practical application for. Of the same make as other settlers, except for venturing the limited risks of a small business, responding alone to unknowns taxed untried depths of a will he wasn't sure of possessing. To surrender his office was no disgrace. Having sacrificed as much as he did was commendable. Never would he accuse his neighbors of innuendoes. And never again would the chance to pull a coup from such a shambles occur. An ordinary man, satisfied with life and himself, a good citizen and friend, that spark innate in all men had gotten the affair this far, and, by thunder, would get it the rest of the way.

In the face of his wife's and mother-in-law's protests, despite middle-of-the-road sense, up went his house and business for a mortgage. A legerdemain he, after the fact, applauded his having put a scratch for nest egg in a fund needed for a sweep of eastern cities. To sell Sam was his transmogrified grail.

Being untroubled by much overhead also elucidated a lack of means. Squeezing resources, Boy Scout tight, by pushing himself, no snug ad man suspected the problems besetting the natty sharp salesman who punctually showed his finest at every appointment.

Wise to the laundry-list tactics of a correspondence sales course, in spite of great strides in skill, perpetual noncommittal wore his patience and wallet thin. Open dealings had too far ingrained themselves in a country's constitution. Pushing away from a desk, crossing arms, gruff comments, and snappy snatches at the time didn't mean trying and sell me, but go away to Jadiah. With no brochure to support a crazy idea, the more he railed, the more despondent he became.

Down came the winter, and letters were received at home about successes the writer penned after hours of picking up jobs. During work and in the evenings, his style was gone over and over again. Until, when he thought the secret in hand, new rounds were made with a fattened purse and confidence. Should the prospect be a clinger to habits, he would demonstrate how an enriched valley would be good for his company. Minimizing the plan's novelty got the attention of those adjudged too timid to make decisions. Leaving the neurotic scrooges alone, time was available to boost other customers' sense of importance. By making them believe in their superiority did an encouraging number took the matter to lay out artists and production assistants. After which Jadiah hit upon skirting such middlemen altogether. Secretaries to top ad agencies and investment brokers bade him into their bosses' offices. Where hoped-for deals were agreed upon, signed, and delivered first crack.

Back, Jadiah came hailed as a financial whiz. In the last weeks of March, Jackson grew more than in all its history. Rexburg and Casper bankers sent runners to negotiate their board's faith in big business acumen. Liberal loans floated to whomever needed capital as the distant east was introduced to intriguing advertisements. Something of a Paul Bunyon, American apple pie to the core romance was rising out of the west. As a parable, Sam meant something special to generations weaned on Horatio Alger. In a land of Christian ethics, there couldn't be too many examples of what good comes from hard work and diligence. And with Teddy in the public eye, the Wild West Show the darling of civilization, what sour soul dared repute the brilliance of that ass's life?

About Jackson Hole, Jadiah strode as decorously as a general. An aide was needed to arrange details he, as supervisor, chief consultant, and whatnot, couldn't fit into his schedule. Include the families of hurried laborers, and a boom town equal to any of Colorado's silver beset was a fact. Only a mining engineer could tell the truth about the mines as they were.

Like island-stranded sailors did an exponentially increased populace awaited the coming of a salvation.

Centuries of progress gulfed the modes of transportation conveying benefactors. Lookouts on Signal Mountain must have tingled the same hearing the chug of a motorcade as Defoe's Crusoe had to sails poking into the sky. South of the Continental Divide, on a mud road, when tourists in coaches and autos reached Moose, the word was long since there. Nobility are seldom so received as those in a vanguard heralding the coming of a main body that didn't quit. The rest of the spring, all summer, and into the fall.

Like that, the Hole came alive as not to be imagined. Shops and hotels spilled over with spenders. Goods couldn't be kept on the shelves. Yarn weavers Rip Van Winkle to exhaustion. And no original was safe from being revered as the epitome of the American Gothic that never really was.

Nothing veered from unfolding finer than a dream. On the tide's crest, credit was granted to mere whims. Even Wall Street was touched. Not until the roaring Florida trade were wheeler dealers taken by a place so remote. Action was to be had in northwestern Wyoming; a number were intent upon getting.

Into the Hole went their feelers. Feedback being favorable, a titan or two wired to make offers. Schematically, the probers worked toward securing a monopoly. Wringing meanings from compiled data, ouijaing which enterprises upheld the works, the proprietors asked, not one gave an affirmative answer.

The wonder attached to Sam by the visitors was not unrelated to the wonder attached to his creator by those in on the secret. Jadiah's counsel was in every case sought. Pell mell, a pattern was discerned and neutralized. Advertising each to refrain from commitment, he also asked them to return for a meeting. Out of which came more than a resolution to hold onto some property. The pride of having started from nothing was tantamount to confessing a much greater love for the site of their struggle. Winning a close contest invests in the victor a need to discover the ins and outs of his competitor. Up to the crests to see for miles, a sublime tie, soon or late, infused each with a humor their children were born with. It was that platoon, unjaded by the windfall, whose intractable innocence pushed Jadiah into summoning the meeting that made others recognize the obvious.

By hepping the put-on people were stomping fragile meadows to death. Their autos ruining night quiet, careless with campsites and littering like pigs, it was a Coney Island, entertain me, attitude which palled the value of profits. The excitement of a bonanza was not worth such blithe disregard. Enough became too much from patronizing snobs who would have paid for a piggy back up to a mine if the service were offered. But an army was needed to enforce regulations existing only as individual good wills.

Seeing the shambles, counting the lawsuits of those whose stupidity got them mauled by bears, a lot of money went a long way to push for federalization as a national park. All winter, even the former detractors of government infringement hung on the outcome.

At the onset of spring's tide were the defeated petitioners and an incognito twist. Through a breached local resistance, the masses adequately masked the slick maneuvering and candid questioning of two men. They snooped and spent a lot of time at the mines and left nobody knew when.

A new age was awakening with the century. Men with resolve were fighting free from enforced existences and exposing duplicity wherever suspected. Muck raking was becoming less the avant-garde and more the overwhelming practice. Practitioners abounded with the no-holds-barred ideals of the mining engineer and writer who had descended upon Jackson Hole.

It was first detected in the coolness of once generous bank officers. Tourists inexplicably didn't show. The bustle was a rustle when the word befell the good folks; they were God's disgrace, a bane to the purity of the pioneering spirit. Technicalities of the chicanery were amazingly accurate. The worship of Sam took a satanic turn.

Though Jadiah wasn't pilloried, when the fun seekers decamped, down came the symbol of his mistake. Those sunk by overextension were buoyed by those who emerged intact. Every vestige of the debacle in time was disassembled or destroyed. Things were reverting to as they were. To a point. Exact recovery was not possible, not after two years of sensations.

Indigenous to fame was publicity. Favorable or un makes no difference. To get in print, that is all that matters. The combination of fame and infamy, putting the Hole on the map, had attracted those whose moral parameters were different from the rest. These people reaped different meanings from the reports or, having gone there, found in their bones the need to return.

Reduced by multiples, the numbers who walked the towns and meadows over-tramped neither. A religious respect-imposed self-restraint whenever necessary for the good of a preservationist sentiment. And when more seasons passed and quite a few of those, constituting a nucleus of similar thinkers, traded the epithet of visitor for resident action action-backed codes put to paper. Naturally, the dude ranches were frequented by those with as much money as time to spend it. But, in the main, most who came did so to deal in first-person rather than vicarious adventures. Living closer to their wallets, they enjoyed more by going hiking, climbing, and doing stripped to the essentials, knowing the open sesame to delight was fitness and an attitude reveling, not the goal, but every moment getting there. As is always the case, the equilibrium shifted to the good by leaving well enough alone. To the resident's satisfaction. To Jadiah's immense relief, and for the benefit of everything and body involved, except a mule who had passed his mortality ignorant of the fuss to come.

OCCUPATIONS

Hidden Falls didn't monopolize the tourists' attention. Cameras aimed at the water invariably were trained on the rocks to the left. From the fringes of the rainbow west, to a perpendicular cliff, climbers swarmed over the rocks to make them come alive.

Barrages of clicks and whirs recorded what the cameramen thought was unadulterated adventure. Ropes and gear draped across the slopes were reminiscent of historic sieges. Each climbing class was applauded as it snaked its way to the base of the training slopes. Novices were afforded the same respect as experts. The sightseers didn't know who was who, or what was what.

That kind of ignorance wasn't shared by the climbers. A couple of pitches were all that was needed for the dullest novice to appreciate what the intermediate and advanced classes were about. The spectators didn't know that when the tyros weren't climbing, they were ogling their betters. If they had, they too would have ogled them.

The slopes the small advanced class maneuvered on, whether viewed from near or far, appeared formidable. Its fewer members could not entirely explain why it had outdistanced all other classes. Despite stopping to learn a new technique, practice a complicated move, or listen to climbing lore, it still kept ahead. The distance lost taking turns with direct aid, reviewing chock placement, and doing special problems was made up with only a little difficulty. The adept class was able to rappel the intermediate's drop before the intermediates arrived.

The spare time left before calling it a day was used to challenge the experts. The climb that was unanimously assented to had the assenters and themselves swallowing in awe. The perpendicular cliff bounding the west end of the escarpment was well named. Impossible Wall carried the National Climbing Classification System rating of F 10, meaning that a free, unaided ascent was, by and large, a wish.

The students remained demure while their guide rigged an overhead belay. The levity preceding previous climbs was conspicuously absent. The importance of this climb was overwhelming. The exactitude the guide had demanded was finally understood. The climb was what climbing was all about.

"The only thing to worry about is the rope breaking," quipped the guide. (The rope could support an elephant.) His affection for the climb couldn't be concealed. He was familiar with the slightest detail of it. The first climber was directed to reach for indentations even he could hardly see. The trust acquired earlier kept the climber responsive to everything the guide said. Amazingly, the climber progressed up the sheer face, like a drugged insect, struggling for each inch. Up to a point, he made the summit look reachable.

The advance came to an abrupt end on a hand ledge. The climber didn't have the spider-like dexterity required for getting his feet where his hands were. The jackhammer effect of his forearms showed how much his subsequent fall was from inability rather than heart. The next student didn't get nearly as high. Even with Chounards with which to smear footholds, he quickly was separated from the rock. Repeated tries were less and less successful. The remaining students couldn't master the tricky start. They'd slip off as if on purpose.

The classes that arrived to rappel the neighboring slope might have thought the experts were playing swing. The time an anchoring sling saved only increased the number of attempts. There was no improvement.

The guide took his turn while his students recuperated. His acrobatics drew praise from the growing crowd. He distracted the onlookers of the rappel and an adjacent, moderately difficult pitch that the intermediates had set upon.

The awe of the advanced class set the mood for the rest. The guide slipped across the hand ledge with ease. Only his fellow guides could accurately gauge his headway. They knew him; they knew the climb; and they knew how economical his moves were. Stopping, shaking one hand while gripping with the other, scanning what was above, then committing himself with a diminishing vigor, inexorably separated him from the bottom by a few more feet.

He skewed to a dike, clambered up it, then ranged diagonally across the face, ever so slowly, deliberately advancing. There was no warning of his fall. It appeared intentional.

The scratches suffered while falling through the slack the belayer let accumulate weren't on the guide's mind at the bottom. "Arms blown," he gasped. "Too close to lunch. Blood not circulated."

Though he was near collapse, not one contradiction was heard.

Impossible Wall profited from the esteem the man was held. The defeat was conclusive, and would have been put out of mind had another guide not taken the first's place. The game was on.

No excuse was offered when, despite coaching and encouragement, he failed. Another's excuse about not being in good climbing condition damaged his reputation. A fourth's apologetic eyes won him the hearts of the overly sentimental.

On lesser climbs, none of the guides had been daunted. Their various styles looked effective. Whether convulsive, rhythmic, or in between, each had gotten the job done.

Its guides' reputation was behind the climbing school's success. They were the best. Nature just wasn't to be conquered in this case. It accidentally came out that only the first guide had ever made the traverse. His reticence was understandable if it was known what a purist he was and how he had to resort to a previously embedded piton. Impossible Wall was aptly named.

Their mutual defeat strengthened the guides' camaraderie. As a source of amusement, their fallibility brought them closer to their students. Quips came from the crowd. Taken in the spirit in which they were given, repartees were generally clever. The one that wasn't called attention to whom it was aimed.

Except for his class, nobody knew why the individual was singled out. A devastating salvo elucidated matters. Second takes were required to believe he was one of them. The Youth's face was so pure, so unblemished, completely untroubled. It was classic. Underneath a floppy hat, the youth radiated a gentleness befitting a cherub.

He lacked the bravado as well as the age of his colleagues. The years of hazardous living, of responsibilities only combat sergeants know about, and exposure to an unemasculated world hadn't adversely affected him. Attributes his crusty colleagues had he also had, but without the bitterness. The disarming charm nature had kissed him with won him the instant respect of the strangers.

Unmerciful teasing clued the crowd to the youth's reputation. A lot of self-efficacy got into his smile of surrender to the goading.

With but one reservation, the spectators braced themselves for a treat. His lithe, bronzed body wasn't bulky with the muscles Superman was supposed to have. Only

Tarzan was thought to be able to master the climb. The boy wasn't. The tourist in the students couldn't be eradicated in a single day, in a single season.

Disproving one of the spectators' prejudices didn't change them, but it helped. The moment the youth touched the wall, their conception of manhood took an unexpected turn.

He was in his element. Witnessing the rare event of a man and his work complementing each other underlined how rare it was.

His initial moves presaged what was to come. Right off, he negotiated the start differently from what the first guide advocated. From the beginning, he embarrassed his predecessors. He glided across the face, astonishingly, even with stops, moving in what would later be sworn as a continuous motion. His virtuosity drew raves from his elders. He outclassed everybody, not making the climb look easy so much as making it look boring. The belay rope seemed superfluous.

"He's an animal" was a popular refrain. There was style, grace, and culture in his ascent. A definite statement was made about sports for the sake of sports, aesthetics for the sake of aesthetics. The appreciation fans have for excellence was commingled with the excitement of reaching a goal. The youth had won for his discipline a following of dillentants.

That it was inconceivable for him to parlay such a performance into cash showed how ignorant people are about the sport. The public would have to have its tastes reprogrammed before it hailed a climber as a somebody. The outdoor gymnast had a long way to go before the conquest of a rock could seem as consequential as running around a field. Without a ball to manipulate, even the agile youth was at a disadvantage.

Dry throats distorted the shouts raised upon the acrobat's reaching the top. A shy wave was for an acknowledgement. Complaints about the cost of the school vanished. A new hero was born.

Touching down signaled an ovation. The hero's shyness prematurely ended the hysterics. With only one exception, he was allowed his privacy. That one person was immune to his sensitivity. He hounded the hero, shamelessly worshipping him. Immune to the hero's feelings, he was also immune to the crowd's feelings. Heroes were to be congratulated; they had earned the honor. It was the way of the world. The hero's discomfiture was misinterpreted as modesty...the appropriate reaction of a hero.

The arrival of more classes made a promoter out of the nuisance. The annals of sports had another great moment after his briefings. Some of the hero's glory was appropriated by broadcasting about it. More was appropriated by satisfying a sudden demand for a biography. The promoter was a conduit for information between the guides and the students. The re-routing of the flow of facts to accommodate all interested perturbed him.

The congestion in front of the Impossible Wall might have been irritating. Beginners rappelling a couple of times each to a lower slope, and intermediates on their F6 slope, got in each other's way. Narratives about the hero soothed jangled nerves. A captive audience was soon won over. A few facts whetted people's appetites for more facts. The scenery and informality helped the listeners reach insights that classrooms couldn't possibly duplicate. Aspects heretofore unknown about the real nature of heroism were come across with astonishing ease. The hero was revealed to be more than a hero than they at first realized.

Climbers who had teethed on the Andes and were instrumental in the golden age of Yosemite climbing unanimously raised the hero's past above their own. A senior guide with a resume that included a K2 expedition and ascents of the Eiger, El Capitan, and Tahquitz Rock, and whose anecdotes could have, as they often had, entertained the students, instead chose to expound about the man of the hour. It wasn't his derring-do or his accomplishments that merited his horn being blown. Neither were they remarkable, per se. It was his style. Throughout the climbing community, his name was an eponym for style.

He was a paradigm for manners and etiquette. If ever a mountaineer was in a quandary about climbing ethics, as the adage went, he only had to guess what he would do. The ethos of climbing was too sacrosanct for him to shamelessly collect credits. A glance at any handbook to the Teton and Wind River ranges would disclose where his mind was. His first ascents were legion among those intimate with the area. What experience did for others, genius did for him. His gift for discovering challenging routes was uncanny. Without making the kind of history scaling the Grand Teton's north face makes, his personality colored the ranges more than anyone else's. Knowledgeable climbers climbed his routes first, and rejoiced whenever he turned up something new.

No clearer statement of a mountaineer's ethos was possible than that made by his climbs. They were practical but elegant, difficult yet fair. Their most appealing aspects were life's most appealing aspects. Those who tested themselves in his footsteps had to reach inside themselves for attributes that the clutter of life rusts. Cleared minds and straightened perspectives always accompanied the thrill of completing an ascent. What wise people aspire to be, climbers successful on the hero's routes were.

The hero was a leader by example, a Gandhi whose passivity was his chief strength, and whose legend was cast throughout the high country.

More than just altitude differentiates the mountains from the plains. A different value system operates where the air is rarefied. A brotherhood forms against the vagaries of nature. Personal grievances, greed, or petty jealousy do not exist above the tree line. Professions, social status, and the appurtenances of civilization are left below, where they belong.When plying their trade, the guides are looked to by the most hopeless tourist as saints.

Their aura wanes the closer they get to sea level, and nature doesn't prey upon people's minds. People demand instead of begging for their time. Their prerogatives diminish where the populations increase. The deeper they sink into society, the less they are appreciated until, as it turns out, their profession is their woe.

Because of what has to be given up to devote one's to the vertical environment, the brotherhood is very protective of its members. Lower altitude air wasn't allowed to infest the upper altitude. The two societies are mutually exclusive, totally unable to comprehend the other. It wasn't atypical of the tourists to think of the hero as being uneducated or, like they, skilled only at what put bread on the table. His multifaceted talents weren't visible. His reticence to flout them was in keeping with his colleagues' reticence. They had no urge to prove themselves.

The hero's degree in hard science wasn't identical to most. The name of an Ivy League school wasn't printed on the parchment. An abridgement of his life wouldn't mention personages such as Ansel Adams, as would on mathematician-photographer-mountaineer.

His resume' was a collage, indicative of what he did to supplement his small compensation as a guide. To all but the most liberal metropolitan employer he was a bad bet.

It wasn't his fault. The ideal career for him hadn't been invented yet. If only being a guide was as profitable and as durable as a typical profession.

The absence of a solid secondary occupation forced him to acquire a telic attitude. Many concessions had to be accepted ever since he chose to let his skill rather than his education feed him. His references were excellent only so far as his climbing was concerned. Referrals for carpentry work and the like were not to be depended upon, not where he lived. Carpenters are overabundant in economics geared for free spirits. It took three years to get hired by the guide service. Luck had more to do with a job at the ski patrol than perseverance or ability. The odds of ever becoming more than, say, a four-dollar-an-hour ranger were slim.

The attitude necessary for mountaineering prevented "winter" from being dirty work. He could handle adversity. It was pointless to hope the guide service would expand to include arctic mountaineering. Because seniority was the principal method of selection, he knew his application to another year-round school would rot before it was reviewed.

With only two seasons in the mountains: fall and winter, and it already being late August, in light of what has been said, it was understandable why his feat wasn't on the hero's mind at the end of the day. The droning of the promoter screened out real disturbances. Holding negative thoughts at bay afflicted his usually cheery spirits. Life without school wasn't much fun. It was what kept him together. He relied upon it as an alcoholic relies upon a bottle.

The banality of the exchanges as the students departed was no indication of superficiality. The hero was hurt to see them go. Watching people improve was both a pleasure and an inspiration. Over and over, ordinary persons reaffirmed their faith in humanity. Modular relationships were anathema to him. His inability to nurture lasting friendships was an unfortunate facet of his job. He liked people. Even the inconsiderate promoter was taken without cynicism. He just had an irksome way of expressing himself. He probably had the time of his life, that's all.

Seeing his students off was the worst part of the hero's day. The local storekeeper could tell how business was by how often he bought notebooks. Hardly a county in the country wasn't represented by an address in his black book.

Although the promoter kept him unusually late, little was abnormal. He had been kept late before, and by more obnoxious people. He was ill-prepared for what was to confront him at headquarters.

Normally, the warmth of the company he sought radiated from the log cabin. When it didn't, what had been taboo to think about came immediately to mind. Works weren't needed to communicate the extent of the catastrophe. The absence of memorabilia and sentiments gave the cabin a stark aspect. It was unfamiliar, cold, and alien. The clean paint behind the removed pictures was disturbingly incongruous. Removing the knick-knacks undid the manly impression the place conveyed. Without a theme, the place was a sty. It was symbolic of what would happen to the climbers should their avocation cease being their vocation.

Times had changed. The world had gotten very complicated. The school couldn't make do on the principles it had been founded upon. Its ethos, as reflected by the simplicity and functionality of its furniture, was passé. Traditions such as putting profits into expeditions or the hands of a financially ailing employee were not well advised.

The pioneer attributes that got Jackson Hole on its feet in ranching were cracking under the onslaught of tourism. The Hole's business climate was becoming more attractive than its scenery. In adjusting to its changing economy, the community was torn this way and that. The number of transient employees serving their companies' interests equaled the number of natives. Traditions had toppled. Dude ranching was a safer bet than real ranching. Dudes wintered better than livestock. People-pleasing enterprises had all but strangled the industries that had once served the town. Curio shops, restaurants, theatres, motels, and realtors had swallowed dry goods and hardware establishments. Coney Island had gone west.

The fierce competition and the smell of money engendered in town seldom spread to the provinces. When it did, a hamlet conveniently sprang up. The businesses in serene Teton Village aren't altruistic about who gets how much of the skier's dollar. The threat of financial ruin hung as heavily over the inhabitants as had violent death over the first white man.

Entrepreneurs are just as sneaky at legalistics as Indians were at ambushes. When they aren't by design, they often are by accident.

Prohibitive insurance rates have threatened the outdoor recreation industry since its inception. Rafting, horseback riding, and mountain climbing outfits were in particular jeopardy. More business meant a shift in the bell-shaped curve that actuaries derive the law of averages from. Suits from accident victims or their families had irrepressibly weeded out the least stable companies. A point was reached when only Lloyds of London would handle them. The group plans tried once, Lloyds, too, dumped them, hadn't worked. Fighting unfriendly takeovers by corporations in the early days had proven ruinously expensive. The proprietors' independence was unmistakably their woe.

The hero typified all climbers by not letting the matter dishearten him. Problems that couldn't be directly dealt with weren't given top priority. After all, life and limb weren't imperiled. The dour faces of the hero's colleagues wouldn't last. They were just stunned by the speed of their dispossession. There were other schools and other ways to support one's addiction to the mountains. Being steeled to whatever nature threw at them steeled them to whatever society could do, too.

The fraternity was resolute. It was unnecessary to ask the members to join hands in a communal relationship. The proceeds from the sale of the building and land went for the purchase of an "A" frame on an inexpensive tract. Savings were compiled and apportioned according to need. The burden of ideological defeat kept bachelor and married men together. Both emotional and material needs were taken care of. To the extent possible, they flourished.

No simple reason could be fingered for their eventual breakup. It didn't have to do with personalities. Their protean ability to tolerate idiosyncrasies was remarkable. Mundane "civilian" jobs didn't fester them. Labels such as "Salesman" or "distributo" weren't uncomfortable to wear. They weren't important enough to be considered.

For several, the transition was just too hard. For others, the sacrifices that had to be made for the common good were too much. Whatever it was that impelled them to forsake the middle class impelled them to forsake their new arrangement. Mountaineers kept away from the mountains but for weekends act in aberrant ways.

The hero was the first to go. He was the youngest, and therefore the most naïve guide. Life hadn't battered him badly enough to tarnish his ideals. Misfortune hadn't scared away the fearlessness responsible for his virtuosity. It was no wonder he was touchy about having to make compromises.

The pilot's license he had earned did little good once the scenic raft companies were liquidated. The challenges the fickle Snake was noted for might have satisfied him. Pretending he could live in it was impossible. Being submerged in it rather than on the periphery gave him an altogether different perspective of it.

Jackson Hole ran on A.R.V. fumes. It was a stationary rendezvous, a place where latter-day trappers came to get bilked. It was a parody of itself, where the yet-to-have-it-made

Spent a week and they have already retired. Condominiums, mansions, and country clubs cast huge shadows. Anything authentic was either a historical site or was lost. "Frontierland" was inhospitable to people trained to see things as they are.

The hero had to resort to looking up contacts. The greeting he received from Royal Robbins himself was a welcome change from what he normally had to put up with. The famous mountaineer's hospitality is at his disposal. It was awkward for the hero to ask about a job. It might not have been brought up at all had the great man not brought it up. The climbing community's grapevine had spread the word of his troubles. It had also notified him of similar occurrences elsewhere. The applicant could not be offered a job at his Rockcraft school. It wouldn't have been fair to the others who would sooner or later apply. Royal Robbins couldn't afford any friction. Friction breeds publicity, and publicity was to be guarded against. Not being jeopardized by insurance companies or harassed by Dunn and Bradstreet was possible only by remaining unnoticed.

The profession, as an industry, didn't exist.

Emotions that immobilize urbanites do not affect mountaineers. They are the envy of ulcer victims. Disappointments are too much a part of their lives to warrant much concern. Poker faces are emblematic of the profession. What the hero's fortunes were was impossible for a casual observer to tell. His employment search was often mistaken for a vacation.

Vagabondage wore well on him. He had always been an untried wanderer. Up, down, across the continent, alternately hitching rides and taking buses, he sought that elusive dream of meaningful work. Discouragement was an impetus to try harder. He didn't become bitter as it became evident his skill was in as much demand as a phrenologist's or a sorcerer's.

Often, Mr. Robbing's addresses were antiquated, his leads erroneous. Proprietors of failed outdoor businesses do not remain at he scene of their failure. Forwarding addresses had to be coaxed from religious fanatics, hippies, and other assorted squatters.

Funding his search put him should to with a variety of types. Driving cars from Seattle wharfs to dealerships, picking apples in Washington groves, and shoveling coal in Gary, Indiana, introduced him to people as they normally are, not as they are on vacation.

Spare money went for needed vacations. He leapt at opportunities. A hike in the Tennessee Smokies became a job repairing trails at the other end of the Appalachian Trail. By following up on tips, he uncovered a school in upstate New York, where climbing was reported to be the rage. A stint there for almost nothing, followed by a few leads that led nowhere, left him broke.

Desperately soliciting his services as an independent guide put enough dollars in his pocket to buy a suit. The gamble that a prosperous appearance would lure a "yes" from loan officers didn't work. Their syrupy rejections encouraged him to keep dreaming of becoming at least an outfitter. He computed impressive statistics as evidence for the feasibility of a school. A persistent sharper could have put his case across for him. The hero needed an agent. He was too modest and too callow to guess how the game worked.

Loan agencies, with their less gentlemanly money changers, attacked his self-image with aspersions about his lack of collateral. The chances of him counterattacking were nil. The financial currents pulsating along the eastern seacoast wouldn't let him have a sip. His calculations wound up in the trash.

The distaste acquired for manual labor, coupled with the realization society had at once taken away his niche and roasted him for not finding another, tried his patience. Being so ineffectual was maddening. He did not know how to look out for his best interests. His brain needed reprogramming if he was to function in the environment he found himself in.

A donor was needed, someone molded and shaped as vigorously by civilization as the hero was by the mountains. Seeing the world through a mountaineer's eyes, describing it with a mountaineer's vocabulary, and listening to it with an ear attuned to the sounds he was familiar with were handicaps. Being unaware of his uniqueness was more serious.

He could clumsily handle the externals of society. The internals, society's philosophy, was different, very different.

Too bad no well-heeled urbanite advised him. He needed to be warned of the dangers of a reconnaissance. The urban world swallows people who come too close. The hero didn't know how big his first timid steps were.

Without notice, seconds become years in the city. The metropolis is a universe, with its infinite field of time and space.

Modern transportation has fused all metropolises into one. The voids between them have only supportive roles. Rural philosophies get no hearings. The noise of rush hour drowns them out.

It was inevitable that the hero's self-image as a leader wouldn't last. Self-images are malleable. They have to be in the city. It is anachronistic to think in terms of job permanence. Elasticity, not specialization, is the secret to survival. Only the urban setting remains unchanged in the working lives of urbanites. Rapid turnover is a cosmopolitan ethic.

A glance at a Sunday's employment section was all that it took for the truth to win out. Employment compatible with the hero's interests was nonexistent. No position was one he'd normally look twice at. Besides tradesmen, salesmen and retailers were the only people in demand.

His degree was his edge in the competition. How a degree in science qualified him wasn't ruminated upon. He had no reason to question the way the city operated. He respected it. He respected success. Success, to him, was the only valid criterion for making judgments. The faults of the city must have their tremendous energy amended.

It was regenerative. It was seductive. Its complexity was inspirational. It was fetched by cajolery and fiat. It talked the hero into lowering his guard, into trusting it. Nothing he could perceive looked inimical. He had taken a fork in the trail and had come across a new land.

Playing by new rules didn't bother him. Different ascents required different techniques to surmount. Weather changes had to always be watched for. Companions had to be kept congenial. Whatever had to be confronted was confronted with his welfare in mind. Having little idea what he was getting into had the tinge of adventure to it. Nothing he had yet come up against had done him over.

He envisioned himself hand in hand with a team of dedicated colleagues performing socially critical functions. He wasn't going to be knocked about willy-nilly. He figured retailers in the outdoor sports field would benefit the most from his expertise. He had a lot to offer. His fit body and remarkable mind were two pluses to be confident of.

Neither his physical nor mental attributes entered into his first job interview. Only later, after his rejection, did it occur to the hero how irrelevant his credentials were. All the obese, amiable manager wanted was someone knowledgeable about deep water fishing. The new line of special paraphernalia needed a promoter. An entire career, the second item mentioned in an obituary, relied upon what fishing bums possess.

The model's salary was twice what the hero was used to living on. There was a communication barrier. The interviewer didn't respond to his unpretentious claims of familiarity with other sports that the company dwelt with. Their hero's demure nature worked against him. The euphemisms mountaineers traffic in were taken at face value by the weekend adventurer.

The sugar-coated rejection left a pleasant taste in the job seeker's mouth. No regret about having wasted the day ruined his disposition. Pragmatically, he concentrated upon seeking a place for the night.

His budget kept him from all places but a "Y" near dilapidated subsidized housing. He considered himself fortunate to procure one of the few vacant cells. It was doubtful any of the rooms ever entertained as much activity as that one room that one night. By morning, the market supplements of all the dailies were riddled with holes and defaced by ink. The contrast between the dismal building and the nattily attired businessman who emerged from it was striking.

The hero remained conspicuous until reaching the outskirts of the business district. There, no one thought he hadn't arrived by train or by car. No one thought of him at all, except for—maybe—a cabbie who cut a corner too sharply.

His destination was a typical building, if a copper-paneled building could be called typical. The hustle outside was going on inside. The innovative twist that the wholesale-retail company used to undercut its retail competition was almost physical. Free enterprise at its competitive best was blatantly flaunted.

Judging from their consternation, the forms the immaculately dressed aspirants poured over could have been professional boards. By mentioning how glad he was to see the applicants, even the janitor exhibited the go-getter that everyone else exhibited. More managers meant growth. Growth was the catchword implied in each question the interviewer asked the hero when it was his turn to sell himself. The interviewer knew his business. His grilling extracted the truth from the hero. He had no heart for, hence no business being in, the trade. No refugee from the suburban takeover of Jackson Hole could hide his aversion to retail.

The interviewer could have done the hero a great service had he said what he knew, with emphasis. The amiable parting belied the interviewer's true sentiments. The hero was a Misfit. Had he an ear for listening between sentences, he would have understood that. As it was, it was his turn to misinterpret euphemisms.

The subsequent interviews differed only in the particulars. The similarities were so apparent that a sharp picture of the suit and tie world started to develop.

His policy on privacy didn't prevent him from sneaking peeks at his competitors' applications. They were as uniform as their three-piece suits.

Hailing from the metropolis, having graduated in business or the humanities from metropolitan schools, and having listed the reason why they left their last job as a lack of opportunity for advancement, stamped them as of the same ilk. Their conversations were money-deep. They were born into the game and had never experimented with anything else. They had the same advantage the hero would have had had the playing field been close to the timber line. They were better fit to be asked for second interviews.

Professional help was a must. The blank spaces in the want ads were soon where employment agencies that advertised their services.

He did not get beyond the first one he walked into. Once the chore of filling out several identical applications was completed, his counselor whisked him to her desk. She wasn't about to let him go. She was his surrogate mother, his coach, his pal. She devoted herself to him. Her practiced hand retouched his applications to make them passable. Her confidence in the interviewing techniques she outlined was convincing. She told him what he was interested in doing and groomed him toward those ends.

She had him memorize lists of dos and don'ts, memorize the histories of companies he'd ask to get hired by, and escorted him in and out of intra-office workshops. She corrected his posture, taught him about body language, and how to differentiate key, make-or-break questions from flak. Her vivacity was infectious. Thanks to her, jobs were considered more like rewards than grim necessities. The hero was well-prepared to meet the companies whenever their representatives arrived.

The wiles his doting sounselor drummed into him stood him well during the fury of "visitation day." It was combat, with each side sniffing out, sizing up, white lying to, and waving its respective attributes. Various executives of the employment agency were installed in a room away from the front line. Battle-fatigued job seekers sought rest and inspiration there. Self-awareness films were on tap, as was coffee. But it was the executives who were the most informative and stimulating. Their confidential asides, by putting careers into perspective, put the job seekers at ease. The younger personnel, manning the forward edge of the battlefield, might have been surprised to hear what the old guard had to say. The go-getters' injunctions to outprofessional the professionals, their harping about the sacrifices getting to the top necessitates, and their claims that position dictates worth were concepts the executives disproved.

A difference of opinion prevailed across the generation gap. Heresies such as the remark that jobs were just means to support a person's avocations came from the mouths of those nearing retirement.

The haphazard method by which the prospects were wedded to companies lent validity to the elders' claims. Personality was paramount. The electricity every successful candidate had created was behind their acceptance, not their resume, references, or transcript. The most productive part of a person's life began completely arbitrarily.

If given more than a short dose of the elders, their audience might have slunk out of the agency. However, the applicants were fed only enough pessimism to put them at ease. Rejuvenated job seekers returned to the fray.

The next bunch of battle-beaten prospects crowded out the malingerers from the previous bunch. The hero was shoved back into action.

He heard himself parrot what he had been trained to parrot. The need for money and his rapport with his counsel conspired against a crop of reasons begging him to flee.

The combat brought what he had and hadn't looked for in a job into focus. The antithesis of what he believed in had to stare him in the face before he knew what he did believe in. Not until their hopeless loss was he aware of how vital the satisfactions his former career afforded. Having to part with his talent without compensation for

It was purely malicious. He had been hoodwinked into mediocrity.

Putting up a belated fight worked against him. His disgruntlement turned people off. Blaming the people around him compounded the problem. A panic about returning to the mountains only for vacation was behind the disturbance he was causing.

His counsel surreptitiously removed him from the firing lines. A cadgy reprimand left him feeling he had wronged her. By glorifying their artificial relationship, she preyed upon his sense of honor. The mountains faded away, and with them, his aggravations. Reiterating her faith in him restored the self-esteem she had previously sabotaged. A much more resolute individual was sent back to do good.

He held up through the fusillades from the interviewers he hadn't alienated. His analytical mind was sharp when it didn't detract from it. He just knew what to say and how to say it. Wise interviewers examined him from the standpoint of him someday being their boss. Only the incompetent couldn't distinguish him from the general cut.

He didn't have to pretend, as he went from station to station, he was interested in each prospective employer as he came to them. For him, it was a buyer's market. He went to the highest bidder, to the man whose sale sheet proved his top salesmen made a fortune.

The ringing of a toy bell, signifying someone landing a job, was a jolt. The cuteness of it was repulsive. The glit and tinsel he had been talked out of seeing, the bell forced him to see. He was a leashed and muzzled wolf among sheep.

The receptionist's more ringing of the bell taunted him. He was losing control, and might have lost control, to storm out of the office, out of the city, and back to the high country had his counselor not gotten hold of him. News of his success had beaten him back. His counselor was ecstatic about his good luck. She grabbed him by his Achilles' heel.

His largeness was his weakness. Making somebody else happy made him happy. It disarmed him. He wasn't nauseated by talk about the good pay, benefits, and upward mobility the firm was noted for. The elation of narby counselors tore his defenses to shreds.

The hero was once more honored. The praise soothed him. Not knowing what to think, he let others do the chore for him. A new person came into existence. The agency had successfully crammed a round peg into a square hole.

The transition from looking for work to working was smooth, so smooth that their interchangeability was unmistakable. There was no opportunity to reflect upon what was happening. He was shunted inside another building where smiling faces and glad hands marshaled him through antiseptic room after antiseptic room. Musac prevented him from thinking deeper than completing the paperwork handed to him when he was left alone. Indoctrination tapes assured him that the glad tidings he received during the in-processing would remain throughout, and after, his term of service. A smorgasbord of benefits was gone over, point by tedious point, to show how well the company took care of its people.

The price for protection from life's hard knocks wasn't skipped over. What was expected from each of the firm's representatives was explicitly detailed. Words of encouragement followed next. Conversations the hero overheard confirmed his suspicion that all hirlings were treated as if they were special. Superlatives were too overworked to mean anything. That everyone was required to excel in the image of the company was what it all came down to.

Not since the days of his climbing classes was friendship so easily acquired. Such amiability was rare, or so it seemed. Had he not been from a foreign culture, he might have copied his fellow inductees and taken it all in.

The difference being in a subordinate rather than a dominant position wasn't subtle. The hero knew what an obligation it was to justify a superior's friendship. That was why he had made his students look at him as a tutor, not a professor. Now, with everybody who was established in the company a superior, the pressure was oppressive.

The air of promiscuity permeating the offices had to be lived with. The hero accepted his colleagues' puffy, uncared-for bodies, their monetary minds. He had to. He kept quiet about the phoniness of the macho wall decorations. The coyote howls a row of wizened clerks set up in response to his introduction, causing him to bite his tongue.

A painted lady congratulated him on his choice of companies. A sales manager gloated about how well he would fit in. He was baptized, in the sense that his past was wiped away. His future was to be written on company stationery.

To ensure that his record would start in italics, his boss ushered him into a private suite. A trace of recognition caused a remark about how people use only a tenth of their capacities to tail off. The hero discounted his first impression, too. With a presence of mind that forgets about nuisances, he wasn't likely to remember the promoter. Because the hero was so far out of his element, his former promoter wasn't about to ask him to identify himself. Coincidences that rare belong in mediocre fiction.

The promoter's climbing experience was his only taste of adventure since, like so many his age, the Second World War. He hadn't changed upon his return to thicker air. His feats had been mentioned primarily to accentuate her feat. It had received a premier reportage. The carnage of acquaintances bored to death by it was awful.

The promoter might have kept quiet about his climbing had his new employee shared his penchant for the usual spectator sports. Seeking a common interest proved to be laborious. Not only did the employee know who won the last Super Bowl, but he also didn't know who Arnold Palmer was. He didn't play golf, or tennis for that matter. He didn't seem to do much of anything.

The Dale Carnegie course that the firm had the former promoter take encouraged him to probe deeper. It was out of desperation that climbing was touched upon. The mere mention of an interest in it got the promoter going. The hero had no chance to explain the nature of this interest. His boss wasn't about to give up the floor. The hero had feigned interest and not exaggerated or made mistakes. Having to stoke his boss's ego kept the man going, on and on, until the hero had no false impression about what he had gotten into. But there was no alternative.

ENGLISH-AMERICAN INCOHERENCE

Two young adults meet outside a restaurant. The attractive woman collapses her umbrella.

Woman: Where is the bin for my brolly? You must be David Anderson from Ensaw.

Man: I must. And you are Olivia Hastings, from Farrady.

They shake hands. Her grip is dainty.

Olivia: Glad my office found this restaurant.

David: It is swell, especially as a last-minute substitute.

Olivia: As we were.

Maitre d' checks their reservation. They are led to their seats. David attempts to pull the chair back for her. She sits herself.

David: We're both last-minute fill-ins.

Olivia: I was knackered when I got the call.

David: I thought they were yanking my chain. I put out so many fires ought to call my office ladder seventeen.

Olivia: We're expected to touch base. My office believed I could best meet this moment, demonstrate Farrady's commitment to fairness and equality in the merger.

David: Ensaw is all in too.

Olivia: Right. We must move the needle together.

David: Be two peas in a pod.

Olivia: I supervise three departments, so what comes of this dinner will have consequences.

David: I'll stay on point, and make sure the VPs I report to will get the skinny.

They look at the wine list.

Olivia (to server): What year is this Sauvignon Blanc?

Server: I don't know but I will find out.

Olivia: Do that, love.

Dave: Not for nothing were we chosen as replacements. Knew we could get er done.

Olivia: At the end of the day we need to review compatibilities and redundancies.

Dave: Show what we need to do. Be able to work smarter, not harder.

Olivia: Precisely, so we won't be as bog standard as our competitors.

Dave: Don't want to jump the gun. Need to get to know each other better, beyond ebitda, mission statement, franchise fees, roi, market share, you know, brain storm.

Olivia: Right, let's start with organization.

Dave: We're mostly horizontal, cross trained.

Olivia: Sounds off license, a recipe for meddling. When everyone is responsible no one takes responsibility.

Dave: Everyone knows his place.

Olivia: His?

Dave: Their

She sighs

Dave: I keep my ear to the ground.

Olivia: So you know your onions.

Dave: Everyone from my neck of the woods does. Came from top schools. Especially the women, who we have more of than men.

Olivia: Does that surprise you? There are more women in university than men. England has always been at the vanguard of social evolution. You, yanks are just following suit.

Dave: Soccer has never caught on here.

Olivia: In important things. Leaning in will be normative, populating the suites.

Dave: Glass ceilings will be a mirage. Everyone knows you have what it takes.

Olivia: We will stretch the boundaries of possibility.

Dave: We'll help you through the bottleneck, thread that needle, and the rest will be history.

Olivia: Together we can meet this moment, demonstrate our commitments to justice and women's rights, and effect change. End the patriarchy.

Dave: You can look under any stone in our company, and you won't find it.

Olivia: Patriarchy is endemic in the business world. No one admits it. The assurances I heard a fortnight ago, at a conference call, was bullocks. No one could explain why we have only one female VP.

Dave: Let me guess. Human Resources. Should be able to keep her position.

Olivia: Why wouldn't she?

Dave: She?

Olivia stares at him.

Dave: I'm sure I was handed the football to put your mind at ease. So we don't jump the shark.

Olivia: Only I can put my mind at ease. You provide input for me to consider. What we need is a consensus so invigorating public perception of it would provide a positive impact. Make it a done deal, as you would say.

Dave: With you controlling the optics we'll show the world we can crush it.

Olivia: Ensure a paradigm shift.

Dave: Empower those women.

Olivia: Sounds condescending.

Dave: I am just championing the ladies I work with.

Olivia: Sounds misogynistic.

Dave: You'll be Joan of Arc.

Olivia: Sounds dodgy.

Dave: You'll lead the herd to the hilltop. Be the cat's meow.

Olivia (confused) You mean go pear-shaped?

Dave: I mean you will be a rock star, leading those women to the promised land.

Olivia: Overegging the pudding, aren't we?

Dave: We men will be in awe of you. It is what it is. All we'll see is your dust.

Olivia: I might have to contact H.R. The Chinese whispers I hears about you are spot on.

Dave: Let's circle back. I apparently am not cutting the mustard.

Olivia: What mustard?

Dave: The mustard.

Olivia: That doesn't make any sense.

Dave (frustrated): It makes perfect sense. If you can't see it you have to be full of beans.

Olivia: I should hope so.

Dave: It wasn't a compliment.

Olivia: So that was some sort of derisive comment?

Dave: Let's get back on track.

Olivia: What track?

Dave: The track.

Olivia: I hope not the one you men have predetermined for us.

Dave: The one I am being railroaded on.

Olivia: Where you're making a dog's dinner out of this dinner.

Dave: Where you're thinking so far out of the box you don't even know where the box is.

Olivia: I know where the box is and it is off limits to you.

Dave: That's cheeky of you to think I would want it.

Olivia: So you say.

Dave: In your own language.

Olivia: Maybe you weren't here to reach out so much as to grab.

Dave: In your dreams.

Olivia: Codswallopper.

Dave: Snot.

Olivia: Tosser

Dave: Witch.

Olivia: Pea souper.

Dave: Pin head.

Olivia: Wanker.

Dave: Token.

Olivia: Git.

Dave signals for the check. Olivia throws her napkin onto her plate. Dave receives the check and flips it to Olivia.

Dave: Here, you want to be important.

Dave stalks off. Olivia looks stunned, gets mad, but recovers as she thumbs through her purse for her wallet. She composes herself and proudly hands the waiter her corporate card. She then eyes the glass of wine, sniffs it, swirls it, holds it briefly to her lips, and takes a sip. After swallowing, she admires it, saying: "mint."

ABOUT THE AUTHOR

I'm a Yankee who became a damn Yankee when I wouldn't leave the South. When I did leave, it was overseas, where I comfortably acquired the moniker of "Yank". I have two bachelor's degrees. The one in geology I used to support myself, the one in history showed I am curious about human nature. This curiosity culminated in *Thunder in the Wind* after I found out about a Cree named Almighty Voice while I was engaged in geologic fieldwork in Montana. His revolt almost united the tribes, as had Pontiac's and Tecumseh's before him. I was predisposed to write about Indians, as, being from Northwest Indiana, I grew up on their lore and history. I even achieved the rank of Eagle Boy Scout, where my advancement mirrored the age societies of most tribes. I defended Kansas from the communists as a 1st Lieutenant in the Army and was a junior golf champion who got to play with the University of Houston golf team. I've been a journalist and wrote copious op-eds, dozens of short stories, and at least 10 books, mostly fiction. I've put four up for sale. *Thunder in the Wind* won a Best Western award. I am a member of the Writers Guild of America Divorced, I supported myself as an oilfield geologist, often overseas.

9 781967 375165